SEIZED

HOSTAGE RESCUE TEAM SERIES

KAYLEA CROSS

SEIZED

Copyright © 2015
by Kaylea Cross

* * * * *

Cover Art & Formatting by
Sweet 'N Spicy Designs

* * * * *

ISBN: 978-1519599766

Dedication

To all those men and women in the world out there working hard to safeguard the rest of us. Your efforts and dedication are so appreciated.

Kaylea

Author's Note

Vance's story is finally here! The basic conflict between him and Carmela was set up in the previous book (*Exposed*), but "falling in love with your best friend's sister" is one of my very favorite friends-to-lovers tropes in romance, and these two are definitely meant to be together.

Some of you may remember that hubby and I went on an Alaskan cruise together this past summer. It was actually a secret research trip! Thankfully, our cruise was both peaceful and uneventful. Unfortunately I can't say the same for poor Carmela.

I hope this one keeps you on the edge of your seat!

Happy reading!

Kaylea Cross

Prologue

Miami, FL

Carmela Cruz rushed toward the rear entrance of Jackson Memorial Hospital, panic beating inside her like a frantic bird's wings.

Please let him be okay. He has to be okay.

An agent had just informed them that her brother Ethan, a member of the FBI's elite Hostage Rescue Team, had been injured while rescuing a hostage from a drug cartel. No one she'd talked to since had any more details and she hadn't been able to reach Ethan or any of his teammates by phone, so she was here to get answers herself and find out how badly he'd been injured.

It was all over the news. She'd been listening to updates on her car radio on the drive here and now she was half frantic. At least one suspect was dead, another missing. An FBI agent and one victim—her brother and his girlfriend, Marisol—had been transported here by ambulance.

And Jackson Memorial housed the only level one adult trauma center in Miami-Dade County.

The rapid snap of her flip-flops against the asphalt barely registered over the thud of her pulse in her ears. Had Ethan been shot? It terrified her. He could be in surgery right now, fighting for his life.

She refused to even entertain the thought that he might be gone. She'd dropped her mom at the front entrance before parking—she'd tried three different lots before finding a freaking spot—so hopefully her mom would know where Ethan was by the time Carmela met up with her at the information desk.

The automatic doors whooshed open when she stepped on the pressure sensor. A wave of air-conditioned air hit her. Inside the entryway she glanced left then right, and spotted a familiar face coming toward her down the right hand hallway. Her heart careened in her chest.

Sawyer.

Relief crashed through her at the same time tears pricked the backs of her eyes. He was still in his fatigues, must have come straight here from the op. He and Ethan were best friends, he'd know exactly what had happened to her brother.

He started to smile as she tore toward him, flip-flops slapping on the linoleum floor, her belly a giant knot of fear. A million questions crowded her mind.

He towered above her, the top of her head barely reaching his chin. "Hey," he said, concern on his face when he saw how panicked she was. He stepped forward to catch her by the upper arms but she latched onto his broad shoulders and started firing questions at him.

"What's happened? Where's Ethan? And Marisol?" She scanned his dark eyes anxiously, her entire body vibrating with tension. "The agents at Mrs. Lorenzo's said there'd been a firefight and that they'd both been injured. It was all over the news but no one would tell us anything.

Where—"

"Whoa, slow down," he said gently.

The thin hold she had over her temper snapped. She dug her fingers harder into the solid muscle of his shoulders, narrowed her eyes at him and leaned in to snarl right in his face. "Don't you dare do that 'speak softly and don't make any sudden moves' thing with me. I want to know what the hell happened to my brother."

"No, listen, he's okay." He squeezed her upper arms gently to reinforce his words.

She shook her head, frustration about to make her explode. "He's *not* okay. If he was okay he wouldn't be here, and they would've told me what happened." Why else bring him by ambulance to a level one trauma center?

He started to shake his head. "Just calm down a sec and—"

"No, I won't stop!" Tears flooded her eyes and she held on tighter. They were close friends, it wasn't like him to hide something so important from her. "Why won't you just tell me what happened? He must be hurt badly, otherwise—"

Her impatient words were cut off when he suddenly took her face in his hands and kissed her.

She jerked in shock, her eyes flying wide in surprise. What the hell? And this wasn't just a simple peck on the lips.

It felt like a claiming. One she'd been dreaming of for almost two years.

Only not under these circumstances.

He cradled her face between his big hands like he needed her. Cherished her. She was too stunned to respond but for just an instant she let herself soften. Allowed her eyelids to flutter closed.

His big hands slid into her hair to cradle the back of her head and he slanted his mouth over hers. Her belly fluttered.

The tiny part of her brain that was still functioning confirmed that this must mean Ethan really was okay. Sawyer would never cross the line between friends and more than friends at a time like this otherwise. Still, his actions confused her. Was he keyed up from the op and seeking reassurance from her too? The thought made her melt a little.

More relief slid through her, taking the strength out of her already rubbery legs. She made a small mewling sound and leaned into him, pressing against that rock hard chest while her lips parted. He slid his tongue along her lower lip, making her shiver before stealing inside the warmth of her mouth.

A soft, quick taste. Not nearly enough to satisfy her, not after how long she'd wanted him, but now wasn't the time or place to figure out why he'd had the sudden change of heart.

When he lifted his head a moment later they were both breathing faster. But then she noticed his eyes were clear, his gaze too sharp and alert for someone who'd supposedly just been so overcome with the need to kiss her that he hadn't been able to contain himself.

The romantic fog instantly cleared from her brain, and she narrowed her eyes at him in suspicion as a humiliating possibility hit her right in the face. "Wait. Did you just kiss me to shut me up?" she demanded, completely insulted that he would do such a thing. If he'd kissed her to stop her questions, it had definitely worked.

But if it was true then she was embarrassed on top of being mad and worried about Ethan.

"No, now listen to me." He slid his fingers through her hair and held her gaze. She didn't believe him, was still angry with him, but he kept on talking. "Your brother's okay, and so is Soli. Ethan had to have a routine CT scan to make sure the bump on his head didn't cause any damage, and Soli had some minor cuts that needed to be cleaned up. Mostly they wanted to bring her here to get her hydrated and bring her core temp back up. She got thrown into the water for a bit. That and the shock of everything that happened meant she needed a doctor to check her out, and they both had a lot of questions to answer."

Fake kiss put aside for the moment, Carmela blinked at him as she absorbed all that. My God, what the hell had happened out there today? "So they're both okay," she repeated, watching him warily, unsure whether he was lying to make her feel better, make her think everything was okay just so she wouldn't freak out. "You're certain."

He nodded, his gaze steady. "Yeah."

She lifted her chin, hating that her face was still hot, broadcasting her embarrassment. "Swear on my mother's life that they're both okay."

"I swear," he said without hesitation.

Okay, he wouldn't lie under that kind of oath. Not where her mother was concerned. Everyone knew how much Sawyer adored and worshipped Mama Cruz, and vice versa.

She closed her eyes for a second and heaved a sigh of relief, then reached for him, needing the physical reassurance of his embrace. A tiny shudder ripped through her when those heavy arms wrapped around her back and pulled her close to him, seeking the comfort she'd needed so badly.

Sawyer hugged her close, his strong, solid frame supporting her as her knees seemed to sag. He smelled like fresh air, the salty scent of the ocean, and an underlying delicious scent that was all him.

Ethan's okay, and so is Soli. That's all that matters. She kept repeating that to herself as her heartbeat slowed.

"Okay now?" he murmured against her hair a minute later. He dwarfed her, the feel of his strong arms around her every bit as wonderful as she'd imagined over the past couple of years.

But that kiss bothered her. Made her feel cheated and self-conscious. He'd manipulated her, something she'd never thought him capable of.

She nodded against his shoulder, conflicting emotions battering her. "Yeah, better. Thanks."

He pressed a kiss to the top of her head and released her when she eased back. The moment she stepped out of his embrace she felt colder.

Carmela cleared her throat and looked at the floor, suddenly unsure of herself. She could feel she was still blushing and she couldn't quite meet his eyes. God, why had he played her like that? "So, can I see them both?" She wanted to see them for herself, hug them both.

Sawyer seemed to hesitate a moment before nodding. "Yeah. But come with me to grab a cup of coffee first."

She shot him an uncertain look, still agitated and off-balance. Seeing her brother was priority one, and besides, the idea of being alone with Sawyer any longer made her uncomfortable. She'd never imagined feeling awkward around him until now and she hated it. "I don't know, I'd rather be upstairs in case they need me…"

"They're both talking with investigators right now anyway, and honey, I'm so tired I'm about to drop face first onto this no-wax floor. So come with me while I get some caffeine into my system and then I'll take you up to see them both in a little while."

Studying him now, for the first time she noticed how tired he looked. His eyes were bloodshot and lines of fatigue bracketed his eyes and mouth. A sexy mouth outlined by a neatly trimmed black goatee that made him look even more rugged and masculine.

Whatever had happened today behind the scenes, it must have been bad. He was on the same assault team as Ethan so he would have been directly involved in the operation, would probably have seen Ethan get hurt. Since the two of them were closer than a lot of brothers she knew, that had to have weighed heavy on him. It made her want to hug him all over again.

But she wouldn't touch him again now, not when she was feeling so raw.

"Okay," she relented, but looked away again, avoiding his gaze. She didn't know what to think, except that he'd clearly taken advantage of her feelings for him. Those old, well-developed protective instincts sprang to life inside her.

Pretend you don't care. Don't let him see he got to you.

She'd learned an important lesson today, one she wouldn't forget. And it was past time she got over him anyway.

She turned on her heel and responded with a muttered, "One quick cup of coffee."

Chapter One

Seattle, ten weeks later

His damn shoulder was killing him and they hadn't even begun the hard part of the op yet.

At the south entrance of the building, Special Agent Sawyer Vance pushed the pain from his mind and stood on the mobile ramp behind his teammate, Adam Blackwell, as they approached the doorway. The warehouse was dark inside and appeared deserted, with just enough ambient light in there for them to see clearly through their NVGs once they entered.

But it wasn't deserted.

Four of the FBI's most wanted were inside, all of them radical Islamist terrorists plotting to launch a huge attack on U.S. soil within the next few days. And there were female civilians mixed in with them. Because the bastards thought that would protect them from attack.

They thought wrong.

Sawyer kept his gaze locked on the door while Blackwell planted the explosive charge, then turned his head toward the far end of the building. Tuck, their team leader, placed another charge on the north door. Through various means they'd been studying and watching the building since early last night. Now that the main players were here, all that critical preparation was about to pay off.

The seconds crawled past as they waited. He was already sweating lightly in his utilities. It was surprisingly hot and muggy for Seattle in early September. A bead of sweat rolled down his face but he didn't move, staying locked in position. He and the rest of the boys were ready to rock.

But Tuck didn't give the signal. Sawyer wasn't sure what he was waiting for but didn't question his team leader. He stood still behind Blackwell, waiting for the order to execute, and for a moment he let his mind drift to thoughts of Carmela.

He missed her like hell, felt like he was living with a hole inside him since he'd ruined their relationship with that kiss. As much as he'd been dying to kiss her and holding back his true feelings for her, he couldn't say that one moment of bliss had been worth it. Not when the consequence was losing her. He had to fix it somehow.

"On my count," Tuck murmured into the team's comms, his Alabama drawl making his voice sound even calmer. "Three. Two. One. *Execute*."

Tuck and Blackwell simultaneously blew the charges on both doors. Sawyer swung past his teammate to deliver a punishing blow to the ruined door with the breaching tool.

The tendons in his shoulder screamed in protest with the motion and impact but he ignored it. One more ram and the steel reinforced door flew inward, clearing the way for the assaulters.

Blackwell led the way, Sawyer directly behind him and then Evers, M4s to their shoulders. At the north end of the building, their four remaining teammates stormed the front of the warehouse.

Blackwell and Tuck started yelling as they breached the building. "FBI, everybody down!"

Female screams pierced the air, mixed with male shouts as everyone in the building scrambled. Seconds later, gunfire erupted from the north. Sawyer saw two armed men jump out at the end of a row of pallets. He and Blackwell both fired two shots at the same time, taking them down in a matter of seconds.

In his peripheral he caught movement to his left. He spun to meet the threat but Evers had already taken the shot, dropping the guy.

Out of sight in the distance, more rounds fired. Sawyer kept his eyes on the remaining tangos' hands as they headed for the back of the building, watching for weapons. Evers took point while Blackwell covered their six.

They turned past a stack of pallets and a woman stood there, frozen, her eyes wide above the veil that covered the rest of her face.

"Hands up *now!*" He wasn't fucking around. A terrorist was a terrorist, no matter what gender they were.

Slowly, the woman raised her hands, revealing something clutched tightly in one fist.

He recognized it instantly and his heart seemed to stop in mid-beat. *Shit.* "Grenade!"

Blackwell stopped short and turned back to him while Evers scanned behind them for more threats. The woman didn't move. She seemed frozen, unsure what to do, only her eyes visible above the veil.

Sawyer made a split second decision and dove at her.

He tackled her to the concrete floor, grabbed her hand in a punishing grip and wrenched the grenade free. The pin was still in it, thank God. He handed it up to Blackwell, who stood behind him, his weapon aimed dead center at the woman's chest.

She didn't struggle, didn't make a sound as Sawyer checked her for more weapons then flipped her onto her belly and secured her hands behind her back. For good measure he bound her ankles as well. She wasn't going anywhere.

"All clear here," he said into his comm to update the others. "Two tangos down, another secured."

Blackwell nodded once and continued past him, scanning the interior of the warehouse as he followed their other teammates.

"North side secure," Tuck murmured from somewhere up front. "Heading into the rear room now."

"We copy," Sawyer answered, climbing to his feet. "Moving in behind you now."

Fifteen yards ahead of him, Bauer stood guard at the entrance to the back room. Even with the limited light provided by the NVGs it was impossible to mistake him. The former SEAL was the biggest guy on the team, bigger even than Sawyer. His huge shoulders filled the opening as he stood there keeping an extra eye on the rear of the warehouse.

A sudden, short burst of rounds came from the back room. Sawyer rushed forward as Bauer swung around and stormed into the room.

"Three tangos down, back room secure," Ethan Cruz, Sawyer's best friend, announced a moment later.

Sawyer relaxed and stayed near the doorway, stopping outside the door. Tuck appeared a minute later, his weapon lowered across his chest. "All clear. Spread out and sweep for weapons," he said to the team.

The seven of them fanned out and began a thorough search for weapons and booby traps. They found a decent-size cache of rifles in a lock box back in the rear room where someone had hidden it, but it would take a long while to check the stacks of pallets and containers crammed into the building. So far, though, no sign of the chemical weapons they'd been warned might be on the premises.

Which should have made him breathe easier.

But it didn't, not with the massive threat still looming over the West Coast.

It was only a few days until the anniversary of 9/11, and a recent massive uptick in chatter warned of an unknown terror organization planning to attack the West Coast. No one knew where or what the target was, what sort of attack it might be or even how many attacks were planned, but the thinking was something big. Chemical, maybe even nuclear, either in LA, San Fran or possibly Seattle.

That's why they were here, hunting suspects in an effort to thwart a major terrorist attack on U.S. soil before it happened.

"Got a positive ID for three of them," Tuck said into his radio, talking to some of the AICs outside. Then he got on comms again. "All right, let's get this place secured and bring the forensics teams in here." He strode for the north door with a male prisoner in tow, hands bound behind him and a hood over his head.

Within minutes they had the building secured and all the tangos—dead and alive— handed over to another team of waiting FBI agents. Four dead and three captured, including the female Sawyer had apprehended. Portable fingerprint scanners confirmed that three of the men were on the Most Wanted list, all linked to the guy they were after—a Saudi national named Aziz.

A successful op all around, even if they hadn't yet found the chemical or nuclear weapons purported to be out there.

The team gathered at a building close to Boeing Field, where the company had given them permission to practice on an old 747 while they were in town. They'd been rehearsing a takedown on the aircraft when the intel had come in about the terrorists operating out of the warehouse.

Ethan appeared near the back of the group and Sawyer saw the mark on the left shoulder strap of his Kevlar vest where a round had either hit or ricocheted off him. "What happened to you?" he asked his buddy.

Ethan threw him a dark look as he removed his helmet. "Pretty self-explanatory, doncha think?"

The others smirked and Schroder, the team's medical expert, slapped him on the back. "It's all good, man. Even if it had gone through you'd be okay. Pretty close to the glenohumeral joint though. Would have messed up your career big time."

Ethan turned a quelling glare on Schroder.

Unfazed, the former PJ grinned and slapped him again. "Since Cruzie got himself shot, he buys the first round." The others all cheered. Ethan grumbled under his breath at them, but Sawyer could tell he didn't mind the teasing because of the half smirk on his lips.

They headed inside for debriefing with various officials and their commander, DeLuca. Over an hour later they piled into the two waiting Bureau-issued SUVs and headed back to the hotel where they were staying. Normally when training or conducting exercises with another unit they'd stay on a military base, which here meant Joint Base Lewis-McChord. But this time they'd been given the upgrade of a cushy hotel, two guys per room. As usual, Sawyer was rooming with Ethan.

In the back of the SUV while Bauer drove and Evers rode shotgun, Ethan grinned as he read whatever message he'd found on his phone.

"What?" Sawyer asked.

He started typing a response, that grin still quirking his lips. "Soli's here."

Ethan's fiancée. "Here, as in, Seattle?"

Ethan nodded. "Wanted to surprise me and I told her a few days ago we'd likely have the night off."

Lucky they'd just taken down a nest of tangos, then, and actually did have the night off. Unless something else came up. "You still coming out for dinner with us?"

"Yeah, I'm gonna text her the address once we get there and she'll meet us."

Looked like Sawyer was going to have a room to himself tonight. "Cool."

"Yeah." His smile was full of anticipation and Sawyer was glad for him. Marisol had given up her job with the U.S. Attorney's Office in Miami and moved in with Ethan just three days before the team had left for Seattle. But with this threat hanging over them, if Marisol had been Sawyer's fiancée, he'd have put her on a plane back to the East Coast that night. Better safe than sorry.

Up in the hotel room Sawyer stripped off his sweaty clothes and stepped under the cool spray of the shower, groaning in relief. It had been a long week and his right shoulder was bugging the hell out of him again from an old rotator cuff injury he'd sustained back in his SF days. He was only thirty-two but most days his body felt much older. Right now his shoulder felt like it was eighty.

It wasn't the worst kind of flare-up this time, thank God, otherwise he'd barely be able to move his arm at all. But if it got to the point that he couldn't perform as well as the others, he'd have to tell DeLuca, who would rightly pull him. He'd already been sidelined a year ago from a busted ankle and had no desire to be benched from the team again. So having the night off to chill and unwind with the guys was a blessing in itself.

He popped a couple anti-inflammatories before joining the others, then they drove to a place near the water. A two-story brick building near Safeco Field that had once been an old warehouse and now was one of the most popular places in the city to grab dinner and a beer or two. Music from the live blues band filtered out into the street as they approached the entrance.

At a table near the back where they all had clear sightlines of the place and easy access to the nearby exit— something they all did automatically—they settled in and ordered their food. The waitress brought out plate after plate of burgers, wings, beers and wood-fire oven pizzas. After he ate, Sawyer accepted a game of pool against Blackwell while Evers came over to watch and the others continued eating.

He'd just racked up the balls and taken his first shot when the front door opened and Marisol walked in looking like a little ray of sunshine in a bright yellow sundress. Ethan launched off his chair and rushed for her, the humungous smile on his face making Sawyer grin as well even as a strange pang twinged in his chest.

Something close to envy, but more like loneliness as he took in the happy reunion.

He watched his buddy pick Marisol up in a bear hug and twirl her around, both of them laughing, before he set her down and kissed her right in the middle of the restaurant. Over at the table some of the guys began whistling and shouting at them to get a room.

Marisol pulled away, blushing, and gave them a wave with a shy smile. Sawyer lifted a hand to wave back, set his pool cue down with the intent to go over and hug her, and stopped when his gaze slid to someone else slipping in the front door. A tingle of awareness started at the back of his neck and worked up to his scalp.

The woman emerged from the shadows into the dim lighting inside the pub and every muscle in Sawyer's body tightened as shock tore through him.

Ethan's sister.

The one woman who threatened his control, the woman he'd been trying like hell to forget about these past few months, was standing less than sixty feet away

15

from him. While his brain processed that impossible fact, he raked his gaze over her like a starved man, taking in every detail. And he couldn't look away.

Luscious. That was the only word that could come close to describing Carmela Cruz. Her height was the only average thing about her, because everything else drew his attention like steel shavings to a magnet.

Her long, chocolate-brown hair was loose in slight waves around her bronzed shoulders, that soft pink dress leaving her arms and calves bare to his ravenous gaze. And her curves. Sweet baby Jesus, her *curves*.

The generous swell of her breasts was outlined perfectly by the cut of her dress, which fit her snugly around the chest and waist before flaring out to drape over her hips and ended just below her knees. The outfit was pretty and feminine, could have been on the demure side on someone else, but on her it screamed sex.

She looked like a pin-up model and in those heels that accentuated the muscles in her lower legs, she was the hottest thing he'd ever seen. The confident set of her shoulders, the way she owned a room the moment she set foot in it, that worked for him in a major way.

Seeing her made him ache with the need to follow the shape of those curves with his hands, then his mouth, watch her beautiful golden-brown eyes go heavy-lidded with need and arousal while he stripped her slowly and revealed every inch of her smooth skin.

Never gonna happen, man. Get over it.

She headed toward the table. Ethan had stopped and turned back to her, a surprised smile on his face. Apparently he hadn't known she was coming either.

She hugged her brother, smiled at whatever Ethan said, then followed him toward the table, glancing around the bar as she walked. Sawyer stood rooted to the spot, practically paralyzed with a combination of dread and excitement, heart thudding with it.

The last time they'd seen each other he'd crossed a line he never should have crossed and kissed her at that hospital in Miami. Since then things had been…awkward between them, to say the least.

And Ethan didn't know about it. Could never know. If he found out there'd be hell to pay and Sawyer would lose everyone he—

His gut twisted at the thought. *No.* He couldn't let that happen. Not ever.

As if sensing his stare, Carmela glanced over and spotted him beside the pool table. Her stride faltered for an instant. Then she put on a smile he could tell was forced and nodded at him once before turning her head and walking on by without a second glance.

The combination of her stiffness and that dismissal made him feel even shittier.

He watched her glide past him, a sense of dread invading him.

At the hospital that day he'd wanted way more than a kiss from her, and he was pretty sure she'd wanted to give him more, but they couldn't have it. And since then he'd been careful to keep his distance from her. She'd obviously taken the hint because she hadn't e-mailed or called once, when they'd normally talked at least once a week and had for almost two years.

He felt like shit about that too.

"You wanna take a break?"

Sawyer glanced over at Blackwell, who was standing next to the pool table waiting for Sawyer to take his turn. He could tell from his teammate's wry grin that he'd seen why Sawyer's concentration was shot all to hell. "In a minute, yeah. I'll take my shot, then go say hi."

He rounded the end of the table to take his shot, his hand curled around his pool cue, fingers clenching tight as an ache bloomed in the center of his chest. Christ, he'd made a hell of a mess of things. He couldn't undo what he'd already done, and to be fair to her he knew he should just let it be, let her think he didn't want anything more to do with her.

Problem was, that was a lie he wasn't prepared to live with.

Chapter Two

C armela hugged her shocked brother and tried to pretend that Sawyer wasn't standing in the corner of the pub, just forty feet away. But he was, and the image of him was now seared into her brain.

Wearing his trademark black Stetson and at over six feet tall, he was impossible to miss. Combined with that white T-shirt that emphasized the rich brown of his skin and hugged every inch of his muscular torso and a pair of faded jeans that clung to his powerful thighs, he was mouthwatering.

She could feel the weight of his dark brown stare from clear across the room. The back of her neck tingled with an awareness she was determined to ignore but her stomach buzzed with nerves.

Ethan released her and stepped back with a grin. "What are you doing here?"

"She dragged me along for the ride," Carmela said, throwing a pointed look at Marisol. Marisol had begged her to come to the pub, and to be fair, Marisol had no idea about the tension between her and Sawyer.

Carmela hadn't said anything and was still ecstatic

that Marisol and her brother had gotten together in the first place. So when he'd called home a week ago to inform her and her mom that they'd gotten engaged, they'd both started crying, thrilled that Ethan had chosen someone as awesome as Soli. Also, Carmela knew she was lucky to have a future sister-in-law she'd known for most of her life, let alone someone she genuinely adored.

Ethan blinked at her in surprise. "Really? You flew all the way to Seattle just to see me?"

"No, other way around," Marisol laughed, winding an arm around his waist and resting her cheek on his chest as he hugged her close. Her brand new diamond engagement ring sparkled in the lights hanging above the bar. "She was flying here anyway, and since I knew you'd be here a couple more days I decided to tag along to surprise you."

"You made my whole week." Ethan squeezed his fiancée and threw Carmela a curious look. "So what did you come to Seattle for? Business?"

"No, I'm taking Mom on a cruise to Alaska. It was a last minute thing," she added when her brother's eyebrows shot up. "My company offered it to me on Wednesday as a reward for being their top pharmaceutical rep last month." She shrugged. She'd been in a kind of funk lately over the whole Sawyer thing and hoped this would help get her out of it. "So I took it."

"Wow, that's awesome, Carm."

"Yeah, Mom's pretty excited."

"What, and you're not?"

Sawyer was still over there in by the pool table watching her, she could see him out of the corner of her eye. She refused to acknowledge him again. He'd already hurt her once and she wasn't going to give him the opportunity to do it again. "I'm looking forward to a holiday and spending time with Mom one-on-one, but you know I don't like being on a boat. I only accepted it because she's always wanted to go on a cruise."

He laughed. "Well this time your 'boat' is huge, so you'll barely notice it moving. Are you going up the Inside Passage?"

"Yes. One way up to Anchorage, then we're flying back."

"Then you won't have a problem with rough water or motion sickness for most of the cruise, since you'll be in sheltered waters until you head out on the last leg to Anchorage. And the weather's pretty good this time of year anyhow. You'll be fine."

"Yeah, it'll be great." Mostly she just hoped the Alaskan ports of call and spectacular scenery would help take her mind off her bruised heart so she could get back to being her happy self again. Because she'd felt anything but bubbly lately, and her friends and coworkers had noticed.

She'd been going nuts at home in Miami, coming back to an empty apartment every night, tormenting herself by remembering every detail about the man she'd stupidly gone and fallen in love with over the past year. So stupid of her.

One-sided love was the *worst* and she had nobody to blame for this situation but herself. Looking back, Sawyer had never given any indication that he wanted anything more than friendship. But he also hadn't discouraged her when she'd begun flirting with him after he'd broken up with his ex-fiancée. It had given her hope.

And then he'd gone and kissed her. To shut her up.

The humiliation was almost as painful as the ache in her heart. Since that day they hadn't said a word to each other.

Normally they exchanged e-mails, texted or talked on the phone at least once a week, even before his breakup with Trina. Just checking in with each other, sharing jokes, talking about their favorite TV show. They used to text each other after every episode on Sunday nights to discuss the zombie apocalypse neither one of them could get enough of. Other times she'd tell him something funny about her day, maybe something her mom had done.

So many times she'd thought of him these past few months, picked up her phone to shoot him a message and then remembered they were no longer close and stopped herself. Since that shut-up-kiss, there'd been total radio silence from him. And she sure as hell wasn't going to be the one to reach out now.

"Have you guys eaten?" Ethan asked her and Marisol, steering them both to the table where some of his teammates sat. Carmela knew them all, since they'd been to her mom's place in Miami back in June for a cookout.

"No, and we're starving," Carmela answered. She took a seat in the chair Schroder pulled out for her, and after they gave their orders, set about making small talk with the guys until the waitress brought their food out.

She ate her spinach salad with bacon and barbecued chicken in silence, painfully aware that Sawyer was now seated at the far end of the long table. He just had this…presence about him that made him impossible to ignore.

When she glanced up and caught him watching her again, she quickly averted her gaze. It hurt way too much to look at him. The small, white gold crucifix necklace he'd given her last Christmas seemed heavy against her skin. It was such a sweet gift, something beautiful just from him and a respectful acknowledgment of her Catholic faith, she couldn't bear to take it off even if they weren't on speaking terms anymore.

Ten more minutes, she told herself. That was all she had to get through. She'd finish her meal, put on a smile, say goodbye to everyone, and catch a cab back to the hotel where she could finally relax. Maybe she'd go down to the pool and soak in the hot tub for a bit.

Suddenly Sawyer got up and rounded the end of the table. A quick glance his way warned her he was headed straight for her.

Her stomach fisted tight and she had to force the bite of salad down her throat.

He dragged a chair over from the next table, insinuating himself between her and Marisol. She stiffened as he swung it around and straddled the seat in a casual, masculine pose, resting his thick forearms along the back.

Close enough that there was no way she could ignore him without coming off as a total bitch in front of the others. Then they'd all know something was up and wonder why, and Ethan would start asking questions she'd be forced to lie about.

No thank you. Right now her brother was too wrapped up in Soli to notice something was wrong between her and Sawyer and she hoped it stayed that way.

Sawyer's big frame seemed to take up all the space beside her, making every cell in her body vibrate with his nearness. His clean, citrusy scent teased her, his sheer size and presence making it impossible to avoid looking at him. When she finally glanced over and met that espresso-brown gaze, a jagged pain tore through her chest. God, the sight of him was like a punch to her senses.

"Hey," he said softly.

"Hey," she answered, her tone wooden. She would be polite, but no more than that. He'd hurt her, plain and simple, and hadn't done a damn thing to rectify that. She wasn't willing to pretend they were still friends, not even to avoid Ethan's wrath if he suspected something was up between them and started digging until he found out why.

Fortunately he was still too busy making googly-eyes at his fiancée at the moment to be paying any attention to her. Or anyone else at the table, for that matter.

"So, what brings you to Seattle?" Sawyer asked, the deep timbre of his voice making her belly flip-flop.

"Alaskan cruise with my mom." For appearance's sake she gave him an abbreviated version of what she'd told Ethan and left it at that, glancing around the table so she wouldn't have to look at him any longer than necessary. Oh yeah, she definitely needed a holiday, time to put aside the sadness that had been hanging over her like a little black cloud these past months.

"Oh, wow, that's good. When does it leave?"

There was no way he didn't notice her disinterest in talking to him. He was pressing because he wanted her to stop freezing him out. Why? Because he couldn't stand the thought of her being mad at him? *Too bad, buddy. You do the crime, you do the time.* She wasn't a woman willing to allow any man to treat her the way he had. "Saturday afternoon."

In her peripheral she saw him nod. "I've always wanted to take that trip. Been to Alaska for mountain training before a couple times, back when I was in the Army. Not the same as having a vacation there though."

She realized he was extending a verbal peace offering, even put a smile in his voice. Trying to mend the damage he'd done, wanting to just pretend it had never happened and carry on as if everything was normal.

Well too bad for him, because it *had* happened. And dammit, she hated that he'd been totally unaffected by that kiss when she'd been just the opposite. The moment his lips touched hers, the entire world had shifted on its axis for her, a year's worth of pent-up longing exploding in a single moment of pure bliss. It had taken her only a moment once he'd lifted his head to realize it was anything but the first kiss she'd fantasized about sharing with him.

"No, I guess not." She grabbed her sparkling water and took a few sips, but it didn't ease the dryness in her throat. Why had she let Marisol talk her into coming down here?

A taut, uncomfortable silence spread between them. They both focused on other conversations going on around them but didn't join in, and the awkwardness grew until it was nearly unbearable.

She shifted in her chair, her entire body stiff. God, she couldn't do this, pretend she didn't care and didn't still want him.

She breathed a sigh of relief when the band on stage started up at last, filling the tense void with music. A solid rock and roll beat pulsed through the bar, drawing couples onto the dance floor, including Ethan and Marisol.

Carmela watched them for a minute and tried to suppress the pang of envy she felt. Watching her brother dance with the love of his life, both of them smiling and lost in each other, only emphasized how much she craved the same and how she'd dreamed of finding it with Sawyer. Which only made her feel even more stupid.

A few minutes later, several of the guys stood up and waved their goodbyes to her. It was still early evening but apparently they had other plans because Tuck, the team leader, came over and bent to shout at Sawyer over the loud music, his dark blond hair glinting in the overhead lights.

"We're heading out. You coming?"

Sawyer shook his head. "Nah, think I'll stay for a bit. I'll catch a ride back with Cruzie later."

A ball of dread formed in Carmela's stomach. If he'd just leave, she'd be able to relax and try to enjoy the rest of the night without having her stomach in knots. Surely he didn't expect her to just hang out with him like old times after what had happened?

"Sure." Tuck handed him a set of keys and followed the others out of the building.

Then Sawyer half turned in his seat to shift his

attention to her.

Before he could say anything Carmela grabbed her purse from where she'd slung it over the back of her chair, and stood. "I'm going too."

She'd catch a cab back to the hotel. She had no desire to sit here like a fifth wheel and watch her brother bask in true love's bliss while she was totally miserable and the object of her unrequited love was right next to her, rubbing imaginary salt into her invisible wound.

Sawyer surprised her by reaching out and grasping her forearm gently. "Wait."

His touch froze her. Made every muscle in her body tighten.

She stilled, swallowing at the invisible sparks that shot up her arm and made her nipples tighten against the cups of her bra. The sexy black lace push-up bra she'd worn purposely beneath the dress she had on, the one that pushed up her girls and showed off her best physical…assets. If she had to see Sawyer tonight, she'd wanted him to see exactly what he was missing. Not exactly mature of her, but there it was. And he could plainly see she was still wearing his necklace.

"Don't go," he said.

Gathering her nerve, she forced herself to meet his gaze. "I should leave. I'm tired."

His grip tightened a little. Not so much that it hurt, but there was a definite command to it. And maybe a plea as well. "Carm. Stay a while longer."

She raised an eyebrow, refusing to cave to the earnestness on his face. "Why?" She wasn't going to make this easy on him.

He knew she'd been into him and he'd not only played with her emotions, something she'd never imagined he'd do, but then cut all contact afterward. No, she hadn't contacted him either, but in light of how things had ended, he should have been the one to reach out. She wasn't going to put her heart out there so he could stomp on it a second time.

"Because it's been too long since we've seen each other," he said over the music, then added, "and because we need to talk." To his credit, he didn't look away as he said it.

She hadn't expected him to be so direct.

She opened her mouth to say that's the last thing on earth she wanted to do, but that look on his face stopped her. He might be over six feet and be built like an NFL linebacker, but he had an inner softness to him that turned her to mush whenever he let her see it. Right now those dark brown eyes reminded her of a puppy dog's. And in that moment she remembered all the times he'd spent with her and her family in Miami, when he and Ethan could get the time off.

Christmas. Easter. Her last birthday when Sawyer had surprised her two days later by showing up at her door with a cupcake he'd grabbed at the store, a pink candle burning in the center. Trips to the beach together with Ethan. Going to a Dolphins game together. Staying up way too late and laughing together while they all played poker or Risk as a family. Special times that forged a bond she couldn't ignore, let alone forget.

Dammit, she thought with a sigh. Upset as she was, she didn't have the heart to say something nasty just to hurt him back and then walk away. She couldn't do that to him.

"I don't think that's a good idea," she told him instead over the music. At this volume, they couldn't have a meaningful conversation even if she'd been willing to.

He scooted his chair closer and swiveled it to face her fully, his knees almost touching hers. She would have backed up but he still had hold of her arm. "We need to talk," he told her.

He was right, but she wasn't in the mood for this

conversation right now. *I'm sorry, Carm, I never should have kissed you. Can we still be friends?*

No thank you. She sent a longing glance toward the front doors.

His long fingers wrapped around her wrist now, and he leaned in until his mouthwatering scent filled the space between them. Lemon and something else spicy that was uniquely him.

The low pitch of his voice resonated deep inside her as he spoke close to her ear. "Please, Carm," he murmured, his grip on her arm gentling, almost a caress.

He was so big and powerful, yet always gentle with her. His touch used to give her butterflies. Now it made her ache for what would never be and what she could never have. And that *please* hit her square in her stupid, squishy heart.

She reluctantly lowered herself into her chair once more, then glanced over her shoulder. Out on the dance floor, Ethan and Marisol were still completely lost in their own world. She could leave now but it might make Ethan suspicious that something was wrong.

Exhaling, she gave Sawyer a stiff nod. "Fine, but not here." Better to go someplace where they could have at least a semblance of privacy and get this over with so they could both put it behind them.

"Then come on," he said, releasing her as he stood, the brim of his hat casting a shadow over his face.

Ignoring the hand he offered to help her up, she pushed to her feet and headed for the door without looking back, all too aware of how closely he followed behind her.

****

Surabaya, Java
As usual, his visit home had passed far too quickly.

Wira Tedja patted his elderly mother's hand and pushed from the edge of the bed to his feet, a familiar heaviness settling in his chest. She'd begun to go downhill right after Leo disappeared last year but she'd gotten so weak the past few days, it worried him.

Looking at her now, it was impossible to ignore the possibility that this might be the last time he saw her. In the morning he'd be on another plane headed back to the States. The day after that he'd report to the docks and board the cruise liner for another contract at sea.

Ten months of twelve-hour long shifts, with only a half day off per week. Ten months of sleeping in the crowded bowel of the cruise ship and helping keep rich westerners safe during their lavish vacation. They made him sick.

"I'll miss you," his mother said with a sad smile, her voice weak.

"I'll miss you too. But don't worry, you know I'll contact you whenever I get the chance."

Her eyes shone with the unswerving love that had made her such a phenomenal mother, and person in general. "You're so good to me."

He shrugged off the praise. She was counting on him and he would not fail her. "You're my mother."

Those deep brown eyes glistened with tears. "You're a good man, Wira. I'm so proud of you."

He glanced away as guilt seeped into his heart. She'd raised him to be a good, loving man. This upcoming mission went against all that, but there was no other choice. This was the only way.

Putting on a smile, he turned his gaze on her once more. "Do you need anything before I leave?"

"No. Your brothers are here to help me. And we all appreciate the sacrifices you make for the rest of us."

His job, she meant, and the long absences from home. A job he hated but kept taking because of the money. The pay was good and he sent almost every bit of it home to support his mother and younger brothers. The only two brothers he had left.

You don't know that for sure. Leo could still be alive. He prayed it was so, that the mission wouldn't come too late. "You've all made plenty of sacrifices too," he said.

She inclined her head, looking exhausted. Her face was pale and she had dark circles beneath her eyes. The doctors hadn't found anything to explain why she'd suddenly deteriorated like this. Even though they insisted it wasn't, he was still concerned it might be cancer and they just hadn't been able to detect it yet. "Yes. May God be with you, my son."

"And with you."

He slipped from the house and stepped into the front garden, breathing in a deep lungful of the fragrant evening air. His childhood home was small, but he was deeply attached to the little bungalow with its walled yard. Other than her sons and her devotion to God, the garden was his mother's pride and joy. Banana trees, palms and a plumeria in the corner provided privacy and structure, and the many orchids his mother favored bloomed in a riot of color all over the yard.

His brothers would be back from the market soon. He wanted to be long gone by then. He didn't like drawn-out goodbyes, and since this might be the last time he saw his family, he didn't want to tip any of them off that something was wrong. They had no idea what he was about to do.

Casting one last look at the house from the sidewalk, he drank in the sight of it, committing every detail to memory before walking to his car. He'd just climbed behind the wheel when his phone rang. He didn't recognize the number, but the country code told him it had to be someone from the organization, so he answered.

"When do you leave?" the man asked, someone Wira had spoken to several times before. They always spoke in English, since it was common to them both. Wira spoke it fluently in addition to Javanese, Malay and some French, but no Arabic as this man did.

"In the morning. I'll be in the States by tomorrow night, Pacific time."

"Good. And what about the others?"

"Either en route or already there. We board Saturday morning." As a long-time and trusted member of the cruise line staff, he had some authority in terms of who was placed under his command. For this voyage he'd made sure to select two members of their group to be on his team. Men he knew personally from secretly training with in a militant camp outside of Jakarta last year.

But someone powerful behind the scenes had been pulling strings to make this operation possible as well. The *Mawla*. The figurehead of this cell, respected and revered by all, but especially by him.

This particular cruise happened to have the highest density of their members on the crew, which is why the organization had chosen this one, with the added bonus of some of the passengers on board and the timing. Several American fat cats were scheduled to be aboard, all the better to leverage ransom with if they decided to go that route. And the anniversary of 9/11 was next week. The significance of the date would give their message even more media attention around the world.

His contact made a satisfied noise. "Your equipment has already arrived in port and is scheduled to be loaded at the time given in our last correspondence."

"Perfect." He glanced around to make sure no one was watching him. So far he hadn't noticed anything unusual, but he couldn't be too careful. One slip up, one whisper in the international intelligence community and he'd either wind up dead or face the same fate as Leo.

Taken in the middle of the night by American commandos and whisked to a secret CIA "black" holding facility somewhere in Eastern Europe.

The U.S. continually denied the existence of such places, but a few had recently come to light in places like Vilnius, Lithuania. Though the Americans kept denying they had anything to do with Leo's disappearance, Wira knew better.

They were only half-brothers, both having different fathers. Wira's mother had given birth to Leo when she was very young and unmarried. Leo's father had taken him away shortly after he'd been born, and Wira's mother hadn't seen him until a few years ago when Leo had reestablished contact with her.

Half-siblings or not, Wira had instantly bonded with his older brother, who'd been a huge influence in his life ever since. They believed in the same things and thought the same way. Because of his ties to an Indonesian terror group Leo had been on the U.S. terror watch list for months before he was taken, but since he and Wira had different surnames and hadn't grown up together, so far Wira had managed to avoid any attention from authorities.

Their mistake. Now he had new and powerful allies around the globe helping him.

The Americans might deny being involved with Leo's disappearance, but the Russians had video evidence of a group of heavily armed men in military-style fatigues taking a group of hooded prisoners into an abandoned building in the outskirts of Riga, Latvia. The Russians had enough evidence to believe that one of them was Leo.

"I'm ready," Wira told his contact. He would either get to Riga and free his brother personally along with his hand-picked team, or die trying.

And if he died on this mission, at least his death would shine a spotlight on his brother's disappearance. People would demand answers. If Leo was still alive, maybe after this incident there would be enough pressure that the Americans would release him.

"I'll be in touch before I board the ship," he said.

"May the blessings of Allah be upon you, brother."

"And you also."

After tucking his phone back into his jacket pocket, Wira started the engine and pulled away from the curb, heading for the airport where he'd spend the night before catching his flight overseas.

The Alaskan cruise season lasted from May to late September and he'd endured it a dozen times before. But this last voyage would be unlike any other he'd ever taken.

A little over a week from now, he'd finally get his revenge. And maybe, just maybe, he'd see his brother again.

Chapter Three

S hit, he'd hurt her. More than he'd realized, and hurting Carmela was the last thing he'd ever intended. Even if he'd been the one to allow the distance between them to grow to this extent. That bothered him. He wanted back what he'd lost—her trust and friendship. She was important to him, he missed being able to talk to her, missed the way they used to be so comfortable around each other.

You blew that all to hell when you put your mouth on hers.

Sawyer stayed close to her as they exited the pub and stepped out into the cool night air. The sun had set so it had a damp, chilly edge to it, and he could smell the briny scent of the water close by.

Carmela got as far as the sidewalk before stopping and looking back at him. She had her arms wrapped around her ribs, a purely defensive gesture that pierced him with sharp little needles of guilt. He didn't ever want her feeling like she had to protect herself from him.

He had no intention of talking to her out here in plain

view of anyone that cared to watch, and he didn't want to take the chance that Ethan would come looking for either of them to see what was going on. Sawyer had told him on the way out that he was driving Carmela back to the hotel, but maybe his worries were unfounded because Ethan had barely been able to tear his attention off Marisol long enough to nod at him.

"Truck's parked over that way," he said, jerking his chin down the street behind her.

She threw him an are-you-kidding-me look. "You think I want to get into a vehicle with you right now?" Normally she gestured with her hands a lot while she spoke, especially when she got excited or worked up about something, and he missed that animated quirk now. Now she was reserved, hesitant around him, still had her arms wrapped around herself.

"I think you'd rather talk in private than out here in the open."

She cast a glance around at the people walking on the sidewalk nearby, and relented with a muttered, "Fine."

Sawyer walked past her and led the way toward the parking garage where they'd left one of the SUVs earlier, frantically thinking of what the hell to say to ease this tension between them. He'd gotten so used to Carm being open and friendly—okay, more than friendly—with him, this cool and aloof side of her drove him nuts. He'd allowed it because he kept telling himself that her distancing herself from him was for the best.

But now he realized he was at risk of losing her for good, and that was something he couldn't handle.

Her heels clicked on the pavement as she walked a few steps behind him. He wanted her beside him where she belonged but didn't say anything. He knew he had to apologize for his behavior, but didn't know how much else he should tell her. The less she knew about his true feelings, the better. Talking about deep, emotional stuff wasn't his strong suit at the best of times.

In all honesty, he was far more comfortable talking to a group of village elders in the most remote part of Afghanistan than he was trying to defuse a situation like this with a woman he cared about. Just one of the many reasons why he'd broken up with Trina; her constant complaints, criticism, and demands for him to become something he wasn't had begun to make him resentful. And thankfully he'd been smart enough to realize that meant he needed to walk away, before it was too late.

He'd just never expected the fallout that came afterward.

He turned sideways to allow a couple to squeeze past him on the sidewalk and took a right down a side street toward the parking garage. When he reached it he opened the door for the stairwell and held it for her. Carmela studiously avoided looking at him as she stepped past, giving him a wide berth so he could lead the way up the stairs.

Halfway to the fourth floor, the metal door above suddenly banged open and angry male voices reached them.

"Stay the fuck away from me!"

"Come back here, asshole," another man growled in reply.

Carmela stopped dead and Sawyer turned back to her, automatically placing himself between her and the men above them. Grunts and the sounds of shuffling feet told him a scuffle had broken out.

Without a word he put a hand on the center of Carmela's back and propelled her back the way they'd come. Before they'd taken three steps, a man tumbled down the concrete steps behind them. He hit the landing with a thud and quickly jumped to his feet, a pained grimace on his face.

His clothes were dirty and worn, and his hair and

beard were unkempt. He froze when he saw Sawyer there, darted a glance between him and whoever had just thrown him down the steps.

And then that feral gaze locked on Sawyer and the desperate light he saw there put him on immediate alert.

"What are you looking at, asshole?" the man sneered. Blood seeped down his cheek from a cut near his right eyebrow, and his eyes were bloodshot, the pupils unnaturally dilated. Definitely high on something, and from the looks of the lesions on his face, Sawyer was betting crystal meth.

The man's hand swept upward, the overhead light glinting off the switchblade he held in his fist.

Sawyer tensed and Carmela sucked in a breath behind him. He was armed but he would only draw his weapon as a last resort because if he drew it, it meant he intended to fire. And if he fired, it would be to kill. If things got ugly, he didn't want Carmela to see any of that.

"Carm, get outside," he commanded in a low voice, never taking his eyes off the guy. He wanted her to get to safety so he could defuse this without having to reach for the weapon at the small of his back.

A second man suddenly stuck his head over the side of the railing to see what was going on. When he saw Sawyer blocking the other guy's path, his smile was pure evil.

Carmela still hadn't moved but Sawyer couldn't risk taking his eyes off the man in front of him. A sheen of sweat beaded the guy's upper lip and forehead and his eyes had a frantic light to them now. He was either going to try to shove past Sawyer and Carmela, or run the gauntlet of the man waiting for him above.

Sawyer slowly raised his hands in a non-threatening gesture and took a step back, not bothering to say anything. Words would only escalate the situation, since the guy was already freaked and obviously not operating with a full deck.

Carmela moved with him, one hand fisting the back of his leather jacket. He wished she'd run when he'd told her, but he wasn't surprised that she was still there. Carmela wasn't the type to bail if she thought someone needed her, no matter the danger. Part of him admired the hell out of that. The other part wanted her as far away from this unstable asshole as she could get.

The trapped man's gaze darted between Sawyer and the threat waiting above, weighing his options. Sawyer knew the moment he made the decision to run at them.

Carmela had only taken a step when the guy suddenly whirled and lunged down the stairs toward them, blade held high in one dirty fist.

"Look out," she cried, but Sawyer was already moving.

He twisted to push her out of the way with his body and turned to confront the threat, knocking his hat free so the brim wouldn't impede his vision. This asshole wasn't getting past him with Carmela standing unprotected a few feet away. The man snarled and swiped the blade at him. Sawyer jerked backward, narrowly avoiding the knife as it sliced past his chest in a wicked arc.

"No!" Carmela lunged for him, grabbed the back of his jacket again and pulled hard.

Sawyer bit back a curse but couldn't risk taking his attention off the attacker to push her out of harm's way. Rage exploded inside him when the man slashed the blade toward him again, this time managing to slice across his left shoulder.

He barely felt the burn, all his focus on taking this bastard down before he hurt Carmela. Before the guy could bring his hand back up for another try, Sawyer stepped in close to take away his leverage and grabbed his knife arm in a bruising grip. The man shouted in surprise and pain as Sawyer wrenched it up and back in a quick twist, at the same time pivoting to lock his free arm around the man's neck and squeezing tight.

The knife hit the ground and bounced down the first couple of steps. Carmela finally let go of Sawyer's jacket and ran down to kick it away from them, sending it clattering to the floor beside the door.

Locked in Sawyer's grip, the man clawed at Sawyer's arm with his free hand, his face turning bright red as the circulation to his brain was cut off. Sawyer held the blood choke, dividing his attention between Carmela, standing on the lower landing, her wide eyes locked on him, and the other man above him.

The man in his hold struggled for a few seconds longer but quickly grew weak. As soon as he sagged, Sawyer dropped him where he stood then whirled and headed for Carmela. She'd backed herself against the concrete wall, her eyes huge.

He reached down with his good arm to snag his hat. "Come on," he told her, taking her by the forearm on his way to the door. No telling what that guy would do when he gained consciousness, and Sawyer had no interest in sticking around to see if the other guy came after them now.

She didn't argue, jogging alongside him in her heels to keep up with his quick strides. He hurried around to the front entrance and took the ramp this time to the level the SUV was parked on.

Using the keyfob he remotely unlocked the doors and put her in the front passenger seat, still keeping an eye on their surroundings. No one was coming after them yet but that didn't mean they were clear if that second guy had a gun and was hiding somewhere waiting to take a potshot at them.

He slid behind the wheel and shut the door, removing his pistol from the holster at the small of his back and placing it on the center console before starting the engine.

He and the others always combat parked to save time in case they needed to make a hasty exit, and it came in handy in cases like this.

No other cars were waiting in line at the exit, but until he made it out onto the street safely the danger wasn't over yet. He lowered his window partway to get the ticket in, his gaze darting toward the entrance to the stairwell. The automated arm began to lift just as the stairwell door pushed open and Sawyer recognized the second man. He was staring at them intently and there was something in his hand.

Sawyer reached out to grab the back of Carmela's head. "Get down," he barked, stomping on the accelerator and raised the window just as a bullet hit the back window with a crack. Carmela cried out and bent lower in her seat.

He shifted his hand to her upper back and pushed downward as he tore out of the garage with a squeal of tires. Pedestrians jumped out of the way and yelled but Sawyer didn't even glance at them.

As soon as they were partway up the street, he relaxed a little. A quick glance in the rearview showed their tail was clear so he let go of Carmela and pulled out his phone. She sat up, swiveling around to look at where the bullet had impacted the rear window.

"Glass is bullet resistant," he said. And thank God for that. She turned her eyes on him and wrapped her arms around herself. "You okay?"

She nodded once, face pale, and raked her gaze over him as she dug out her cell phone. "We need to call the—" She gasped and reached across him for his left arm. He twitched. "You're bleeding."

He glanced down at his left shoulder. It stung, but the knife hadn't done any serious damage. "I'm fine."

"Like hell you are," she argued, peeling his jacket off. He covered a wince as the wound burned. She leaned across him to get a better look, the position awkward.

"Okay, that's deep," she murmured, sitting up to dig in her purse for something.

"I've got to report this to the cops." When he stopped for the next red light he looked down. The wound was deeper than he'd realized, about seven inches long because of the way the blade had sliced along his skin, and bleeding enough that pressure wasn't going to stop it completely.

Hell.

Carmela scooted beneath his right arm and leaned across him to press a wad of tissues to his shoulder. It was sweet of her to take care of him, but Kleenex wasn't going to do the trick. Also, he had no intention of spending hours in an ER just to get a few sutures. Thankfully he had options. He'd talk to the cops, get stitched up, then call his commander.

Ignoring Carmela's efforts to stop the bleeding, he picked up his cell and dialed 911. After reporting what had happened, giving his information and agreeing to meet with officers back at the hotel while he was receiving medical treatment, he called Schroder. "Hey, Doc, I need a favor," he said when the former PJ answered.

"Sure, what's up?"

"I think I need a couple stitches." Carmela's gaze flashed upward, her expression one of consternation. Okay, maybe more than a couple stitches.

Silence for a moment. "What happened?"

"Got too close to a switchblade."

"What? Who'd you piss off in the twenty minutes since I last saw you?"

"Some junkie in the parking lot stairwell." Cops were en route now to hunt the assholes down. "Can you meet me in my hotel room? I don't want the guys knowing about this yet." They'd find out soon enough but he didn't want any more drama than they'd already had tonight.

And he sure as hell wanted DeLuca to find out from him, not one of the guys. He didn't think the knife wound would keep him sidelined, but until Doc verified that, he wanted to downplay the situation to their commander, just in case.

"Sure, man. Text me when you get here."

"Roger that." He ended the call and set the phone into the cup holder, then switched his grip so that his right hand was back on the wheel again.

Carmela grunted in annoyance, a fierce frown on her face as she tried to stem the bleeding. Her fingers were already stained red and he could feel the blood seeping down his arm, over his ribs. "Think you can stop using this arm for a few minutes now?" she said, her voice testy.

"Yeah." He didn't tell her to stop the pressure or not to worry about him. She was a caretaker and he knew that giving her the chance to do something to help was way more therapeutic than any words he could offer right now. "Well, there's no way to hide that bullet hole in the window. I'm gonna have to make an official report to the Bureau as well."

She nodded, her gaze still on where she was pressing tissues to the cut. "I know."

He glanced down at her. "Not exactly how I wanted to spend our time together tonight."

Her lips quirked in a small smile. "Well, tough. And why the hell did you confront him like that instead of just getting out the door? He could have stabbed you in the neck or the chest." Her voice shook a little but the pressure of her fingers was steady. He knew she'd seen her fair share of blood in her work as a senior orthopedic specialist when she went into the operating room with the surgeons to show them how her company's surgical implants worked.

The chances of that meth-head doing him serious damage was unlikely, given Sawyer's training, but he didn't say it aloud. She was shaken, no matter how well she was holding it together.

He wanted to put his arm around her and draw her close to comfort her but didn't dare. Things were too fragile between them now. He had to be careful in how he handled this.

"Because I didn't want you to get hurt," he answered.

Her eyes flashed up to his again. "What?"

He drew in a breath, seeking patience. "If he got past me, he could have hurt you. That wasn't happening."

Something softened in her gaze. She shook her head and turned her attention back to slowing the bleeding. "Sometimes I think you forget the neighborhood I grew up in. I was ready to kick him in the balls if he came close enough, but thank you. And I'm mad at you for getting sliced up to protect me."

He hid a smile. Annoyed and talking to him was a million times better than hurt and silent. "How mad? Madder than you already were before the whole parking garage thing?" At least she still wore his necklace. She didn't hate him so much that she'd gotten rid of it.

"Different kind of mad," she answered, and he respected that she didn't dance around it or try to deny that she had a problem with him.

"So I'm really in the doghouse then, huh?" he said after a moment. The hotel was only a few blocks away now.

One side of her mouth quirked up. "Yeah. And you're making it worse every time you move and bleed more."

"Sorry," he mumbled, and made an effort to stay still for her. Neither of them said anything more for a few minutes. Hell, he couldn't stand knowing he'd hurt her. He might as well just clear the air once and for all, start a meaningful dialogue between them. "Look, about what happened at the hospital—"

43

She made a negative sound and shook her head. "Can we not do this right now? You're bleeding all over the seat and it's pretty much all I can think about at the moment. Give me at least until after Schroder fixes you up and we talk to the police before you go there."

Much as he'd rather avoid this conversation altogether, his instinct was not to let this go yet. But she seemed pretty upset about him getting sliced and he didn't want to make it worse for her. "Okay."

As long as he knew he had a shot at resolving this mess before the night was over, he could wait a little while longer.

Chapter Four

Cops and forensics people were crowded around the damaged SUV in the underground parking lot of their hotel. A flash strobed as someone took a series of pictures of the damage.

Special Agent Adam Blackwell let out a low whistle when he finally saw the mark where the bullet had impacted the rear window of their Bureau-issued SUV. Dead center on the driver's side. Large caliber, for a pistol. Looked like it might be from a .45. "Holy shit."

When Vance had told him and Evers that someone had taken a potshot at them at the parking garage downtown, Adam hadn't expected this. If not for the bullet-resistant glass, Vance might have suffered something far more serious than the gash he was currently having sutured upstairs, which was bad enough.

"Whoa." Evers stepped closer to get a glimpse of the damage, then circled the back of the vehicle, looking for other marks while staying out of the cops' way. Adam hadn't noticed any other bullet holes but he hadn't given the SUV a thorough once-over because of the officers busy cataloguing the damage and taking samples and pictures as evidence for their investigation. "That's not what I was picturing when Vance said they'd had a run-in with someone."

Yeah, me neither.

When one of the forensics guys moved aside for a moment, Adam peered into the open driver's side door and immediately saw the drying blood streaks on the seat. More blood stained the floor mat in the foot well. Ethan's sister had told him the worst of the blood was on Vance, but the interior was going to need a deep clean once they took it in.

He stepped back, moving out of the way and pulled out his ID to show the cop coming toward him. Someone else had already checked their ID when they'd come out of the stairwell. The officer checked it again now, looked at him to verify, and nodded. "You guys taking her back to the Bureau when we're done?" He indicated the SUV with a nod.

"That's the plan."

"Almost done here. Shouldn't be too much longer, just a few minutes."

"No worries." Adam looked at Evers. "Wanna grab a coffee or something while we wait?" There was a café around the corner. They could grab something and be back within ten minutes, tops.

"Sure."

They were partway up the ramp to the exit when a large SUV pulled up at the curb just outside the underground parking.

The Suburban came through the gate, slowed to a stop, then the back door opened. Supervisory Special Agent Matt DeLuca stepped out. He'd no doubt heard about the situation from Vance by now. Adam and Evers stopped and waited for him.

DeLuca walked toward them as two other men Adam didn't recognize slid out of the vehicle and headed for the stairwell entrance. "What's up, boys?" he said to him and Evers.

His smile surprised Adam, given that Vance had been sliced up. "Just waiting to run the SUV back," Adam said.

DeLuca looked confused. "Back? Back where?"

Adam frowned. "To the Seattle office."

DeLuca frowned too and continued past them, following the other two men up the ramp toward the stairwell entrance. "Meeting tomorrow at oh-seven-hundred. Tell the guys to—" He stopped suddenly, his gaze zeroing in on the crowd of cops surrounding their SUV, now visible from his position on the ramp.

Before Adam could think of what to say, DeLuca swung around and divided a hard look between him and Evers. "What the hell's this?"

Uh... Adam scratched his nose. "Guess you didn't hear about Vance yet then?"

"No." He started back toward them. "Dammit, he called me during the meeting and I didn't get around to calling him back yet. What happened?"

"He had a little run-in with some drug dealers earlier tonight after he left the place where we ate," he said. "And Cruzie's sister was there too," he added.

Something was brewing between those two. Adam didn't know how serious it was, but he knew Vance well enough to know that he wouldn't fuck around with Cruzie's sister unless she meant something to him. So if anything romantic or hormonal was going on with them, he doubted it was casual. As far as he knew Vance didn't have a death wish and had to know Cruzie would kill him if Vance messed around with Carmela just for kicks.

DeLuca was already pulling out his cell. He put the phone to his ear, listened a moment, then his lips thinned and he ended the call. "Voicemail. So is Vance okay?"

"Got his shoulder sliced open."

DeLuca's jaw clenched, his gaze turning flat. "Shit. He's talked to the cops?" He nodded at the vehicle still surrounded by a swarm of cops.

Adam nodded. "A couple of cops were up in our room talking to him when we left."

He set his hands on his hips. "Where's Cruzie? He know about it?"

"Yes. He's at Marisol's hotel, a couple blocks away."

"Vance still in the room?" DeLuca demanded impatiently.

"Think so."

"How bad a slice is it? Did he get checked out?"

"Doc's treating him right now," Evers said. "Vance said he didn't want to waste time sitting in the ER."

DeLuca swung his gaze on him now, his face darkening like a thundercloud. "For Christ's sake," he muttered, jaw tight, then leveled that green gaze on Adam. "How *bad*?" he repeated.

It was like being hit with high-powered lasers. Adam understood why DeLuca was so concerned. Yeah, he was worried about one of his agents being injured, but he also had to be worried it would sideline Vance and they could be called out at any time to go on another mission.

"Nothing too serious," Adam said quickly, which was technically true. Vance could still use his arm and everything. Couldn't be too bad. "You can go see them if you want to…" He trailed off, not knowing how to finish.

"Oh, I want to. *Dammit*." DeLuca muttered and stalked past them toward the stairwell. He took two steps then stopped to look at them over his shoulder. "Tell the SAC at the field office I'll be in touch shortly. And bring me back a copy of all the paperwork so I can clear up everything with headquarters," he ordered.

"Roger that." Once the stairwell door clanged shut, Adam exchanged a loaded look with Evers. "Wouldn't want to be Vance right now."

"Nope," Evers agreed with a grin, slipping his hands into his pockets. "Let's just hope he's not benched because of this. We need him."

It was true. Vance was a great operator, but more than that, he was an integral member of their team. The reason why they were so good at what they did was because of the guys and the countless hours they put into training and keeping their skills sharp as possible. They knew each other inside and out, could read each other and anticipate each other's moves on an op. Losing Vance now would be a big blow to the team.

"Should we warn him?" He reached into his jeans pocket for his cell.

Evers waved away his concern. "Nah, him and Doc'll probably both have their hands too full to answer anyway."

"I feel bad for the guy." DeLuca was a fair boss, but he bore the responsibility of making the tough calls. If he thought Vance wasn't physically able to perform his duties, he'd pull him without hesitation. Vance would hate that. Hell, any of them would.

"Agent Blackwell?"

Adam turned at the male voice behind him. The lead investigator was walking down the ramp toward them, stripping off his gloves as he approached. "We're all done here. We'll send a copy of our report to local headquarters, and one to Agent Vance as well."

"Sounds good, thanks."

The cop handed Adam the keys. "She's all yours. You guys have a good night."

"You too," Adam replied, and walked back up the ramp to the SUV.

Agents at the Seattle office would issue them a new ride and start the process of their own report, then get the damaged SUV fixed and cleaned. The paperwork for the new vehicle was already in the works. But he sure as hell wasn't sitting on that seat without putting something down first.

He fished through the glove compartment and came up with a folded map. After spreading it across the seat he started to slide his phone into the cup holder, but it rang in his hand. The name on the display froze him for a moment. Dread and hope twined inside him, a squeezing pressure he'd become all too familiar with over the past few months.

He glanced at Evers, careful to keep his expression neutral. "I should probably take this."

"Yeah, sure, go ahead."

Adam climbed out of the SUV and went into the privacy of the stairwell DeLuca had just gone up before answering, trying to ignore the way his heart thumped against his sternum. This could be good news or it could be the news he'd been dreading for a while now. "Hey."

"Hi." His wife's voice was soft, almost hesitant. "Did I catch you at a bad time?"

"No, it's fine." He shifted the phone to his other hand, his wedding band glinting in the bright halogen lighting overhead. Every time he looked at it he felt a kind of numbness. And there was no avoiding the truth anymore.

His marriage was on life support, being kept alive with a metaphorical ventilator. Had been for a while now, even if he didn't want to admit it. He'd even agreed to try counseling in a last ditch effort to salvage everything, but the results had been lukewarm at best and they'd both been relieved when they'd stopped going two months ago.

Summer was so distant now, pretty much a stranger to him at this point. As he was to her. The distance between them had expanded to the point where neither of them had the first freaking clue how to bridge the gap anymore. "Are you back on the East Coast?"

"Flew in from Karachi earlier tonight."

He frowned. She'd be exhausted after that long flight, and yet here she was calling him in the middle of the night. "It's one in the morning there. Everything okay?" His hand tightened around the phone as he braced himself for the words he'd been preparing himself for.

It's over, Adam. I'm sorry.

"Yeah, everything's good. I was just... I was in meetings and briefings all day about the situation out there on the West Coast. You've been on my mind all day and I wanted to check and make sure you were all right."

Surprise and relief crashed through him. So she wasn't leaving him then. Wasn't filing for separation. Even more astounding, she'd reached out because she'd been worried about him.

It had to mean something. Had to.

Adam closed his eyes, his chest expanding on a painful breath. He'd never known hope could be so painful until his marriage had begun to unravel.

In spite of everything, he knew she still loved him. That was the hell of it. They both still loved each other. Maybe they weren't *in love* anymore, but somehow that critical foundation, no matter how rocky and unstable it had become, was still holding.

He just didn't know if that was enough to save their marriage.

Adam considered his words before answering. As a veteran Defense Intelligence Agency officer, Summer knew exactly how severe the looming terror threat was that they were trying to thwart. "I'm okay, doll."

A beat of silence passed and he could tell he'd surprised her by using the endearment. But fuck it. She'd extended the olive branch by making this call. He was sick of this. Done with always holding himself in check around her, afraid of being hurt or rejected. Tired of the walls they'd built between them, fed up with the emotional divide that kept them apart.

He was a fighter by nature. He was good at it too, good enough that he'd even made a career out of it. And in a fight he never quit.

In that moment he came to a decision. He couldn't speak for Summer, but he wasn't giving up on them without a fight. As soon as he got home after this situation on the coast was over with, he was taking one last shot at saving their marriage.

And if it turned out to be his last stand instead, well… At least he would know he went down swinging.

"You sure?" she prompted, sounding worried. "I mean the chatter level is…"

Unprecedented. Yeah, he knew. "I'm sure. So how did it go at the summit over there?"

His question wasn't just an attempt to spur more polite conversation. After over two weeks without hearing her voice, almost five since he'd last seen her, he missed her, dammit. And maybe it was just asking for more heartache, but he hoped like hell she missed him on some level too.

Summer sighed and he could picture her dropping her forehead into her hand, her red hair falling forward like a curtain. "Frustrating. Our so-called 'allies' speaking out of both sides of their mouth, as usual. Saying one thing and secretly doing another behind our backs. You know how it is."

Yeah, unfortunately he did. Most of his Special Forces career had been spent in deployments around the Middle East and south Asia. Attempting to gain the trust of various warlords or militant groups who could help American interests. After all, *the enemy of my enemy is my friend*, or however the saying went. "Yeah, I do."

I do. As soon as they were out of his mouth the words echoed deep inside him.

He'd said those exact words to her on their wedding

day, had meant them with every bit of conviction he possessed. And she'd vowed the same to him in turn. Yet here they were, on the verge of divorce. They'd made so many mistakes along the way.

Like shutting each other out when they should have turned to each other to deal with their pain. They were both so fucking proud and independent, and that had cost them.

"So there's been a development at work I wanted to tell you about," she finally said.

"What's that?" he asked casually.

"My boss is talking to his contacts at the Bureau, DHS and NSA, but there's a link between someone we've been watching and what's going on there on the West Coast."

Something inside him hardened at the news. She said she'd called to check up on him, but now he realized it was probably just a way to work up to this. He shifted his stance, clenched his jaw once. "I'm listening." They both had high security clearances, so she was free to share information with him about a case.

"We've been tracking several links between things happening in Amman and Jakarta. You've heard of a player named Aziz?"

"Yes." The guy suspected of bankrolling whatever plot his sick and twisted little cell had cooked up. Intel said the guy was already somewhere in the Seattle area, which might be a signal that the attack was about to go down.

"We think he's linked to the cell leader we've been investigating in Jakarta. He's been transferring large sums of money to offshore accounts and we think that's where the flow is going to. From tracing phone records and unscrambling encrypted messages we're sure there's a solid link there, we're still trying to nail down the specifics."

"I'll mention it to my commander, and Alex Rycroft is here as well." The guy was former SF, like him and Vance, and a legendary NSA agent.

She let out a relieved sigh. "Great. I know they've been in communication."

"Any idea when you'll be coming home?" she asked, sounding a little guarded now.

He dragged a hand through his short hair. Her question sounded sincere enough, but he was a little surprised she'd care if she'd called solely to deliver the news. "Not yet. But we should be flying back as soon as we wrap up things here."

After hopefully capturing the wastes of skin behind whatever attacks were planned for the West Coast. "Will you be there?" He didn't ask her to come out to see him. He would be wrapped up with work anyway and he didn't want her here with such a dangerous threat hanging over them all.

"Should be. I don't have any more trips scheduled for another couple weeks."

"Okay, that's good then." Was it? Hell, he didn't know anymore. But they had to do something about the state of their marriage. Maybe they could steal a couple days away together or... God, he didn't know if she'd even be up for that. There were so many things he wanted to say but wouldn't. Not over the phone when they were thousands of miles apart. Not until he knew his heart wouldn't get smashed by her rejection.

"All right, well... Take care then."

"Yeah. You too. I'll be home soon." He hoped it was true.

He disconnected and headed back to the SUV, feeling like a lead weight was squashing his ribcage. He'd tell DeLuca about what Summer had told him once they got back. Right now he needed time to himself.

He climbed into the driver's seat, felt the way Evers

was watching him as he turned the ignition over.

"That Summer?"

He hadn't said much about his crumbling marriage except to Cruz a couple months back, but all the guys knew things weren't going well at home for him and hadn't been for a while. "Yeah." The terse answer did the trick because Evers didn't say anything else on the subject. In fact, he didn't say anything at all on the drive to the Seattle field office.

Which was good. Because Adam didn't feel like talking to anyone at the moment; not even one of his teammates.

****

It wasn't the first time he'd needed sewing up, and it probably wouldn't be the last.

Sawyer sat motionless on the edge of the tub in the hotel room Schroder was sharing with Blackwell while the team medic stitched up his shoulder. What had taken Schroder less than ten minutes so far now that the cops had gone would have likely taken hours at the hospital, when he took into account the long wait and all the paperwork involved there. Besides, Doc did great stitching.

It was always weird to feel the thread pulling through his skin but not feel any pain each time the needle pierced his skin. He'd been stitched up without freezing before out in the field, which was no fun at all, so he was glad Schroder had been able to inject some lidocaine in there before starting. And this way he didn't have to sweat and grit his teeth for each stitch while Carmela was watching.

Out in the bedroom she was perched on the foot of one of the queen size beds, watching the process through the open doorway with a concerned expression. He knew she wasn't squeamish about blood but he could tell she was trying not to wince each time Schroder poked the suture needle through his skin. She'd been out there since the cops had left after taking their initial reports. Ethan had offered to come get her but she'd declined.

Either because she didn't want to ruin her brother's night with Marisol, or maybe because she hadn't wanted to leave Sawyer. Secretly he hoped it was the latter.

He was as conflicted about her as ever and still didn't know what to do about it. His past had taught him the perils of getting involved with Carmela, and that old fear wasn't letting go. While Schroder stitched him up his thoughts drifted back to a memory of when he was a kid.

The catcalls and threats started the instant he stepped off the road and into the glade of trees he had to pass through to reach the edge of his father's ranch.

Sawyer gritted his teeth and walked faster down the pathway, his fist tightening around the strap of his backpack. Every day when he stepped off the bus, he braced for this. Some days he beat the other boys here, but unfortunately today he wasn't that lucky.

"Vance, you black piece of shit, get over here!"

Laughter and more insults followed him, the voices growing louder. He pretended to ignore them, even though he heard every vile word and ugly name they called him. It didn't hurt him the way it used to, but the fear was still there, curdling in his stomach like sour milk. If he could just reach the fence line and get through it before the pack of bullies reached him, he'd be in the clear. Even Richard Allen and his gang of thugs weren't stupid enough to come after him on his father's land.

He maintained his brisk pace, refusing to look over his shoulder or let them know how scared he was, his boots crunching over the carpet of fallen autumn leaves. His breathing was a bit shallow, his senses heightened. The sounds of nature faded beneath the taunts being shouted at him. He knew every inch of this place, knew all the shortcuts, none of which would help him now. At ten he was already an expert hunter, tracker and stalker.

But since school had begun a few weeks ago without his best friend there to run interference, he'd become the prey.

His father's stern voice sounded in his head. A real man doesn't have to use violence to prove himself. A real man has the strength to walk away from a fight.

But Sawyer had tried walking away many times before and it never worked. And he wasn't his father.

The voices behind him drew closer, then the sound of running footsteps reached him. Sawyer tensed. Through the trees up ahead in the distance he could make out the northernmost boundary of his father's property. He'd never reach it before they caught him.

But he refused to run from these assholes. If they wanted a fight, he'd give it to them, even if it meant he'd have to face all four of them alone and getting the shit kicked out of him again.

When the footsteps got close he dropped his backpack and whirled around to face the threat. Richard and three of his goons, all bearing down on him. The tallest one ran straight for Sawyer, tried to tackle him. Sawyer caught him around the waist with a growl and threw him over his shoulder onto the leaf-strewn ground.

Then it was on.

The remaining three converged on him in a flurry of fists and feet. Sawyer held his own until one of them slammed a fist into his mouth, busting his lip open. He stumbled back and another one of them knocked him to the ground. Now all four of them were on him, throwing punches and kicking at his ribs while he curled into a defensive position and covered his head with his arms.

Then a yelp of surprise and pain rang out. In the lull of punches that followed, Sawyer struggled to his knees and saw his best friend, Danny, standing there like an avenging angel. Two years older than Sawyer and in junior high now, he was taller and stronger than the gang of bullies.

Danny went right for Richard, slamming a fist into his nose with a crack. Richard let out a sharp, shrill scream and fell to his knees, blood gushing out beneath his hands as he held his busted nose. The others all backed away warily, their bloodlust rapidly vanishing now that Danny had stepped in to even the odds and their leader was out of action.

"Get the fuck outta here before I bust all your faces in," Danny snarled, fists raised as he stared them all down.

The boys dragged Richard up, who was still bawling as he covered his nose with both hands, and beat a hasty retreat back down the pathway.

Panting and trembling under the whiplash of adrenaline still coursing through his veins, Sawyer winced and pressed a hand to his left side where someone had kicked him in the ribs. Danny turned to face him and held out a hand. Sawyer took it and allowed his friend to haul him to his feet. "Thanks," he mumbled, grateful but ashamed that he'd needed the backup.

Danny shook his head, his blue eyes burning with frustration. "I always got your back, you know that. Dammit, I wish you'd tell somebody about this." He stared at Sawyer, taking in the damage, then shook his head. Despite the age difference and them being in different schools now, Danny never treated him any differently just because he was black, and younger. They were still best friends, no matter what. "This is bullshit, Saw. You need to at least tell your dad what's going on."

"No." His dad would either give him hell for fighting, or cause so much trouble with the other boys' parents that Sawyer would be bullied for the rest of his life. "I can handle them." Every time they came after him he got better. A little tougher, a little faster with his fists.

He was tall for ten, but given his dad's size, he had a lot of growing left to do. Soon he'd be big enough that the bullies would stop picking on him and look for an easier target.

"Yeah, because four against one is a real fair fight," Danny said, his voice dripping with derision. "Seriously, what do you care what happens to them once your dad finds out what they've been doing? They're all racist assholes. They deserve to be punished."

Because their parents were racist assholes too. But fortunately not everyone around here was like them. "I don't want my dad involved with this." He had enough crap to deal with as it was, and it would be embarrassing for Sawyer to have his dad step in and take care of something he needed to handle himself. Some people around here still treated them like second-class citizens just because of the color of their skin. As one of the only black ranchers in the area, his father didn't need any more problems with the locals.

Danny grunted in disgust and bent to grab Sawyer's backpack, eyeing him as he straightened. "Got a spare shirt to change into before you go home?"

Sawyer glanced down to see the blood staining the front of his T-shirt. Hell. Once his dad saw that, there'd be hell to pay.

Danny slung Sawyer's backpack over one shoulder and beckoned with a jerk of his head. "Come on. You can come home with me. We'll get you cleaned up and I'll lend you one of my shirts." Then he grinned and added, "My mom's making meatloaf for supper."

As if he'd needed another thing to tempt Sawyer with.

Despite the pain in his split lip, Sawyer grinned back. Danny was a great guy and his family was awesome. Since he and Danny had become friends four years ago they'd always welcomed Sawyer at their house. A few times a week he came over after school and did his homework at the big, wooden farmhouse table with Danny, eating homemade chocolate chip cookies Danny's mother served warm from the oven.

To Sawyer, being at their house was like living in a dream world, and he savored his time there the way most boys his age savored a new video game.

Those days he went over after school he enjoyed homemade treats and drank glasses of cold milk while finishing his assignments, stalling to stretch out the time as long as possible, knowing that Mrs. Decker would probably invite him to stay for dinner if he was there long enough. He'd eat with the family, help clear the table afterward and do dishes with Danny and his sister, Trina.

Sometimes he even volunteered to wash the kitchen floor after, or help Mr. Decker and Danny with the animals. Anything that allowed him to stay in that warm, safe environment for a little while longer before he had to walk home to the cold, rigid home he shared with his controlling father.

"Okay," he said, already feeling warmer inside at the thought of going there instead of home.

Danny gave him a friendly slap on the shoulder and they walked out of the trees together. At the fork they turned right, taking the path that would lead to the Decker's place. Sawyer's second home, but the one place where he felt welcome.

The only place he'd ever felt truly loved.

"Dude, you're zoning out on me. You okay?"

Schroder's words yanked him out of the bittersweet memory. These days he chose to remember the good times with Danny, instead of dwelling on the bad. "Yeah, I'm good."

"Well, we always knew you had thick skin," the medic murmured as he pulled the thread taut on the next stitch. "This just confirms it."

Sawyer grunted. "Okay, you're enjoying this way too much, man." Must be some weird medic thing.

The former PJ grinned but didn't look up from his work, needle driver in one latex-gloved hand and a curved suture needle in the other. They'd chosen to use the bathtub for easy cleanup. Sawyer had ditched his ruined shirt in the trash and his chest and stomach were smeared with blood.

"Lucky for you, I'm handy with a needle and thread. And bonus that I'm not doing this while under fire. Means I can take the time to make the stitches all pretty for you. Pretty stitches make for pretty scars."

He didn't care if it was pretty or not, he just wanted to get the bleeding stopped so he could get to the nearest police station to give his statement then talk to Carmela, alone.

She sat up straight when someone knocked on the door. "Should I get that?"

"Yeah, sure," Sawyer told her. Had to be one of the guys coming to check on him.

She went to the door and looked through the peephole before opening it. Through the open bathroom door he saw DeLuca stood in the opening, the brim of his Chargers cap pulled low enough to shadow the upper portion of his forehead, but Sawyer could already tell he was scowling.

"Hi," Carmela murmured and stepped back.

"Hi." After the terse greeting their commander walked past her and headed straight for the bathroom. He paused to lean against the doorframe and folded his arms over his chest, regarding the two of them with a stony expression. "What the hell happened?" he said to Sawyer.

Schroder shot him a *good luck, dude* look and kept on working. "Stumbled upon some kind of a drug deal gone bad in the parking lot stairwell," Sawyer answered. "Guy had a switchblade."

"And a pistol, I noticed," DeLuca finished, his expression closed.

Oh yeah, the boss was pissed. Either he'd seen the SUV or one of the guys had already told him. "I left you a voicemail. But no, that was the other guy he'd been fighting with when we showed up. Evers and Blackwell are taking care of the SUV for me right now."

"Yeah, that's how I found out, I saw them in the underground parking."

"I called you."

"I know. I was in a meeting." He sighed then jerked his chin at Sawyer's shoulder and directed his next question to Schroder. "Well, Doc? What's the prognosis?"

"Don't think we'll have to amputate," he joked, pulling another suture through near the end of the gash. "All his shots are up to date, so no tetanus or anything to worry about and I'm gonna give him a shot of antibiotics once I'm done with this. Nineteen stitches in total, but only the upper four inches of the wound was deep. No nerve damage and he'll still have full range of motion, but he'll be sore for a few days. Wouldn't recommend PT or anything for a bit. He's mission ready if we need him though."

DeLuca shifted that penetrating green gaze to Sawyer. One of the deadliest snipers in the world, and he still hadn't lost that edge. All the guys respected the hell out of him, and he was a great guy to work under. "So you're good?"

He nodded, made sure his gaze conveyed his certainty. "I'm good."

DeLuca seemed relieved. He looked over his shoulder at Carmela, poised on the foot of the bed once more. "What about you?"

She blinked once in surprise. "I'm fine. Thanks. Not even a scrape." Her gaze shifted to Sawyer and he saw gratitude there he wasn't sure he deserved.

DeLuca's attention shifted back to him again. "Heard you guys have already talked to the cops?"

"Yeah. They already interviewed us for the basics and their forensics people looked at the SUV. I promised we'd go down to the station to give our official statements as soon as Doc's finished with me."

"Which is in about five seconds," Schroder answered, tying off the last stitch before cutting the thread. Sawyer glanced down. Nineteen neat, perfectly spaced stitches held the edges of his skin together. The whole area was still numb, but he could already see the swelling around it. He was going to be a hurting unit over the next couple days.

Schroder filled a syringe and turned to him with an evil grin. "Drop your drawers, soldier."

"You just said my shots were up to date."

"Yeah, well, this is antibiotics. Lose the pants, my friend."

Sawyer scowled at him and undid his jeans, then rolled them and his boxers down a little on one side to expose the side of his hip. "That's all you're getting. Perv."

"What, you shy with me all of a sudden? I've already seen everything you've got, more times than I wanted to, trust me."

Sawyer's lips twitched in a hint of a smile but he didn't answer as Doc injected the antibiotics into the side of his ass. He barely felt the needle go in.

"Okay, you're good to go." Schroder slapped him on the right shoulder as he stood and Sawyer bit back a growl, narrowing his eyes at his teammate.

Dammit, once the freezing wore off in the stitches, *both* his shoulders were going to ache like a bitch. Sawyer hitched up his pants and did up the fly. This whole night had been one giant goatfuck so far. He just wanted this situation dealt with so he could talk to Carmela, see if he could smooth things over between them. He couldn't stand this.

"Well, good news is as of right now, unless something comes up we've got mostly meetings for the next few days. Whatever exercises we do, if you're not up to them, you tell me right away. Got it?" DeLuca told him.

He'd never jeopardize his teammates' safety by taking part in an exercise or mission if he couldn't physically handle it. But he wasn't going to pussy out because of a few stitches and a possible tear in his rotator cuff, either. "Yes, sir."

The affirmative response and respectful tone seemed to placate his boss. DeLuca nodded and straightened in the doorway. "You need a ride to the station?"

"Nah, but thanks."

"Okay. You need anything else, let me know. *Before* you ask any of the guys next time," he added with a pointed stare.

Sawyer inclined his head and hid a smile. "Will do."

When DeLuca was gone Sawyer and Schroder cleaned up the bathroom and rinsed out the bloody washcloths in the tub. Another knock came at the door a few minutes later and Carmela answered, letting Tuck in.

The team leader handed Sawyer a fresh shirt and did his own visual inspection of the wound. Seeming satisfied with how things had been handled, he left. Sawyer put on the clean shirt, thanked Schroder for his help, and walked down to the lobby with Carmela.

She sat in the back seat beside him, didn't say anything as the cab pulled away from the front of the hotel. The silence became uncomfortable so Sawyer filled it. "This shouldn't take too long, hopefully. I'll have you back to your hotel soon."

She glanced over at him, her features illuminated by the rhythmic flicker of streetlamps they passed. "You sore?"

"Not yet. Still numb."

She turned her head to look out the windshield. "I didn't thank you yet, by the way."

"For what?" Him putting her in a dangerous situation they'd been lucky to get out of with only a scratch? He definitely didn't deserve thanks for that.

"For protecting me," she finished softly, lowering her eyes to where her hands were wrapped around the purse in her lap. "So, thank you."

He should never have allowed them to get into that kind of situation in the first place. "It was nothing," he muttered instead, not wanting to talk about the incident when they had way more important things to discuss.

He couldn't wait to get the damn police statement out of the way so they could get to what really mattered, starting with clearing the air between them once and for all.

Chapter Five

N ow that the freezing had worn off, the wound in his shoulder was throbbing like a freaking toothache.

Sawyer sat beside Carmela at the station while they gave their official statements and answered more questions for the cops involved with the case. Officers had initially responded to the scene of the shooting a few minutes after Sawyer's call from the SUV, and from the security camera footage they'd reviewed, they'd identified both suspects. Both were known to them.

Using mug shot photos, Sawyer and Carmela confirmed the identity of the two men they'd seen in the stairwell. After signing their statements and giving their contact information in case police required anything more, they were free to go.

Finally, Sawyer thought, both dreading and welcoming the coming talk. He was sore and tense and not in the best frame of mind for this conversation, but it had to be done and it had to be now. And if she didn't accept his reasoning about why they couldn't be together, he'd have to tell her about Danny. That old wound that still festered inside him.

Outside the building Carmela headed for the curb, but Sawyer stopped her with a hand on her elbow. "Let's grab a coffee or something," he said. He could use the jolt of caffeine.

For a moment he thought she'd argue but then she nodded and walked beside him down the sidewalk. After what had happened earlier he was hyper-vigilant now, watching for any signs of possible danger. Even when they found a coffee shop and he was sitting in the corner with his back to the wall to provide the best sightline in the place, he still stayed alert.

Nobody was threatening Carmela's safety again, and definitely not on his watch. Once was inexcusable enough.

She slid into the chair opposite him and wrapped her hands around the paper cup holding her skinny vanilla latte, the set of her shoulders tense. "So," she murmured without looking up. "We going to do this now, then?"

"Yes."

Her gaze lifted, that pretty golden brown stare locking with his and he felt that instant punch of connection again, deep in his gut. God, he'd missed her these past couple months. Even just talking, being free to contact her whenever he felt like it, the way things had been before. It was impossible for him to switch off his feelings for her. He just hoped he was hiding them well enough at the moment. Because if he gave her any indication at all about how he really felt for her and what he really wanted, they'd both be screwed.

Carmela was a determined woman. When she wanted something she went after it. If she sensed hesitation or any weakness on his part, she'd push until he gave in, and he couldn't risk putting himself in that position because he was afraid what little resistance he'd managed to hold onto so far would crumble and he'd give in. He couldn't afford to let that happen.

She straightened her shoulders, lifted her chin. "Okay. So. Where do you see us going from here? Because I can't flip some invisible switch and pretend we're back to being just friends now." She shook her head, dark waves moving softly around her face. "I've tried and I just can't do it."

God, when she put it like that he felt even worse.

Under the scrutiny of that stare he struggled not to shift in his seat. His damn shoulder was now hurting enough to irritate him.

Here goes nothing. He made himself look into her eyes as he spoke. "I'm sorry about what happened at the hospital. If I could go back and undo it—"

"Would you?" she demanded, anger and frustration in her gaze. "Do you really regret it that much?"

He wanted to lie, tell her yes, he regretted kissing her that day. But her unrelenting stare made it impossible. Even after all his years in SF and the countless foreign internal defense missions where he'd lived and worked with Afghan villagers and militias, he was still a shitty liar and couldn't pull off a poker face to save his life.

He cleared his throat, tried to figure out what to say that might help salvage their relationship while keeping them firmly in the friend zone, all without hurting her more. God knew both of them were suffering enough right now as it was.

And no matter what, he couldn't let her find out that he secretly craved her with every breath. He knew she'd never let it go if he did.

"I shouldn't have done it. I crossed the line, and for that I'm sorry."

She leaned back and folded her arms across her chest, then simply stared at him for a long moment, studying him. Weighing his words.

He tried like hell not to notice the way the pose

pushed her breasts up and together, but he was only human. And her breasts were something he'd fantasized about more times than he cared to admit.

"Well I'm sorry you're sorry. Because from where I was standing, at the time it didn't feel like a mistake to me."

No, it had felt fucking amazing, and that was the whole problem. He still remembered everything about that kiss. How she'd smelled, felt in his arms. How she'd tasted when she'd softened and melted against him, her lips parting for the stroke of his tongue.

God. He floundered for something decisive and convincing to say, finally came up with, "Things wouldn't have worked out between us anyway."

She arched a brow in silent demand. "Really. You know this because…?"

Yeah, he really was going to have to say all this out loud. He sighed. "Because it would be too complicated." The circumstances around it made a relationship with her impossible.

"Because of my brother?" She didn't sound impressed.

He gave a half-nod of acknowledgement. "For starters, yeah. And my job. I'm gone a lot and can't always tell people where I am or where I'm going, not even someone I'm involved with."

"In case you've forgotten, my brother's job is pretty similar that way," she said wryly. "And yet somehow I've managed to handle it so far, even after what happened with the op in Miami." She raised both eyebrows at him.

"It's different when it's someone you're involved with." Although, yeah, he knew Carmela could handle that part without a problem. She knew how much his job, the team, meant to him and wouldn't make him choose between her and his career. Just another thing that made it so tough to refuse a relationship with her.

Carmela didn't lose her cool or hurl insults at him, as he'd feared. But he definitely saw the hurt that now shadowed her eyes and it made him feel like shit. "What else?"

He should probably shut up now. She'd just shoot holes in whatever argument he put forward and he was running out of plausible excuses to use. "It…wasn't a good idea. You and me. And I'm not ready to be in another relationship anyway." He'd kept telling himself that over the past year, but lately he wasn't so sure about that anymore. Carmela tempted him like crazy.

"So maybe this is about your past and has nothing to do with me at all," she suggested.

The blunt statement was so dead on he sat there staring at her for a long moment, unblinking.

The tension around her mouth and the anger in her gaze told him how pissed she was. "Because you should know me well enough by now to realize I'm nothing like her."

Trina, she meant.

Yes you are, you're too much like her. Her circumstance. Not Carmela as a person. She and Trina were total opposites in most ways, and that was an excellent thing.

He bit the retort back before it could slip out, because she'd interpret the words in a way he didn't mean. She didn't know what he'd gone through. Not really. Even Ethan only knew the basic details about him and Trina, and his buddy had never pried for more. Nope, Sawyer would never again go willingly down that road for any woman. He'd never open himself back up to that kind of betrayal a second time.

Danny's face on the day he'd confronted Sawyer was still crystal clear in his mind. Sawyer had gone over to his friend's place to explain himself, talk it out. He'd never forget the rage and disgust on Danny's face. His friend hadn't been interested in anything he'd had to say.

Get the fuck outta here. You're dead to me. To all of us. Don't ever show your face here again.

And he hadn't just said it out of anger; he'd meant it. Every word. That's what had shocked and hurt him the most. Even though he must have seen things hadn't been right between Sawyer and Trina. It didn't matter.

Sawyer cleared his throat, still smarting inside from that unexpected blow from a man he'd considered his brother. "You're totally different people, yes," he allowed when Carmela kept watching him.

She snorted softly, clearly insulted, and there she went with her hands. He almost smiled. He'd missed watching her wave her hands around when she talked. "It's a hell of a lot more than that, thank you." Then she narrowed her eyes and leaned forward once more, dropping her voice to just above a murmur. "Unless you actually don't like me as a person and you've been faking it this whole time just because you're my brother's best friend?"

"*No.*" God, no, and he never wanted her to think that. That he would play her that way just for kicks or something. "Not at all."

"So what, then? You wish you could undo the kiss, I get it. But the way I see it, we can't go back to the way things were. Where does that leave us?"

In hell.

He blew out a breath and glanced around. This was hard enough to talk about without an audience and a few people were definitely looking at them now.

He grabbed his cup. Schroder had given him some anti-inflammatories to take with him. His shoulder hurt enough that he popped two of them and washed them down with a gulp of coffee hot enough to scald his esophagus. His eyes watered at the burn and he didn't even care that he'd just blistered his upper GI tract. "Let's walk for a bit," he said, climbing to his feet.

"Yeah, all right," Carmela muttered, then followed him outside.

The night air was crisp and had a chilly bite to it now that it was full dark. He'd seen a park a couple blocks back and led them that way.

The sidewalk was quiet, a handful of people going about their business in the residential neighborhood, getting groceries or running errands. Sawyer ditched his almost empty coffee cup in the nearest trashcan and put his hands in the pockets of his leather jacket. It now sported a big hole in the left shoulder but it was his favorite jacket and he'd be damned if he'd throw it out just because some meth-head asshole had sliced a hole in it.

An uncomfortable heaviness settled in his chest as he strode along the sidewalk beside her. He tried to tell himself the distance between them was a good thing, but he wasn't buying it. If things had been different and she wasn't off limits, he would have been free to lace his fingers through hers or wrap an arm around her waist as they walked.

Carmela was sweet. Passionate. And she loved the people closest to her dearly. He used to be one of them. He didn't want to go through life being trapped outside that circle of warmth she created. He was already sacrificing more than he wanted to by keeping his distance, because if they got together he risked losing all the people he cared most about.

"Just tell me one thing, and be straight with me," she finally said at the entrance to the park. A three-quarter moon was rising above the tops of the evergreen trees surrounding the park and a fine layer of mist covered the grass, damp with dew. "Was it all me? I mean, did I just imagine that you were attracted to me up until then?"

Ah, hell. "No," he admitted grudgingly, though it

wasn't easy for him. None of this was.

She stopped walking, looked up at him. Her breath fogged ever so slightly in the cool air. "So you *were* into me up until that kiss?"

Shit, he *knew* he shouldn't have said anything. "Carm—"

"No, seriously, I want to know. Were you?"

Dammit, he couldn't lie to her face about that. He shook his head, determined to stand firm on this. "It doesn't matter whether I was or not."

"It does to me." Her voice had a slight tremor to it.

For the first time he noticed the traces of vulnerability in her, and it floored him. Carmela was one of the strongest women he'd ever met. She always had it together, always came across as composed and confident. It had never occurred to him that she might not feel that way inside.

No. End this now, don't give her any false hope. You've done enough damage already.

Man, when his conscience decided to pull a guilt trip, it didn't pull punches. "I don't want to hurt you more than I already have."

Again he saw a hint of that vulnerability she'd hidden up until now, and maybe a trace of insecurity, too. "Then put me out of my misery and just tell me the truth. I need to know I'm not crazy, that it wasn't one-sided on my part."

He started to reach up a hand to scrub it across his hair but flinched when his stitches pulled tight. Lowering his arm, he met her gaze.

Her face was illuminated by light from a wrought iron lamppost set in the corner of the park, making her bronzed skin glow. It looked so smooth, he ached to lift a hand and cup her cheek, run his thumb across it.

No. He'd confused her enough with his mixed signals and he had to think of her now. He tried to think of how to explain it to her so she'd understand. He wasn't rejecting her, he was rejecting the disaster that would follow if they got together.

"You know my mom took off when I was real young," he began after a moment.

She nodded, watched him closely but didn't say anything. She'd always been a good listener. A great friend. He needed to have that much of her again, at least. Maybe over time the attraction would fade.

And maybe you should get your head checked.

"My dad was real strict but he was a good father to me. Taught me right from wrong, did everything he could to raise me right after she took off. He was never the same after she left. And he's never dated anyone since."

"I know."

"Yeah, well, her leaving…changed both of us. It seemed like everyone else in our town had the perfect family. All my friends had both parents, a mother waiting for them when they came home from school. All my dad and I had was each other."

It made him feel vulnerable as hell to say all this out loud, but he couldn't think of any other way to make her understand. "I guess some part of me always dreamed of having a real family one day. A whole family. Or at least for me to be a part of one."

He saw the understanding dawn in her eyes. "And Trina's family represented that to you."

He nodded. "They seemed like the perfect family. At least to me, looking from the outside in. At first, anyway."

"But then eventually you realized they weren't. Or at least, *she* wasn't what you thought."

"Right." It had taken him far too long to admit that to himself, and longer still to do something about it. To do what was necessary, no matter how it hurt.

Carmela shifted to cup her elbows with her hands. "Why did you break up with her, anyway? You never told me."

He thought about it for a moment. "Things weren't right between us. I knew it in my gut early on but I wasn't ready to let go of her and the people that came with her. There were always problems, signs I can see now when I look back that we weren't right for each other. I ignored them, until I suddenly couldn't anymore."

They'd fought constantly. He wasn't much of an arguer, he preferred peace in his personal relationships, but toward the end even he hadn't been able to stay cool. The constant bickering and her endless criticisms had soured everything, had even made him begin to doubt himself.

"That's when I knew it was over. She wouldn't ever walk away, no matter if things clearly weren't right, not with my ring on her finger and the wedding less than a year away. But I knew it wasn't right. I knew I had to end it."

"And what happened when you broke it off?" she asked softly.

He sighed. "She didn't take it well. Even worse than I expected, actually." She'd vacillated between bouts of rage and bouts of depression where her family had feared she might take her own life. He'd almost gone back to her out of guilt several times.

"I'd only been with the team for a year at that point but she made it clear how much she hated my job and the hours it demanded. She wanted me to quit, wanted me to choose between her and the team. Basically, after I broke up with her, her whole family turned on me. Shut me out, boom. Her parents, extended relatives. Everyone." He swallowed. "Even her brother, Danny."

She sucked in a breath as recognition flared in her eyes. "Your best friend growing up."

"Until the day I broke things off with his sister, yeah." It still hurt, even now. He didn't think the ache would ever completely go away. "We went to school together, became real tight around third grade and did everything together. We lived at each other's places on the weekends and during summer. After graduation we joined the Army and went on to serve together in SF for five years." He'd never imagined anything could ever sever that bond.

He'd thought wrong.

He'd started dating Trina the last year he'd been enlisted, right before he applied to the FBI. "He was more than a friend, he was my brother." It killed him that Danny had turned his back on him, literally cut him out of his life.

She shook her head slowly, her eyes impossibly sad. "Like Ethan is to you now."

He nodded and looked away, a sick feeling in the pit of his stomach and a knot in his throat.

Carmela let out a hard breath, still watching him. "God, Sawyer, my brother would never turn his back on you like that. Not ever."

He'd never thought Danny would, either. Under any circumstance. They'd gone through hell together, fought for their lives and bled together and it still hadn't been enough to make the friendship last after the breakup. "Not even if I hooked up with his sister and then we broke up one day?" he muttered bitterly. "Then what?"

She was silent a long moment, then reached out to place a hand on his forearm. The leather jacket prevented him from feeling the warmth of her hand and the softness of her palm, but the light pressure was unmistakable and it warmed him inside.

"Not even then," she assured him in a quiet, firm tone. "I mean, if you were just screwing around with me and then dumped me, yeah, you'd have a problem. But hypothetically if we got together and things didn't work out later on so we broke up, he'd get over it. He knows

I'm a big girl and that I make my own decisions. He wouldn't judge you based on whatever happened with us."

He faced her now, not believing a word of it. He'd learned that lesson the hard way already. He didn't need to learn it again. "Wouldn't he? And what about you and your mom if we broke up?"

"I…we'd figure it out, make it work somehow." She waved her hands around again. "Are you kidding me? My mother adores you, and you know it. Honestly, Sawyer, we're all grownups. Unless you used me and dumped me or did something totally underhanded, you'd never lose my family because of what happened with me."

He'd like to believe that. But he couldn't. Not anymore. And it wasn't a risk he was willing to take.

He held her gaze, so earnest, so sincere. But talk was cheap and he knew in his gut that when push came to shove, hurt feelings and a broken heart could make people turn on someone they'd once loved. "You don't know what your family means to me," he said finally, his voice rough. "I couldn't go through that again. Not with you guys." He was way closer to the Cruzes than he had been with Trina's family. That terrified him as much as it honored him.

And deep down he knew things would never be the same between him and Carmela from now on. He hated that too.

"You wouldn't, I—"

"*Carm.*" He shook his head sharply. "I can't, okay? I can't go there with you. I'm sorry and I wish things were different for me, but I just…can't."

He knew his words hit home because he saw the light in her eyes dim. And he felt like someone had just punched him in the heart.

He was such a fucking coward.

She lowered her hand from his arm, leaving him cold

on the inside. "Well those weren't the answers I wanted or was expecting, but this time you were straight with me about everything. Thank you for that, at least."

She shook her head, a sad little smile on her face as she looked down at her feet. "I'm leaving in two days' time, and maybe that's for the best for both of us right now."

He could literally feel her closing herself off from him, pulling back emotionally to protect herself and a flare of panic hit him out of nowhere. "I don't want to lose you, Carm." He couldn't bear that.

She pulled in a deep breath, let it out slowly. "Like I said, I can't just flip a switch and shut my feelings off like that, Sawyer. But I've heard you, loud and clear. At least give me some time to adjust, okay?"

She was resigned to accept his decision and forget about ever being together.

He should have been relieved, because isn't that what he'd wanted all along? Instead the victory felt hollow and left him empty inside. The lump in his throat seemed to double in size all of a sudden.

"Yeah," he managed. "Sure."

This is the best for everyone involved. You know it is.

So why did he feel like shit and why was he suddenly so desperate to take it all back? Tell her he'd risk everything so they could be together? Man, she enticed him like no other woman ever could.

She tugged the folds of her sweater tighter around her body and hugged herself, the action as much about self-comfort as it was for warmth. Guilt stabbed at him.

"Let's find a cab so I can get back to my hotel." Her voice sounded tired and the slight smile she put on was totally forced. He hated that he'd hurt her. "And you need some sleep after what happened tonight." She looked pointedly at his shoulder, then turned on her heel and started back toward the park entrance.

Sawyer didn't respond. He'd made his bed, now he had to lie in it. Alone, tormented with countless fantasies about her that would never happen now.

Careful what you wish for, asshole. You just might get it.

With a heavy heart he followed her, staying less than two feet away from her at all times and yet she'd never been farther out of his reach.

Chapter Six

W ira checked the screen of his new burner phone before answering. "Hello?"

"Did you have a restful night?" a male voice asked in heavily accented English. Aziz, Wira thought the man's name was. The one funding this entire operation.

He'd just spoken the key phrase to indicate the caller was from the organization. "Very peaceful," he answered, giving the coded response. With all the recent chatter lately and the media coverage of a large-scale attack expected on the West Coast, they were taking every precaution to remain undetected by authorities.

Wira wasn't sure if the American authorities had learned of his organization's plans yet, or if they expected a different sort of attack, but it didn't change anything for him. He was carrying out this plot regardless. He was finally going to strike back at the U.S. for what they'd done to his brother and shine a global spotlight on his situation.

A cause Wira believed in strongly enough to die for.

"Good. When do you go to work?"

"Tomorrow morning."

"Is Ali with you?"

"Yes." Ali, a new American citizen who'd immigrated to the U.S. from Egypt a few years ago and now worked for the same cruise line Wira did.

On paper, anyway.

Ali was reclined on the bed next to his, reading a section of the Quran on martyrdom they'd been reviewing together when the call came in. It helped to center them both, helped take the fear away that plagued the mortal heart.

"The others have arrived as well?"

"Yes." He'd spoken with three of them an hour ago when they'd arrived at their respective hotels. "Everyone is in Seattle and will report as ordered."

"Excellent. I just spoke to the *Mawla*. The shipment you were promised has arrived also. Everything is waiting at the pick up area."

Wira felt a sharp pang in his chest at the mention of their leader. The shipment was to be placed in a container in the cargo area, at the dock where the cruise liner would be berthed tomorrow morning. "We'll take care of it." He'd already reviewed the procedure with his network. Their cell had far more people on its payroll than just the crew involved on the ship itself. Dozens of people from every walk of life here in the U.S., in transportation, customs, law enforcement, even the longshoreman.

"I'm glad to hear that. Do you need anything else before you leave?"

"No, we've got everything we need." Including all the weapons and ammunition they could want for the upcoming operation. He and Ali had spent a couple hours cleaning and checking their firearms at a cache near the dock before coming back to the hotel for the night.

"You know how to reach us."

Wira made a sound of agreement. "I won't be in

contact until afterward." So, likely not at all. The superiors would learn of the attack from either the news or social media, just like the rest of the world. By then, Wira planned to be well on his way to finding his brother.

"Understood. May Allah be with you."

"And with you."

As he ended the call Ali sat up on his bed, his expression eager. "So we're set?" he asked in English, with barely a trace of an accent.

"It's a go."

Ali flashed him a nervous smile, looking far younger than twenty-six in that moment. He was eight years younger than Wira, and his youth and inexperience could work to Wira's advantage. They were here for different reasons. Ali to wage jihad on enemy soil. Wira and a few others who had known Leo, to avenge him and hopefully locate and free him. Others had joined for the chance to kill Westerners.

There were so many men like Ali in the network. Young men with impassioned hearts were usually easier to control than older men. But having Ali on this op was also a risk. He'd never worked or trained with Ali before. It remained to be seen whether he was brave enough to carry out his duties when the moment came.

If he panicked and tried to flee, Wira would end him before he could do any harm to the operation.

"I just want it to be morning so we can get going. This waiting around makes me nervous," Ali said, rubbing his hands on his thighs.

"It'll be all right. Morning will come soon enough."

He reclined on his comfortable bed—a bed more than twice the size of what he'd be sleeping on for the next week on board the ship—slipped his hands behind his head and watched the news broadcast droning on about the ongoing threat to the West Coast. Excitement tingled through his veins.

The true test still lay ahead of them. Wira would carry out his plans regardless of what happened, alone if necessary. But he didn't think it would come to that.

His men would either follow his orders when he gave the order to attack, or die by his hand.

****

Carmela finished off the last of her martini in a single gulp and for a second contemplated whether it was enough alcohol.

Nope. Not gonna cut it.

She turned back to the bartender to order a shot. She was already feeling the buzz, and planned to consume enough alcohol to take the edge off the gnawing ache in the center of her chest. All day long she'd been down, struggling to come to grips with Sawyer's decision about them. On an intellectual level she understood why he was afraid of having a relationship with her.

But the more she thought about it, the more ridiculous it seemed.

She'd never taken him for a coward before, but that's how he was acting. Before the kiss they'd been close, with a solid base of trust beneath them. They'd become good friends over the past couple years and they got along well. Enjoyed each other's company. And the chemistry? He could hide from it all he wanted, but it was there regardless, and it was the most powerful she'd ever experienced.

The man made her entire body burn just by being near her and she knew damn well he wasn't unaffected by her either. His refusal stung, of course, but for her it went deeper than that, stirring up those damn teenage insecurities that had plagued her high school years.

All courtesy of her overzealous endocrine system that had given her D-cup breasts in eighth grade. The unwanted attention from all the boys who'd catcalled her or tried to cop a feel had taken its toll on her self-esteem.

For the most part she'd conquered it. She was proud of her body, but every now and again her confidence slipped.

God, why was it taking so long to get that shot? After enduring the past few hours in Sawyer's company at dinner along with her mother, brother and Marisol, she was desperate for some emotional numbness. Being rejected last night on top of nursing a bruised heart was punishment enough without having to get through the next few hours sober.

The bartender finally placed the shot glass on the polished surface of the bar in front of her. Carmela downed it with one swallow, trying not to wince at the burn as the alcohol slid down her throat then set the glass back down with a sharp clink and swiveled around on her stool to look at the dance floor.

Being expertly led around the floor by Sawyer, her mother appeared to be having the time of her life, if that wide grin on her face was any indication. There was no doubt those two adored each other and Sawyer and Ethan loved to play up their rivalry in trying to outdo each other in a bid to be Mama Cruz's favorite.

They both knew how ridiculous that was though. Ethan and Carmela might be her babies, but their mom had a huge heart and Sawyer definitely owned a part of it.

Carmela watched as Sawyer lifted an arm to effortlessly spin her mother around in a tight turn, her mom's head thrown back in a joyous laugh. They'd been out there for almost fifteen minutes already. It was good of him to be so sweet to her, but Carmela suspected it had just as much to do with avoiding her as it did with entertaining her mom.

"Didn't know you were a whiskey drinker," Schroder said over the music as he slid onto a stool next to her. He grinned and tipped his beer to his mouth.

"I'm not," she answered. Most of Ethan's team was here. She and the others had come to meet them for a "quick drink" after dinner. Over an hour later, here they were, and her mom showed no sign of slowing down out there.

She eyed her empty shot glass. Should she have another just to make sure it did the job?

No. Last thing she needed was to suffer from a broken heart and a wicked hangover. After a minute she noticed Schroder watching her with a half-amused, half-pitying expression that told her he knew exactly what was bothering her.

"Are we gonna have to carry you out of here later?"

She huffed out a reluctant laugh at his teasing tone, nowhere near tipsy. "No, don't worry." She watched Sawyer move on the dance floor. All sexy masculine grace, surprising in a man his size.

A pleasant warmth flowed through her as the alcohol began to do its thing.

So he didn't want a relationship. What about just straight-up sex, then? She could go for that.

Seriously, what was wrong with friends with benefits? At least for one night. Yeah, that was probably either wishful thinking or the alcohol talking, because she doubted Sawyer would go for that arrangement. To be honest she wasn't sure she could handle that emotionally anyway.

But the need he ignited in her wasn't going away any time soon. She wanted him and only him, period. Couldn't she have him just one time? One little taste? Wouldn't he give her at least that much?

"How about we dance off some of whatever's bothering you instead?" Schroder set down his beer and held out a hand.

Carmela studied him for a moment. With his deep

auburn hair and hazel eyes he was good looking and she liked him a lot, plus she knew he wasn't flirting with her because he'd spent the first ten minutes after she'd arrived at the bar telling her all about his live-in girlfriend, Taya, who sounded amazing.

She lowered her eyes to the strong hand he held out, and gave a mental shrug. Why not? Why shouldn't she at least try to enjoy herself while she was here? "Sure." She slipped her hand into his and slid off the barstool to follow him onto the floor.

Schroder was fun, even more fun than she'd expected. Within minutes he had her laughing and shimmying out there with the others on the floor. Out of the corner of her eye she noticed when Sawyer led her mom back to a table off to the side of the room where Bauer and Blackwell sat, but after that she tuned him out.

She danced three more songs with Schroder then one with Evers before calling it quits and returning to the bar with both of them.

Evers ordered himself a beer. "You guys coming over to the table after, or are you gonna stay here?" he asked over the music.

After giving her a questioning glance, Schroder answered for her. "We'll stay here for a bit."

"Thanks," she told him when Evers left to join the others.

"No worries." He leaned back with his elbows resting on the bar. "So is the plan just for you two to avoid each other all night?"

"Looks that way." Thank God Ethan was still preoccupied with Marisol and hadn't seemed to notice yet what was going on with her and Sawyer.

He nodded, his gaze on the people crowding the dance floor. "You know, if you'd rather leave I can either drive you to your hotel or put you in a cab."

Carmela smiled at him. It was sweet of him to offer.

"Thanks, but it's okay. I'll wait until my mom's done and go back with her." She was out there with Ethan and Marisol now, busting a move in a way that was truly impressive for a woman her age.

"Sure thing. Man, that woman is a live wire," he said with a chuckle.

"Oh yeah." Carmela shook her head fondly. Her mom loved to dance and rarely got the chance to do it anymore. "She's something else." It was messed up, to be jealous of your own mother just because she'd gotten to dance with Sawyer.

"Incoming," Schroder said under his breath a few moments later, and reached for his fresh beer.

Carmela glanced up and followed his gaze across the room, her pulse skipping when she saw Sawyer heading their way. His height and large frame made him stand out in the crowd, but the trademark Stetson was a dead giveaway.

His gaze was locked on her, sending a quiver of awareness up her spine.

She quickly averted her gaze, hating the way her stomach drew tight as he approached. The alcohol was doing its thing, but it still wasn't enough to dull the pain. Just friends, when her body and heart went haywire whenever he was near? How the hell was she supposed to shut that off?

He didn't try to avoid her or use Schroder as a kind of shield. Instead he came over to stand right next to her and lean against the bar, his big body crowding close to her, and dipped his head to speak close to her ear. "Want to dance?"

The question startled her so much she swung her head around to stare at him in shock. "What?"

His dark eyes crinkled slightly at the corners in the hint of a smile and a flash of teeth appeared, bright white against his deep brown skin. "Dance. You and me."

He couldn't be serious. She'd told him she needed time to adjust, which he also should have understood meant space. Dancing with him now would be pure torture, a full sensory teaser of all she couldn't have. "My mom put you up to this, didn't she?"

"No."

She sure as hell had.

Sawyer tossed a loaded look at Schroder that made the medic immediately get off his stool, muttering some excuse about joining the others before walking away, leaving them alone.

Carmela sighed. She knew damn well her mother was watching them from over there at the table. She refused to look over.

"I can finally teach you how to two-step like I promised," he coaxed.

Dammit, he smelled so good and looked even better in those jeans and T-shirt that hugged every muscular plane of his torso.

She wanted to be angry, lash out, but she didn't want to make a scene and the truth was she was more hurt than mad. And that damn, pleading look in his eyes.

This was stupid, she decided suddenly. They were both being stupid. The two of them were both single, unattached adults, and they wanted each other. Because of Sawyer's stubbornness, they were letting the opportunity to get together slip through their fingers. What was so bad about one night of sex between them? The idea was tempting. She wondered what he'd do if she propositioned him here and now.

Fear of being rejected again cooled her off in a hurry.

"Fine." She hopped off the stool and marched onto the floor without looking to see if he was following. Steeling herself, she turned to face him, trying to ignore the pang in her chest when her gaze connected with his up close and that all too familiar sense of connection and rightness hit her right in the heart.

He stepped nearer, until only inches separated them, the toes of his cowboy boots nearly touching the tips of her high-heel sandals. Even in her heels she still had to tilt her head back to look at him.

A frown wrinkled his forehead beneath the brim of his Stetson as he peered down at her. "How much have you had to drink?"

Not nearly enough. "Two drinks. I'm fine."

Looking dubious, he reached for her right hand. And dammit, the instant his fingers touched her, invisible sparks skittered across her skin.

They got worse when he wrapped those long fingers around hers and raised them to shoulder height, then turned into currents of raw electricity when he curved his free hand around to splay across the middle of her back. His healing shoulder had to hurt but he didn't show it. The feel of those strong, solid hands on her even in this platonic way had her entire body buzzing.

His hold felt possessive. Secure.

Except this was as close as she'd ever come to knowing how it would feel to be his.

An unexpected lump formed in her throat and tears burned the backs of her eyes. She looked away so he wouldn't see and stood stiffly in his embrace, ordering herself to get a grip. "This isn't a country song," she managed, still not looking at him.

"Doesn't need to be." The hand holding hers tightened a fraction. "Just dance with me, Carm."

Relenting, she kept her gaze on the center of his broad chest and focused on his steps as he began to move. He started out slow, guiding her through the steps, his hands strong and sure on her, the way he moved sexy as hell. She shook the thought away, concentrated on the footwork, stepping backward each time he stepped forward.

Quick-quick, slow, slow. Quick-quick, slow, slow as he moved her across the floor. He made it seem effortless. Her body automatically moved with his, attuned to his every motion.

The pop song they were dancing to ended abruptly and a slower one came on. The strains of *What I'd Give*, by Sugarland, permeated the air. She stiffened. She loved this song but right now the lyrics hit way too close to home.

Carmela swallowed. This was too intimate. Too painful. She didn't know if she could bear this. She'd dreamed of slow dancing with him like this for over a year and now that she was doing it she felt like crying.

"Hey," he murmured, his lips mere inches from her cheek. "It's all right."

No it wasn't. But the selfish and apparently masochistic part of her wasn't ready to let go yet. The initial buzz from the liquor had faded, reduced to a slight glow in her veins.

And her heart betrayed her. Why shouldn't she take advantage of this? For just a few minutes she could pretend they were more than friends. God knew she'd fantasized about this long enough, of being close to him, feeling his heart beat beneath her cheek as he held her on the dance floor. Just one of the many romantic fantasies she'd spun about him.

Giving into the moment of weakness, she leaned in until her forehead touched the soft cotton of his T-shirt stretched across that wide chest, and closed her eyes.

It had to be her imagination, but the beat of the music seemed to slow down even further. Surrounded by Sawyer's scent, held in the circle of his arms, the club gradually faded away into the background, leaving her solely focused on the man holding her. They were swaying together now, barely moving to the music.

Sawyer seemed to curve himself around her. He

shifted his grip to bring her even closer, slid his hand lower to rest in the dip at the small of her back. The heat of his palm sank through the fabric of her dress as he lowered their joined hands, brought them to rest against his chest close to her cheek. Almost as if he was cradling her.

Carmela exhaled and allowed herself to lean into his embrace. The instant her breasts made contact with his torso the arousal she'd been trying to hold at bay suddenly burst into flame. Every inch they touched tingled and sparked, turning her body into a live electrical wire.

Her nipples pulled tight, igniting a powerful pulse between her legs. And there was no mistaking the thickening bulge pressed against her lower belly. Whether he wanted to face it or not, he still wanted her. She couldn't decide if that made her feel better or worse.

She let herself drift, getting lost in the feel of his arms around her. But there was no way to fight the erotic sensations that zinged through her each time their bodies caressed one another with every step. Her pulse skittered and her belly flipped in a delicious way.

The haze of arousal suddenly evaporated when Sawyer tensed and stopped moving. She raised her head in time to see Ethan weaving his way toward them through the other dancers. Immediately she tried to step back but Sawyer's hands held fast, locking her in place against his hard body.

Her brother walked right up to them, bent his head a little to be heard over the music. "The guys are leaving and I'm staying the night with Marisol at her hotel. We're gonna take mom back with us," he told Carmela, then added to Sawyer, "She said something about you promising her a pair of binos for the cruise? Can you grab them and drop Carm off on your way back? You can take the second SUV."

"Sure, no problem." Sawyer released her hand to

take the keys from him.

"Thanks." He didn't seem suspicious about the way they'd been dancing, or maybe he just didn't think anything of it since Sawyer had danced with their mom earlier. And the grin he shot them told Carmela he was totally preoccupied with spending the night with his fiancée. "See you guys later. Have a good trip if I don't talk to you before you board," he said to her, bending to plant a kiss on her cheek. He turned away before she could answer and disappeared into the crowd.

Awkwardness overcame her. Sawyer's right hand remained firm against her lower back and after slipping the keys into his pocket he took hold of her hand once more.

With the bubble of her fantasy burst, she cleared her throat and stared at his chest. "You don't have to take me back later. I'll just go with them now and save you the trip."

"No."

She looked up at him, startled by the forcefulness of his response.

"I don't mind taking you back later," he said in a softer tone. Something moved in his gaze and his hand tightened around hers. "I want more time with you."

Annoyance pricked at her. Was this some sort of power trip for him? Did he not realize he was hurting her? She let her irritation show in her gaze. "Why?"

He froze, seemed to fight himself for a moment before answering. "I've missed you," he admitted softly, and she saw the mix of regret and longing in his eyes. He knew things would never be the same between them too.

A sweet pain hit her in the chest and she didn't have the heart to pull away. She believed that he had missed her and she'd never get this chance again. Why not enjoy it to the fullest for just a while longer?

When his hands urged her closer she didn't resist,

this time resting her cheek against his chest with a little sigh. The arousal returned, but different now. Deeper, suffusing every part of her body, flowing through her like warm honey. Every shift and press of his thighs against hers, every flex of the muscles beneath her cheek made her feel drunk. By the time the song and the other ballad after it ended, she was melted against his big frame.

The music transitioned into a faster beat of a popular top forty song she recognized. All around them the other couples picked up the pace, energized by the increased tempo, while she and Sawyer stood without moving in the center of the dance floor.

He stared down at her with a powerful mixture of tenderness and arousal that made her breath catch in surprise. His gaze dropped to her lips, a muscle in his jaw bunching before he looked back into her eyes, and the moment was gone. She read the resignation there, and maybe even disappointment. "Wanna get out of here?"

"Yeah," she answered, her voice a little breathless. No surprise, considering how hard her heart was pounding.

This time there were no issues in getting to the vehicle and a few minutes later they were at the team's hotel.

Sawyer looked over at her as he put the truck into park. "You want to wait here, or…?"

"I'll come up with you." She undid her seatbelt and hopped out before he could answer then followed him up to his room, the whole time admiring those wide shoulders and tight butt.

Yeah, based on the way he'd looked at her on the dance floor, friends with benefits was looking better all the time.

He unlocked the door and hit a switch that turned on a small reading lamp in the far corner, bathing the room in a warm, golden glow. "I'll just grab the binos," he murmured, striding past her for the large duffel set against the far wall next to one of the queen-size beds.

Carmela watched from just inside the door as he hunkered down and began rummaging through the bag, the powerful muscles in his back and shoulders shifting as he moved.

She withheld a groan. The man was her fantasy brought to life and she didn't see the point in trying to pretend he wasn't. After dancing with him tonight, feeling his body move against hers, she was revved and aching for him. Either she made a move now or it would be too late.

Binoculars in hand, he straightened and turned around, only to stop dead when he saw the hungry way she was watching him. He didn't say anything, didn't move as the long seconds stretched out.

Carmela straightened her shoulders. When it came to sales, she was an expert. She was a senior orthopedic specialist and her company's best surgical sales rep on the East Coast for a reason. She knew just how to pitch a product to get the sale.

In this case, the product was her. And she wanted Sawyer enough to push her fears aside and give him the best sales pitch of her life.

"I've wanted you for two years now," she told him bluntly. To hell with hiding her feelings. If she wanted him then she had to be bold, blow his reluctance all to hell. "Did you know that?"

Surprise and heat flared in his eyes, quickly followed by dread. He shook his head slowly, his gaze locked with hers.

"I'm not good with hiding how I feel, as you may have noticed, and so I can't pretend I'm okay with just being friends tonight." Then she upped the stakes. "And there's a particular fantasy of you I can't stop thinking about."

His throat bobbed as he swallowed and when he answered his voice sounded strangled. "Carm…"

"No." She was absolutely not giving him room to argue. Not when she sensed she was getting closer to having what she wanted. "We're both adults and we both want each other. You're not ready for a relationship and I get that. But I can't stand here and pretend I don't want you. It's not how I'm built. I'd rather have this than nothing."

"We can't," he said, his voice a low rasp, the tension in his posture telling her he was more than tempted and didn't want to be. "We can't do this." His free hand balled into a fist.

Oh yeah, he wanted her. Wanted her bad, no matter what he said. She tossed her hair back, gaining confidence. "Actually, we can."

He shook his head again, denial and hunger warring on his handsome face. "It's too dangerous."

"Not if we both know and agree to the rules beforehand."

"No."

Stubborn, beautiful man. "I'm a big girl. I can handle this."

"Well I can't. Jesus," he breathed and shook his head again.

"Sawyer, look at me."

A muscle bunched in his jaw and he reluctantly shifted his gaze back to her face.

"I need you."

Now he looked tortured. He swallowed hard. "That's dirty, Carm."

If dirty was what it took, then game on. "No, it's the truth. I *need* you." Couldn't he see what he did to her? "We'll make things crystal clear up front, so there's no confusion or hurt feelings afterward," she pressed before he could argue.

He looked at the ceiling in disbelief, blew out a breath like a prayer. "I can't believe we're even having this conversation."

She took a step toward him. His gaze shot to hers and held, and she saw the way his body tensed. He shook his head in silent warning, his expression wary. "Don't do this, Carm."

But his plea had no conviction behind it. He thought he was protecting her, doing the right thing in turning her down. The honorable thing. Her gaze slid down to the front of his jeans where the outline of his erection was unmistakable.

In reality he was only denying them both something they desperately wanted.

She took another step, undaunted. "One night. We'll be friends with benefits for one night and then go on as if nothing ever happened afterward."

It was almost funny, him stepping back only to come up against the wall. As though he was afraid of her. He lifted an arm, winced a little as he rubbed his hand over his closely-shorn hair and opened his mouth to no doubt argue, but she didn't give him the chance.

"After tonight it'll be a long time until we see each other again, maybe even up to a year if you don't come down to visit with Ethan next time he comes home, so that will make it easier. We'll have time to put this behind us, time for me to let the idea of us go and move on. But I want tonight at least, Sawyer. Don't deprive me of that on top of everything else too."

His shoulders seemed to sag. "Dammit, Carm, I'm trying to protect you. Both of us," he amended. "I don't want to hurt you any more than I already have."

"Then don't say no. Don't send me away tonight."

At her soft words his expression turned tortured. He shook his head. "You're not thinking straight."

"The hell I'm not, I'm stone cold sober, and I've

been thinking about it since last night. I can't walk away from you without asking for at least this."

She caught the longing on his face, quickly masked by skepticism. But he wasn't angrily shutting her down or storming past her in an effort to escape. That had to mean something.

"What about Ethan?" he demanded. "What do you think he'd do if he found out we'd screwed around? It'd be even worse than if we dated then broke up later."

She frowned at his choice of words and his pessimism. If she and Sawyer ever got naked together, it wouldn't result in "screwing around". They both had deep, genuine feelings and respect for one another. Nothing that happened between them in bed would be cheap. "This isn't about him. This is about us, and tonight."

He made a derisive sound. "You think we can hide it from him forever, that I could lie by omission about something like that and be okay with it? He's my best friend."

She didn't care what her brother thought about it because it was none of his business, but she realized Sawyer was asking because he was concerned about losing his best friend over this. "He and my mom will never find out. Unless you plan on telling them?" She knew damn well he wouldn't, and she certainly wasn't going to cause trouble by telling them either.

He gave her a *get-real* look. "I don't want to use you like that, Carm," he argued in an impassioned voice, distress clear on his face. She wanted to cup it between her hands so badly and kiss the doubt and fear away. "You mean too much to me."

"So you'd rather walk away instead? Never know what it would be like between us?"

"I already know what it would be like between us," he muttered, "that's the whole problem." His chest expanded with a big intake of air and he stared at her for a long moment. "And what about you? You're telling me that you're suddenly okay with a one-night stand and then going back to being just friends after." He looked and sounded totally unconvinced.

"Yes." Okay, she wasn't totally sure she could do it but she'd find a way to deal with the emotional aftermath because she'd promised him no-strings and having him once was worth the pain later on. At least she'd have this memory of him, a bittersweet goodbye, as she chose to think of it.

"You were doing shots earlier," he accused.

"I had one, two drinks total, well over an hour ago. And those are my terms." She could feel him wavering. Knew she was close to swaying him. Just a little more pressure, a little more persuasion and desire...

He groaned and put his hands on his lean hips. Hips she wanted to wrap her legs around while he rode her, slow and deep. Her insides curled and heated at the thought.

"God, you're making it really hard for me to do the right thing," he said with a humorless chuckle.

"Good," she fired back, waving her hands as she spoke. "Because I'm not a fan of what you consider to be 'the right thing,'" she said, using finger quotes. "Give me tonight."

His mouth twitched, his eyes warming with humor mixed in with desire. Then he sobered, and she could feel the heat in his gaze from across the room, scorching her where she stood. "What the hell are you doing to me? I should walk away. Hell I should *run* away, but I want you so damn much that I..."

She moved another step closer, stopped within arm's reach of him. His nostrils flared as she lifted a hand and caressed the side of his face. She had every intention of seducing him. He grasped her wrist gently to stop her but didn't push her hand away, staring at her while the air around them crackled with electricity.

Undeterred, she drew her thumb across his lower lip, heard him suck in a sharp breath. "I want to touch you all over. My hands, my mouth. I've fantasized about it forever."

His pupils dilated, swallowing the deep, coffee brown irises until they were almost black. He wasn't the kind of man to back down from a challenge, and she had every intention of pressing each of his buttons until she got what she wanted.

One more push. She was close, she could feel it.

And so she found the courage to once again lay herself bare to the man she wanted more than anything in this world. "Please. I *need* you."

Chapter Seven

S he was killing him, making him crumble, and she damn well knew it. But there was no fucking way he could ignore that plea, not when she was standing there so vulnerable before him. Her saying she needed him sliced through every resistance he had. And he'd already been feeling guilty about not meeting her needs, about putting himself and his own fears first.

Sawyer let out a pained growl and repressed a shudder before sighing and leveled a hard look at her. "One night," he repeated in a stern tone, still unconvinced.

She lifted an eyebrow. "What, you want me to sign a written contract or something?"

He was too revved up to laugh.

She nodded, pulse beating fast in her throat. "One. And maybe if we're lucky, it will get us both out of each other's systems."

He snorted at that, still in disbelief that he was even still considering her proposal. "Just tonight. No regrets, no hurt feelings, we stay friends afterward, and no one ever finds out." He raised his eyebrows to drive the point home. Did she understand what she was doing? What she was saying?

"Right."

He didn't respond, but the molten heat in her eyes made the breath catch in his lungs. The pure hunger there gave his arousal a darker edge. The man standing before her right now was a little dangerous, with layers she hadn't even begun to uncover yet. Was she ready for that?

Bold as ever, Carmela trailed the flat of her hands down his neck to his chest. She paused there, letting him feel the heat of her palms, making him imagine what they'd feel like on his naked skin. His entire body was rigid, his skin too tight, lust and anticipation a dizzying mix.

Holding her gaze, pulse thudding in his ears, he felt the last of his resolve crumble. The rigid set of his shoulders loosened as he accepted defeat.

She smiled in victory, and he knew it was game over.

He didn't even try to stop her when she tipped her head back and went in for the kill by lifting on tiptoe to press her lips to his.

A jolt of sensation ripped through him even as Carmela broke the kiss and moved closer yet. From the way her hips shifted in a deliberately provocative rhythm and her golden eyes glowed with desire, he could tell she was every bit as turned on as he was.

No wonder the woman was a top surgical sales rep for her company. She'd just sold him on something he'd been dead set against twenty minutes ago, even when he knew the consequences of going through with this might be disastrous.

Fortunately he didn't give a shit about consequences at the moment. Not with her standing before him with that look on her face that said she wanted to lick him from head to toe. Not when he was dying to find out what this fantasy she'd spun about him entailed and deliver on every naughty, erotic detail she'd come up with.

There was no way he could have walked away from her when she'd laid herself bare to him like that. He might not be ready to give her the relationship she'd wanted, but he couldn't deny her this. Not full-on sex, though. That was too far if he couldn't give her anything beyond tonight. But enough to take the edge off for her.

He just hoped to hell she knew what she was doing, that she really could handle parting ways after this.

Can you?

He ignored the whisper in his head. Her lips were inches from his, her palms flat against his chest, then she flexed her fingers, the tips sinking into his muscle. A jolt of sensation traveled throughout his body at the simple touch, the heat of her hands seeming to burn his skin.

Oh shit yeah, he was in trouble. He'd always sensed that he and Carm would be off the charts together in bed. He had a feeling they were about to set the sheets on fire.

Assuming they actually made it to the bed, that is.

"Let's get this off you," she said in a sexy murmur and reached for the hem of his shirt.

Sawyer allowed her to peel it up the length of his torso, ignoring the twinge in both his shoulders as she pulled it free of his arms, then grabbed the back of it with one fist and peeled it over his head. He dropped it on the carpet at his feet, a tidal wave of lust crashing over him at the way her eyes heated and raked over the length of his naked torso with pure feminine hunger.

The woman was staring at him like she wanted to eat him alive, and now that he'd made the decision to go through with this, he desperately wanted her to.

She hummed in appreciation and slid her palms over his bare chest, making his pecs twitch, the gentle but possessive caress sending more blood surging to his groin. "Turn around," she murmured, putting her hands on his waist to turn him until he faced away from her. "Hands on the wall."

Raw desire surged through him at her soft command.

He did as she asked, placing his palms flat on the wall and stood there waiting for her next move, the mix of anticipation and uncertainty she created hot as fucking hell. He liked control, enjoyed running things in bed and he'd never received any complaints. But her fantasy was obviously about her having control over him so he was willing to give her that temporary illusion and go along with her commands.

For now.

His pulse beat an erratic rhythm as he stood there, waiting. His dick was already hard and aching and all she'd done was touch his chest.

The room was utterly silent, intensifying the sensual vibe she projected. He heard a whisper of movement behind him then felt the touch of her hands at his waist. They traveled up either side of his spine to glide over the width of his back and across his shoulders, down his arms, her touch reverent but proprietary. And for whatever reason he fucking loved the thought of this woman owning him.

She made a throaty, hungry sound and leaned in to press a kiss to the taut muscles between his shoulder blades. "You have no idea how long I've wanted to do this," she murmured.

I'm guessing for about as long as I've wanted you to do it to me.

Sawyer didn't say it, just closed his eyes so he could absorb every sensation. Her soft palms smoothed gently across his skin, waking every nerve ending, her lips feathering tender kisses across his shoulders and down his spine.

By the time she scooted under one of his arms to stand in front of him, his entire body was on fire for her. He stared down into her eyes, heart thudding and his breath coming faster. She leaned in to press a kiss next to the line of stitches in his shoulder, her gaze flicking up to his as her lips lingered on his fevered skin.

"Hurt?" she murmured, trailing little kisses around his healing wound. Kissing it better but making the hunger raging inside him a hundred times worse.

He almost laughed at the question. Pain couldn't even register with him right now, unless he counted the throbbing ache between his legs. That was becoming damn near unbearable. He shook his head tightly.

Carmela's lips curved in a sultry smile. "Good," she whispered, an instant before she slid her hands up his ribs and leaned up on tiptoe to kiss a fiery path along his jaw, over his short-trimmed goatee to the edge of his mouth. His arm muscles twitched with the need to grab her, fist his hands in her hair and claim those tempting lips teasing him.

"You are so gorgeous," she whispered against the corner of his mouth, just inside the trimmed edge of his goatee where his skin was the most sensitive. Not by accident, he was sure. The woman was trying to drive him insane, purposely testing his limits.

And he was loving every second of it.

His nostrils flared as her scent enveloped him. Coconut and lime. Tropical and sunny, sweet and tart, just like her. It took every bit of willpower he possessed not to break his position or turn his head to cover her mouth with his.

Her soft little tongue darted out to flick at the crease of his lips. He inhaled sharply, his cock surging at the seductive caress. He imagined that tongue exploring him everywhere, those full lips closing around his cock and sucking...

She continued to torment him, brushing tiny, feather-light kisses around the edge of his mouth. He gave a warning growl to let her know his patience was running thin and she responded by plastering those sinful curves flush against the front of his body.

The feel of her full breasts pressed to his chest and her lower belly cradling his engorged cock was too much. Only a breath of air separated their mouths as she stared up at him, her gorgeous eyes molten with desire.

"Carm," he grated out, the need to touch her, claim her, almost overwhelming his control.

"Stay still," she murmured, the hot gleam in her eyes telling him she knew exactly how on edge she had him and was enjoying the hell out of it.

His fingers flexed against the wall, impatient to touch her, peel that sexy dress and whatever she had on underneath it off her so he could finally see the naked body he'd been fantasizing about for far longer than he cared to admit. But he remained in place, palms flat on the wall, dying for her to do more to him.

An appreciative hum sounded in the back of her throat and she finally settled her mouth over his, her hands coming up to cradle his face. He leaned into the kiss, opened for her, unable to keep from doing that much. Her lips were so damn soft, he needed more.

The tender stroke of her tongue along his lower lip made him shudder, then she delved inside to stroke his tongue with hers. Sawyer groaned and pressed his body against hers, crowding her against the wall because he couldn't stop himself. The feel and taste of her went straight to his head, obliterating everything but the insatiable need she'd ignited.

She nipped at his lower lip, the point of his chin, before skimming her lips down his throat and chest, pausing to lap and suck at his left nipple on the way down his torso. All his muscles drew tight. Hell, he was barely breathing by the time she dropped to her knees before him and undid his jeans.

Any remaining blood in his brain surged south.

After helping her remove his boots and socks he

somehow remained still while she eased the denim over his hips and tugged his boxers down to free his cock. It sprang up eagerly, hard and throbbing in front of her face and the way she stared at him, so hungry, made the ache a hundred times worse.

He fisted his hands against the wall and hung on as she wrapped her fingers around the shaft, her touch sending an arrow of pleasure rocketing throughout his entire body.

He focused on her face, every precious detail from the dark curve of her lashes against her cheeks and the full, shiny lips inches from where he was dying to feel them. With one slender hand wrapped around the base of him, she squeezed and leaned forward to brush her lips across the sensitive head.

Sweet baby Jesus.

He hissed in a breath, the muscles in his thighs twitching. He was sweating, panting, unsure how much more of this he could take before he snapped. And she was clearly loving it.

Darting a glance up at him, Carmela licked her lips then lowered her gaze back to his cock and enveloped the crown with her soft lips. Slowly. So slowly he couldn't breathe, thought his heart might stop as the heat of her mouth surrounded him. Scalded him.

He moaned out loud, fighting the urge to thrust into that luscious, hungry mouth.

Sawyer clenched his teeth. Christ. He'd never seen anything as hot as Carmela on her knees for him, fully dressed, her silken mouth wrapped around him. When she sucked on the engorged head lightly, ran her tongue around the lower rim, his control frayed.

His hips rocked forward all on their own, driving his dick deeper between her lush lips. She leaned into the movement, took him deep before lifting her head, her gaze rising to meet his. He growled and flexed his hips again, wanting so badly to wrap his hands in her hair, take control of her movements.

He allowed himself three more slow strokes into her mouth, in and out, and then he was on the edge of coming. It was too good. Too hot. He couldn't stand it.

"Stop." His voice was rough. He lowered one hand to grip her hair, gently pulled that sexy mouth off him. He was shaking slightly, heart pounding.

A shudder ripped through him when he at last pulled free of her lips. His dick was shiny and swollen, desperate. He wanted to make her feel the same way, make her this wild before he finally took her to heaven and back. Make her writhe and sob and come against his tongue, around his fingers.

Make her *his*, even if only for the next few hours.

Sawyer instantly pushed the territorial thought aside. He couldn't think of her in those terms, no matter how much he wanted to. This was a one-time thing, no strings attached. Had to be, to protect both of them from more pain later on. But it was damn hard to remember that when he was so keyed up for her.

Without a word he grabbed her beneath the arms and hauled her to her feet, cutting off the sound of protest she made with a forceful, voracious kiss. He dragged her backward to the bed and kicked off his jeans and underwear, his hands busy pulling the dress up and over her head. His stitches pulled but he barely noticed, too caught up in the tide of desire.

Carmela moved with him, keeping their mouths fused, tongues entwined until he sank onto the edge of the bed and pulled her atop him. She straddled his lap, threw the dress aside and he groaned at the sight of her on display for him.

Her golden skin seemed to glow in the lamplight, those full breasts pushed up in a sexy black lace bra, his necklace dangling between them, her mound covered with matching panties. God, he could already feel her heat through the thin scrap of fabric between her thighs, her center pressed tight to his throbbing cock.

She reached back to unhook her bra, let it fall to the floor and Sawyer was lost as those gorgeous breasts spilled free.

Months, he thought with a low groan. For months and months he'd stolen guilty glances at them when she wasn't looking, had fantasized about what they'd look like, feel like in his hands and mouth. Wondered how sensitive they'd be, what sounds she'd make when he sucked on their tender tips. Now he finally had the chance to find out.

She's your best friend's sister and you're using her.

Sawyer shoved the guilty thought from his mind. She needed him and he needed her too, and in the end he was too much of a selfish asshole to walk away without this.

He cupped the full mounds in his hands, withholding another groan at the weight and feel of them, her light brown nipples so hard, begging for his mouth. She whimpered when he licked at one, closed his mouth around it to suckle.

Her hands came up to grasp the back of his head, pulling him closer, tighter, as if she was afraid he'd stop.

God, baby, I'm not going anywhere, don't worry.

She twisted in his hold. Christ, the sounds she made as he teased and sucked her sensitive flesh. Plaintive, breathless mewls that tied him in knots, made him want to both soothe and drive her insane with pleasure. And the way she squirmed in his lap, the exquisite pressure against his cock, was pushing him steadily toward release.

He feasted on her tender flesh, reveling in every soft groan, every pleading cry he pulled out of her. It wasn't enough to simply make her come. He wanted her desperate, begging, ready to explode before he satisfied her. He had only this one night with her and he was damn well going to make it unforgettable.

She was already impatient for more though. Squirming in his grip, little pleas for more spilling from her lips, Carmela released her hold on his head and seized the waistband of her panties, shifted to shimmy out of them.

He released her nipple, glanced down long enough to get a glimpse of a neatly trimmed strip of dark hair covering her mound and the glistening folds between and his mouth watered, suddenly ravenous for the taste of her.

"Come here, baby," he murmured, stretching out on his back and grabbing her hips to pull her upward toward his waiting mouth.

****

She felt dizzy. Drunk, even though the alcohol had long since worn off. Carmela had never been this turned on in her life and she needed him so desperately her chest and throat were tight.

Her legs trembled as Sawyer pulled her up to straddle his face, the painful ache between her legs unbearable. He had her so worked up she couldn't even think.

Splaying her hands against the headboard she settled her weight onto her knees, gasped as he pulled her closer and raised his head to kiss her swollen, sensitive flesh.

"Closer," he whispered, his big hands gripping her bottom, pulling her flush to his waiting mouth.

She quivered, moaned when his tongue slid up her tender folds to caress her throbbing clit. A slow seduction of gentle circles, tender flicks. Her eyes slid closed.

She dropped one hand down to cup the back of his head, melting from the inside out, her entire body a mass of trembling sensation. Pleasure gathered deep in her core and spread outward in thick, syrupy waves, pushing her higher and higher up the cliff. God, she wanted him inside her, wanted to feel his thick length locked deep in her when she came.

Leaning back, she wrapped her free hand around his erection. He was so thick, it was going to feel amazing when he finally slid into her. He flexed his hips, pushing his erection into her grip, a deep moan of masculine pleasure rumbling up from his chest, vibrating against her core.

His tongue flickered softly at her clit and the looming orgasm rose sharply. "Wait," she gasped out, squirming free of his mouth. He released her and laid his head on the pillow, those dark, fathomless eyes staring up into hers. "I'm on the pill," she managed, and when he didn't argue or try to stop her, she knew it meant they didn't need a condom. Sawyer would have told her otherwise. She completely trusted him in that.

She shimmied down the length of him to straddle his hips. Just the feel of his hot erection against her slick folds was enough to make her shiver with anticipation. But he sat up to reach for her, wrapped his arms around her ribcage to hold her still and sought a nipple with his hungry mouth.

Pleasure coiled tight inside her, a bright silver wire of sensation connecting her nipple to the ache between her legs. She whimpered and clamped one arm around his head, used her free hand to try and position his cock against her entrance. Again, he stopped her, this time with a low sound of denial.

"Now," she whispered, barely able to speak for the need tearing through her. "Please now."

"Not inside you," he argued against her breast.

What? Irritation rose sharp and fast. "Why n—" Her words cut off abruptly when he began sucking on her nipple once more. He slipped a hand between them to cup her sex and began to gently caress the swollen bundle of nerves at the top, and she couldn't think, couldn't breathe.

The fingers of his other hand dug into her back as she moaned and stroked his cock. He stilled, a raw moan ripping free as he tipped his head back. The expression of agonized pleasure on his face snapped the last of her control.

She pumped him slowly with her fist and rocked her hips against his hand, increasing the friction where she needed it most. He slid two fingers into her, easing the terrible ache he'd created, his thumb stroking her clit. And she was lost. Ecstasy shimmered across her skin with each slow motion of her hips.

Sawyer turned his face back toward her breast, his tongue flicking at the rigid nipple before the heat of his mouth engulfed her once more. She cried out and rocked harder in a headlong rush toward the orgasm building deep inside. He held her tight and sucked at her sensitive flesh, his fingers buried inside her.

Her sob of release filled the room as the orgasm hit, an endless tide of pleasure coursing through her. It faded slowly, leaving her trembling and gasping.

Bringing both hands to his head, she lifted Sawyer's face to hers and kissed him. She caressed his tongue with hers, rubbed her breasts against his chest, his fingers still lodged deep inside her. With a groan he leaned backward, taking her with him.

She braced her elbows on either side of his head and kept kissing him, rocking her hips steadily, savoring the little aftershocks. She'd have preferred coming around his cock rather than his fingers but she understood why he'd refused to cross that final line. He'd given her a mind-blowing orgasm and now she wanted to do the same for him.

He withdrew his fingers, slid his hands into her hair and eased her head up until she met his gaze. "Stroke me more," he urged in a tight voice.

She was only too happy to comply. But she'd do

better than just stroke him.

Carmela sat up tall, watched his eyes as she shimmied down the length of his body, striking the most erotic pose she could think of, ass in the air, hair trailing across his muscular thighs.

It seemed to work for him because he sucked in a breath and his jaw flexed, his hands locking around fistfuls of her hair. Then she took him in hand and lowered her mouth to take him inside. A raw, guttural groan exploded from him as she sucked, ran her tongue around the sensitive head.

His face was rigid, the muscles in his chest and arms bunching. "Slowly, baby," he rasped out. "Make me work for it."

He wanted her to draw it out, make it last.

With a tiny smile she did just that, sucking him slow and sexy, adding a little swirl of her tongue that made his breath catch. Enjoyment flowed through her as she pushed him closer to the edge.

It was fascinating and insanely hot to watch his expression change, watch him struggle to stave off the inevitable while she went down on him. Her pulse skipped when he gave a low, tortured moan in the back of his throat, his fingers tightening.

"Harder. Make me come." The words were a desperate plea.

Triumph and tenderness exploded inside her. She'd done this. Made this proud, powerful man feel so good he was begging for release.

Sawyer squeezed his eyes shut, the bite of his hands in her hair telling her just how close he was. He was so gorgeous like this, desperate for her. All hers, even if only this once. But oh, man, it was going to hurt so bad when they said goodbye.

She pushed the desolate thought aside, focused on his face, memorizing him in this moment.

His head tipped back, a throaty growl coming from him. "God, Carm, *now*. Faster, baby, make me come. I need to come."

She lifted her mouth away from him long enough to whisper, "I want to taste you."

With a strangled sound he shifted one hand to the back of her head and held on like a drowning man, gasping at each pull of her mouth. His hips drove up, his whole body rigid. Suddenly he went still, the hand on the back of her head locking her to him. He moaned and arched, and she tasted the slick pulses of his release filling her mouth.

Even when he sagged back against the bed he didn't let go of her hair, holding her close as he came down from the high. She released him and crawled back up to straddle his waist, bending to press her lips to his.

The kiss turned slow and languid, a delicious caress of tongues, hands gliding over damp skin. When her breathing and pulse rate normalized she sighed and rested her cheek against the curve of his shoulder.

Sawyer's heavy arms wrapped around her, cradling her, the thud of his heart soothing beneath her ear. Suddenly, tears burned her eyes. He was everything she'd been waiting for. It was heaven, being here like this with him. So perfect.

Too perfect to last.

And that's when she fully realized what a colossal mistake this had been. The bittersweet goodbye she'd wanted had been far more powerful and tender than she'd bargained for. He'd let himself be vulnerable with her, had given her far more of himself emotionally in bed than she'd expected for what was technically a one-night stand. Apparently no better at hiding his feelings than she was.

She blinked against the sting of tears, determined to hide her reaction and get a grip on herself. If she got emotional now she risked alienating him forever. They'd both agreed to one night. Even if she knew damn well it had been far more than just physical between them, it didn't matter.

He didn't want a relationship and she had to let him go. Had to let this memory of him sustain her going forward and somehow get over him.

But he didn't seem to want to let her go either.

They stayed twined like that for a long time, even dozed for a little while and when she woke with a start she sat up and checked the clock. Almost three in the morning.

She pushed her hair out of her face, aware of the sticky wetness between them where she still straddled him. "I'd better get going."

He ran a palm up and down her spine, his touch soothing and arousing at the same time. Her nipples tightened and she ruthlessly stifled the spike of desire. "We've got a few more hours left if you want to stay longer," he coaxed.

No. Too dangerous to her emotional health. She needed time and distance to shore up her defenses again. "I want to be back before my mom wakes up." She didn't want to have to explain herself or answer questions she didn't have the heart to answer.

"You sure?" He was already hardening against her inner thigh.

The invitation was so damn tempting, lying here with him heaven, but she had to get out of this bed and put some distance—not to mention clothing—between them before her resolve crumbled even further. Because she desperately wanted more, to curl up in his arms and stay there forever. "Yes."

Sawyer was quiet a moment then sat up, helped her off him. She grabbed her clothes from the floor and went to the bathroom, fighting off a wave of self-consciousness when he stared at her naked body and telling herself she was stupid for wishing he'd pushed harder for her to stay.

When she came out a few minutes later after washing up and making herself as presentable as possible he was fully dressed and waiting by the door.

"You sure you don't wanna stay a while longer?" he asked, his eyes steady on hers.

The temptation to slip back into his arms was so strong she almost gave into the need, saved only by the warning blare of the alarm going off in her head.

You have to leave now, before this gets any harder.

She nodded and walked to the dresser to grab her purse. Kinder to both of them if they made a clean break now. If she stayed any longer it would just make things messier. "I'm sure."

Was it her imagination, or did she detect disappointment in his gaze? "Okay then."

Her throat felt tight as she followed him down to the SUV. He drove her to her hotel without speaking, the radio the only relief from the awkward silence. She'd known it would be this way, hadn't wanted to think about it, and now that cold reality had settled over her she regretted that there had to be a goodbye.

It was still full dark when they arrived and something the news announcer on the radio said caught her attention.

"Authorities are still bracing for what they're calling an unprecedented terrorist attack on U.S. soil," the male reported said.

Alarm twisted inside her, as much from the report as she was being on the verge of tears. She was well aware of the possible threat the media had been talking about for the past week, but this sense of impending danger was new and terrible.

Sawyer reached out to change the station but she stopped him with a hand on his forearm and the reporter's voice filled the interior of the SUV. "…officials have not yet released any other information about the suspected attack or the target, though it is believed the West Coast is most at risk. For now the terror level remains at extreme…"

Fear prickled over her skin and she looked at Sawyer. "Is it really as serious as they make it out to be?" she asked him. "The terror threat level hasn't been this high in forever."

He glanced over at her for a second before looking back at the road as he pulled up to the hotel's front entrance. "It's real."

She swallowed, stared at him. "Is this why you guys are in Seattle?" It suddenly made all kinds of sense.

He put the SUV into park. Meeting her gaze, he nodded.

Her stomach balled up. "Well what… Are you…" She stopped herself from saying the rest, because it would make her sound stupid and she already knew the answer anyway.

Of course they were in danger here. Sawyer obviously knew about whatever the threat was, and the HRT would be trying to hunt down whoever was planning the attack before it happened.

Alarm slithered through her. She understood the dangers that came with their job as an HRT member but that didn't mean she liked it. It scared her to think of anything happening to him and her brother. She'd almost lost Ethan when Marisol had been kidnapped.

"Hey." He reached a hand out, cupped the back of her neck, his eyes delving into hers. "It's gonna be okay, sweetheart. Promise."

Tears formed without her permission. God, they'd be so good together as a couple. Couldn't he see that? That a relationship with her would be nothing like the one with his ex? It hurt her and made her so damn angry that he refused to give them a chance because of something that happened with someone else, yet he'd been okay with sleeping with her. There was something so damn unfair about that.

She fought back the surge of raw emotion. "I hate knowing that you'll both be in harm's way." She'd be out on a cruise, her and her mother being waited on hand and foot on a luxury liner while he, Ethan and the others were out hunting terrorists and putting their lives in danger. It felt so wrong.

His fingers squeezed her nape gently. "We have to, it's our job. And we're prepared for it. It's why we train the way we do, why we're always working. And we all look out for each other."

She nodded, forced a smile she knew didn't reach her eyes.

Sawyer made a low sound of reassurance and leaned toward her, his other hand coming up so that he had her face cradled between them, and kissed her. His lips were soft and warm, his tongue tender as it twined with hers. Then he eased back, wiped the tears from her lower lashes with the pads of his thumbs, and smiled a little.

"Call or text me whenever you get into port?"

The abrupt change in subject made her blink in surprise. Hesitant, she frowned at him. "I thought you'd want space now."

He exhaled a hard breath, frowned and shook his head in apparent frustration. "Yeah, I thought I would too, but I don't."

That was just his conscience talking because he felt bad, like he owed her something more because of what they'd shared. But soon enough he'd regret it, feel trapped in a relationship he didn't want and wish he'd never opened his mouth just now.

She deserved better than that. She wouldn't let him do this, not even if it meant a tiny chance to keep him. And she wasn't going to freaking beg him to be with her.

Disappointment speared her, so sharp it was all she

could do not to wince. She pulled free of his gentle hold, looked away. "Look, you don't need to do this, okay? We both knew the score going in and I'm not asking for anything else now. There's nothing for you to feel guilty about. It was a one-time thing, and now we're both moving on."

"I don't feel guilty, dammit. That's not why I said that." He took her face in his hands again, forcing her to meet his eyes. She read the confusion there, the determination.

"I care about you. God, I *more* than just care about you, and I don't know what the hell to do about that. I don't know if I'm ready to be in another relationship and I don't know how to handle things with your brother if he ever found out about us. I don't want to make any promises to you that I can't keep. All I *do* know is that right now I can't stand the thought of letting you go."

Surprise made her heart stutter, and a rapidly inflating bubble of hope pressed against the inside of her ribcage. But he was clearly so conflicted. "So then you want…what?" Because she was totally confused, if elated that there might be a shot for them.

He groaned and kissed her again. "I want you to call me when you have cell service on your trip. Let's start there," he murmured against her lips, pausing to nibble at the lower one. "Because dammit, I already miss you and you're still right here in front of me."

He didn't sound too happy about that. A smile curved her mouth anyway, joy and hope twining in her heart. "I miss you already too."

"God." He wrapped his arms around her back, drew her to him in a strong hug, his hold possessive. "I must sound like a hypocritical asshole saying all that after what I told you earlier." His arms tightened more, those delicious muscles contracting around her, making her feel safe and wanted. Needed. "Damn, I'm sorry. I swear I'm not playing with you. I fucking hate not being able to give you a straight answer about what I want, but the truth is I need…."

"Time," she finished for him. Time to figure out if he could handle facing his fears and risking the same consequences he'd experienced with Trina's family should something go wrong between them.

She couldn't see her family ever doing that to him but it didn't matter what she thought. For him the risks were higher than just potentially breaking up with her someday.

To him, he risked losing his second family as well. And he had to know that was already a risk because of what they'd just done. Even though she had no intention of telling anyone, Ethan and her mom were bound to figure out something had happened between them.

No. He had to make this decision on his own and be comfortable with it, or it wouldn't be right.

Sawyer exhaled noisily against her neck and nodded, his cheek moving against hers. "Yeah," he said, sounding relieved that she understood. "I need time. I'm sorry I—"

She cut off his apology with a shake of her head. She could accept that he needed time to process everything, given the one-eighty he seemed to have turned tonight. She felt his confusion, knew he was probably feeling whiplashed.

"Just don't tell me you're in unless you mean it." She couldn't take him entering into a relationship with her out of guilt, only to break things off later because he'd realized he'd made a mistake. It would gut her.

He pulled back to gaze into her eyes. "I won't," he vowed. After a long moment he released her and leaned back against the seat, then glanced up at the hotel, a slight frown creasing his forehead. "Want me to walk you up?"

She snorted softly. "I can handle my mom on my own if she wakes up when I walk in, don't worry. But I appreciate the offer for backup." She caught his hand in hers, squeezed tight, still worried about him. "Promise me you'll be careful out there, okay?"

He smiled and returned the pressure, his grip solid and warm. "You know I will, and you know I've got your brother's back too. Don't worry. Have a good trip."

She nodded. "I'll call you."

"You'd better."

Grinning, she slid out of the SUV and headed inside, unwilling to pop the bubble of hope rising inside her. Maybe, just maybe, there was still a chance for her and Sawyer after all.

Chapter Eight

S awyer rolled his left shoulder to ease the soreness in his healing muscle tissue and followed Blackwell into the meeting room where DeLuca and some other agents were waiting to do a debriefing.

The op they'd executed on another suspected terrorist's hideout two hours ago had been a bust. They'd received bad intel and arrived several minutes too late to bag him. Somehow he'd slipped out of the apartment he'd been staying in near Tacoma without the surveillance teams noticing. Agents were frantically reviewing CCTV and security camera footage in the area to try and find him, but so far no luck. He had to be getting help from someone skilled in evasion and tradecraft.

Inside the room it was standing room only. The other members of Blue team, including both sniper teams, were already seated before the long rectangular table set at the front when Sawyer walked into the room with Blackwell.

Special Agent Celida Morales, Tuck's fiancée, stood behind the table with her partner, Agent Travers. They were higher ups in the domestic counterterrorism division, so it made sense that they were in attendance.

The back of the room was crowded with agents and officials from various government agencies and local authorities.

Next to Celida at the front of the room stood DeLuca, along with Alex Rycroft, the fiftyish NSA agent who had worked with them on ops before, sharing intel and manpower. Back in December he'd even brought in his own hand-picked private security team to act as protective detail for DeLuca and his now girlfriend, Briar, when they'd run into trouble.

Rycroft might also be former SF and a good guy, but his presence at the meeting made Sawyer uneasy. If he was here in Seattle, then it meant intelligence officials expected the proverbial shit was about to hit the fan. The attack had to be imminent and it frustrated him that they hadn't yet stopped the plot dead in its tracks.

The sense of urgency in the room was palpable. Every person at this meeting was in a race against time to find and capture whoever was planning this strike before it happened.

His thoughts strayed back to Carmela as he threaded his way through the crowd of agents lining the wall next to the door. She'd been on his mind all day. He'd texted her prior to leaving for the op, since he didn't think he'd get the chance to talk to her before her ship left port. He couldn't stop thinking about last night, couldn't stop remembering the feel of her, the taste of her. He wanted more, but he had to be fair to her, get over his baggage and move on first.

In the few hours he'd had to himself after dropping her off, he'd wrestled with what he wanted to do about them. She was exactly what he'd been waiting for, the kind of woman to come home to at the end of the day, share his life with. He'd already been half in love with her, but after last night...

Hell.

He mentally shook his head at himself. He was never getting over her now, and he must have been insane to think he could ever walk away from a chance with her. She already owned part of his heart, and if he let her in a little more, she'd own the whole thing.

Lying on his hotel room bed alone just before dawn this morning after dropping her off, he'd come to a decision. Trina was part of his past, that entire awful situation was behind him, and yet he was still letting old fears control his actions.

To hell with that.

Across the room Sawyer's gaze connected with Ethan's and guilt sliced through him. Shit, did Ethan suspect something was up between him and Carm? He didn't think so but his friend had been uncharacteristically quiet around him today, even on the way back to the hotel after the op. He took the chair beside Ethan that the guys had saved for him and put his personal crisis aside as DeLuca got down to business.

"You guys all remember Agent Rycroft with the NSA. He flew in a few hours ago and just received some fresh intel from his team back at Fort Mead that you all need to know about." He stepped aside to let Rycroft take center stage.

"Thanks, Matt. Morning, all. As you already know, the suspects in custody from your previous op are mid-level players of a cell involved with the plot we're investigating. But we've had our eyes on a bigger prize over the past few days." With the sleeves of his pale blue dress shirt rolled up his forearms, Rycroft tapped a few keys on the laptop before him, brought up an image on the screen mounted on the far wall.

A middle-aged man of Middle Eastern descent with a moderate length beard appeared, wearing white robes. Sawyer didn't recognize him. "Ahmed Aziz," Rycroft said. "That's who we've traced all the threads of this cell back to. He's a Saudi national, an oil magnate currently living in Jordan. Or he was, until last week."

He paused to straighten before continuing, easily commanding the whole room with his presence. "Six days ago he left his home in Amman, after telling everyone he was going on vacation and didn't specify where. He's rich enough that he doesn't answer to anyone. At first we thought he might be simply providing the financial backing to the cell or cells here in the States waiting to take action, but recent intel suggest he could be directly involved as well."

He paused a moment. "We've been monitoring chatter and digging through international security agency databases but until now he's been unaccounted for. Based on recent chatter, the latest thinking was that he'd either adopted a new identity, changed his appearance enough to fly here to the U.S., or he'd simply gone to ground somewhere else.

"I should also mention that before he struck it rich in the oil industry, he worked as a chemical engineer." His grave tone left no doubt how dangerous Aziz might be. And Rycroft knew just how scary this chemical weapons shit was. He and his now wife had been exposed to Sarin gas during an op in Karachi. They'd both barely survived.

Sawyer folded his arms across his chest, his hands curling into fists. A chemical weapons strike on the West Coast would be devastating. Bad enough to think about that kind of carnage unleashed on the population, but knowing Carmela and her mom were here made him feel sick with worry. The sooner her ship left Seattle, the better, and hopefully this situation would be over by the time her cruise was done.

Rycroft typed in something else, brought up another screen showing a map of the greater Seattle area. "Undercover teams have been running surveillance ops on two potential targets in the area where he might have visited yesterday. Shortly before landing in Seattle I got confirmation that one of the men seen leaving a home in Bellevue yesterday evening, was in fact Aziz."

Bellevue was a quick fifteen-minute drive from downtown, across Lake Washington via the floating bridges.

Rycroft nodded at Celida and Travers before continuing. "We've also discovered several phone calls he's made recently from various burner phones, using new, cutting-edge voice recognition software. He only uses them once, then takes out the battery. All the calls are to various numbers in Jakarta. We now think he's taking orders from someone else over there in Indonesia, maybe even the ringleader of the cell, who they call the *Mawla*. Arabic for protector, master or supporter. If we're going to stand a chance in hell of cracking this plot before it happens and finding out who the *Mawla* is, we need to find out who he's taking orders from."

He pulled up another image of Aziz, clean-shaven this time, and dressed in jeans and a button down shirt. "This was taken six minutes ago. Aziz will be armed and he's got a well-trained security team with him. All former Saudi Special Security Forces."

Rycroft's expression was as grim as Sawyer had ever seen it as he braced both hands on the tabletop to address them. "We've got a lock on his current location." His gaze settled on the members of Blue Team. "So we're gonna need you HRT boys to bring him in for questioning *immediately*."

****

Wira adjusted the radio on his belt and took the forward, portside stairs from the lido deck to the navigation deck where the nav bridge was located. The captain was there along with the rest of his officers in

125

charge of the ship for this voyage.

Captain Van Slater smiled at him and nodded. "Wira. Good to see you again."

"You too, sir." They shook hands. Wira had sailed under Van Slater's command seven times before. He was young, for a captain of a cruise ship, early to mid-forties. The man was professional but warm and seemed to make a point of remembering people's names and circumstances. So his next words probably shouldn't have surprised Wira as much as they did.

"I was sorry to hear about your mother. Is she getting better?"

Wira withdrew his hand, his smile stiff. He would likely never see his mother again. But he hated the pity in the other man's eyes. "No, sir. But thank you for asking." There was no way the captain could know that her health had taken a drastic turn immediately after Leo disappeared. It had changed her. In ways that had shocked him at first, but now he loved her all the more for it. Losing Leo had broken her heart.

He's not dead. Wira knew it, no matter what the evidence or anyone else said.

Oblivious to his thoughts, Van Slater clasped his hands behind his back, his feet braced apart out of habit, likely from his years serving in the Royal Netherlands Navy prior to working for the cruise line. "The crew is accounted for and all our supplies have been loaded, I see?"

"Yes. I've checked everything personally." All the crewmembers were aboard and at their stations, including those who belonged to Wira's secret team. "Everyone's getting ready for the muster station drill." Wira's team members were also awaiting the prearranged signal once they left the final port before sailing for Anchorage. The one the *Mawla* would deliver.

"Good." He nodded at the screen displaying the

latest meteorological information. "Looks like we're in for a stretch of good weather for the first week."

He put on another smile. "Smooth sailing, then." The irony of the wording amused him. He felt a tiny bit of guilt about betraying people he's worked with, but quickly dismissed it. Collateral damage was a necessary evil in order to accomplish this mission. He refused to think about the people who would die as a result of the operation. The American people needed to suffer just as his family had. They deserved it.

"Exactly. Anything else to report?"

"No, sir. I was just going to go down to the lower promenade deck but wanted to check in with you first."

"Good, good. Carry on."

Wira left the nav deck, this time taking the aft, starboard side stairwell down to the lower promenade deck where the last of the passengers were boarding the ship via the gangway extending from the cruise ship terminal. He checked in with the crewmembers under his command, observed while they carried out their duties.

The crewmembers screened passengers as they embarked, using their ship ID cards to verify their identity, put them through metal detectors while their personal items were scanned with an X-ray machine much the same as they would be at an airport.

A few minutes later another crewmember entered from the gangway. He paused inside the doorway and removed his sunglasses, his dark gaze connecting with Wira's.

Ali.

Wira gave him a nearly imperceptible nod, but it was enough. The younger man returned the gesture and continued past the others without a word, disappearing into the crowd filing up the amidships stairwell. Wira took a deep breath as relief flooded him.

Ali had just verified that the last piece of their plan

was finally in place, and was still undetected by anyone else.

Wira turned his attention back to the passengers, watched the proceedings and offered a polite smile to everyone who met his gaze. A few older couples filed through the security area, one woman needing assistance without her cane while it was being x-rayed, then an attractive young Hispanic woman in her early thirties came through the metal detector.

When she saw him she flashed him a little smile before turning her head and speaking to a shorter, plumper, middle-aged woman behind her, whom he guessed from certain similarities must be her mother. He glanced over at the monitor as the crewmember standing at the podium checked their photographs against the pictures scanned into the ship's security system with their ship ID cards.

Carmela and Veronica Cruz, from Miami.

Both women nodded to him as they passed by and he did the same, keeping his expression neutral, careful not to betray his growing excitement. The failsafe was now safely aboard and hidden amongst the other supplies they would need when they took the ship. That final measure was in place only as a last resort, in case U.S. authorities tried to launch a counterattack before he and the others were able to safely evacuate the ship.

He shifted his stance and stood tall, hands clasped loosely behind him. With his post and his impeccable service and background records, no one would ever suspect that he was heading up this attack. The entire intelligence community was so focused on a different kind of threat, they'd missed this one entirely.

It made him even prouder. The most powerful nation in the world had missed this op unfolding right under its nose. Leo and the *Mawla* would be proud of him too.

He waited another forty minutes until the crew

withdrew the gangway and untied the moorings. A P.A. announcement described the meanings for the various alarms the ship used. Shortly thereafter, everyone made their way to the upper promenade deck for the mandatory muster station drills.

As the ship's whistle sounded three times to announce it was leaving port, Wira hid a smile and turned toward the aft of the vessel to continue his duties, his pulse thrumming. Everything was going exactly according to plan thus far and he had faith that their plot would remain undetected until it was too late.

Every member of his team was prepared to die in this op if necessary. And once they were within helicopter range, their Russian friends would pick them up and help him on his journey to free his brother.

Chapter Nine

"And what creation is waiting for me tonight?" Dwi, their Indonesian cabin steward, turned and smiled at Carmela as she strode up the hallway toward the cabin she shared with her mother. "You'll have to wait and see," he said with a mysterious grin. "I hope you enjoy it."

"I'm sure I will, I've loved all the others." Little animal creations made out of a hand towel, carefully set on the foot of her bed each night. There'd been a seal, a squid and an elephant. So cute she'd taken pictures of them to send Sawyer.

"Did you have a good night?"

"Yes." She didn't ask if he had, since he started early in the morning and didn't finish his shift until each cabin had been tended to. "When's your next day off?" Well, technically he only got half a day off each week. Which sucked, but she guessed it made sense considering there were only so many crewmembers to do all the jobs aboard ship.

This time his grin was wider, showing his teeth.

"Sunday."

"You're going to call your family, I'll bet?"

"Yes, it's my son's birthday today. I left a special present for him."

It made her sad to know Dwi wouldn't see his little boy for another ten months. "I hope you get to see him open it."

"My wife promised she'd wait until I called."

"Well that's good."

He motioned to the bucket filled with cleaning supplies that he held. "Well, have a good night."

"You too."

Carmela let herself in and shut the door. When she turned around, she laughed out loud at the sight before her. Dwi had somehow fashioned the towel into a monkey, hanging from the clips of a coat hanger by its little hands.

Then with a groan of relief she sat on the foot of her bed and slipped her high heels off. "Oh, God, that feels good," she groaned into the empty cabin, flexing and arching her toes.

She loved sexy shoes, and these ones in particular were downright hot, but man they were a pain. Literally. She'd only been in them for the past three hours because it was a formal night on the ship, and even that was too long.

She and her mom had dined at the ship's fanciest restaurant before taking in a comedy show in the large theater and now she had the cabin to herself for a few blissful hours of quiet. Maybe she'd indulge in a hot bubble bath, or bundle up in the plaid blanket next to the sliding door and sit out on the private balcony for a while, watching the scenery pass by. It was gorgeous out, if a bit rocky on the water, the full moon frosting the mountains and forests on the shoreline with a dusting of silver.

But before enjoying all that, she had an important

call to make.

She leaned over to grab her laptop from the bedside table and fired it up, her heart beating faster as nerves took root. Only five minutes until the Skype session she'd arranged previously with Sawyer. Internet on the ship was insanely slow so she wasn't even sure the call would connect, but it was worth a shot. They'd texted back and forth several times over the past five days but that was it.

Not about anything serious, just friendly chitchat like old times, minus the flirtatious tone she'd been using these past few months. It was hard not to press him for answers about where they stood, but she was doing her best to keep her impatience in check.

Keeping in touch with him during her trip wasn't easy though. Most of the time she didn't get his texts until hours later because they'd been out at sea when he texted, and he'd missed a lot of hers due to work. She didn't know exactly what his team had been up to the past few days but they were still in Seattle as far as she knew, so they must be keeping busy there. That could be good or bad.

When it was time she settled herself against the pillows she'd stacked against he headboard and logged in to her Skype account. Her feelings for him had nervous butterflies swarming in her stomach as she waited for the call to connect. She was so deep into him, had been intimate with him and she was on pins-and-needles hoping that he'd decide he wanted to be with her. It was giving her a complex, all her buried insecurities waiting to pounce on her if he pulled back now.

She pulled in a calming breath. She had to keep things light, not say anything that might be construed as pressuring him for an answer about their status, just like when she'd texted him. And she'd been careful to text Ethan just as often, so as not to rouse her mother's suspicions that anything was going on between them.

Although Carmela was almost certain from the little

comments she'd made now and again that her mother knew exactly what was going on between them, and not only that, *approved*. Carmela still wasn't going to mention anything to her though. If she did, her mom would never let it go.

To her relief, the call went through. Sawyer accepted it and a moment later he appeared on her screen, so handsome he took her breath away. "Hey," he said softly, his deep voice reverberating in the quiet cabin.

"Hey." Maybe it should have embarrassed her that her voice sounded a little breathless, but he always made her feel that way, and without even trying. And now that she'd gotten a taste of him, oh, man. "We finally connected."

He grinned, his teeth bright white against his deep brown skin. "Yeah. So how are things?"

"Great. I'm enjoying myself way more than I thought I would. The water's been pretty calm too, for the most part. The ship's rocking a bit now, but not so much that I want to run down and climb in my life boat."

He chuckled. "That's good. What about your mom?"

"She's loving it. I left her down at the casino, where she'll stay until they close. She's having the time of her life on the ship. Pretty sure we've both gained a few pounds each. The food's been awesome, although mom said she's really missing her beans and rice." Being able to eat whenever you want and however much you wanted was pretty great. She could get used to that.

"Glad to hear it. What did you guys get up to today?"

"We were in Skagway. Learned a lot about the Yukon gold rush, walked through the town, had some lunch then took a train up the White Pass just over the border into B.C. before coming back down. The route the miners took was insane. They had to carry a thousand pounds of supplies up to the top, where the Northwest Mounted Police were waiting to check everything and weigh the supplies. If you were short, they sent you back down. And they treated the horses and other pack animals like crap. There's a huge ravine up here called Dead Horse Gulch, where they shoved sick or injured animals off the side of the trail and down the side of the mountain." She was babbling, she knew she was, but it helped ease the nervous energy inside her.

Sawyer was quiet while she detailed the highlights of the rest of the history lesson she'd found so fascinating. That by the time many of the miners who made it to Bennet Lake and actually managed to build some kind of boat or raft to take them to Dawson City, all the claims were gone. Many had gone to all that trouble and suffering for nothing.

When she finished and finally fell silent she could see Sawyer's mouth twitching. "What?" she asked.

He laughed now, the sound doing funny things to her insides. "I love how you get all animated when you tell a story. How you talk with your hands."

She felt herself flush, but didn't try to deny it. The hand thing was something she'd picked up from her mother, she was sure. "Well, isn't that crazy though? Putting your life at risk and half killing yourself to get to a dangerous place in the middle of nowhere, then find out there are no more claims to be had?"

"Crazy," he agreed, his eyes twinkling as he smiled. "And yesterday you went whale watching?"

"In Juneau. Oh, it was amazing. We started with a lunch of king crab legs right on the dock—best crab I've ever eaten. And we managed to get a sunny afternoon so when we went out on the tour boat it was just gorgeous. We even saw some humpbacks bubble net-lunge feeding. Incredible. I'll send you the video."

"I look forward to it," he said in a tone that held a teasing note.

She shot him a playful scowl and put on a pout. "Are

you making fun of me?"

"No. Seriously, I think it's so damn cute the way you get all excited about stuff."

She shrugged. "Can't help it, I'm Puerto Rican. Passion's in the genes, baby." It was freaking killing her not to express the passion she felt for him.

"Don't I know it," he said in a wry voice. He sat up taller and craned his neck, trying to get a better look at her. "What are you wearing right now, anyway?"

She blinked at the question, then narrowed her eyes in suspicion. "Are you alone?" He had to be, because there was no way in hell he would ever ask such a thing if her brother was around.

"'Course I'm alone. So? What have you got on?"

"It's a dress."

He gave her a bland look. "I can see it's a dress. I want to see the whole thing. Stand up and model it for me."

Not the words of a man who was trying to distance himself from her, yet she told herself not to read too much into it. *Okay then.* She set the laptop on the foot of the bed and climbed to her feet, then proceeded to do a slow twirl in front of the screen.

Sawyer inhaled audibly, the sound incredibly gratifying and a much needed boost to her ego. "Holy hell."

She stopped and looked back at the screen over her shoulder, arching her back a little to stick her ass out as she raised an eyebrow. If he was okay with flirting, then she was on board too.

"You like?" The black-sequin cocktail dress stopped at mid-thigh and had a plunging V neckline that showed off her figure. She'd bought it on a whim prior to leaving Miami because it made her feel sexy. From the look in Sawyer's eyes, it looked as good to him as it made her feel.

"Sweet baby Jesus, yeah."

Even through the monitor she could feel his gaze raking over the length of her body, sending tendrils of heat flowing across her skin. She faced him with a sultry little smile and tossed her hair back over her shoulders. "You should see what I've got on underneath this baby."

He groaned and dragged a hand over his face. "Don't say things like that when I'm stuck here hundreds of miles away from you. It's not fair."

She made a sympathetic face. "Poor baby." She crawled back onto the bed, noting the way his gaze drank in every movement. "How are things there, by the way? I've been keeping tabs on the news and haven't heard about anything bad happening yet." Although she hadn't checked the news since this morning. "The West Coast is still in one piece, I presume?"

"Yeah, it's all good."

His expression was neutral, his tone the same, giving away nothing. He couldn't tell her classified information even if he'd wanted to, so she left it at that. "And what about you? How's your shoulder?"

"Stitches are almost healed up. Doc's gonna take them out in a couple days." He hesitated a moment before adding, "My right shoulder's been bugging me though."

Uh oh. "You mean the rotator cuff issue you were having before?"

He nodded. "Aggravated it, is all. We've been busy around here."

His words erased all traces of teasing and she sobered. "And have you…made any headway in whatever it was you guys were doing?"

"Some. Not as much as we'd like. But enough about that. Tell me more about what you're wearing under that sexy excuse for a dress."

He'd only brought that back up again to distract her. She smiled, her heart warming. Worrying about the security situation and his team's safety was pointless, as there was nothing she could do about either of those things. She'd much rather enjoy Sawyer's appreciative reactions to what she was wearing. "Sure you want me to show you?"

His eyes turned heavy-lidded and his voice dropped an octave. "Not sure I can handle it, actually."

She was about to pull the strap on her left shoulder down when she heard the sound of a door opening and Sawyer's gaze jerked sharply to the left. His face was uncharacteristically stiff as he spoke to whoever had just come in. "Hey, man."

Before she could say anything, another voice came through in the background. "Who you talking to?"

Carmela recognized her brother's voice and withheld a groan. They'd set up this time purposely so they both could do it in secret. *Perfect timing as usual, Ethan.*

"It's Carm."

"Carm's on?" Ethan's face appeared in front of Sawyer's a moment later, close to the screen. His expression of surprise melted away into a grin. "Hey, sis. How's it going?"

"Great." *Nothing to see here, Ethan. It's totally normal for a girl to Skype with her guy* friend *at this time of night while on vacation.*

Not.

"Mom's loving it too and is currently losing the hundred bucks she took with her to the casino."

"No surprise there." His smile vanished. "Glad you're having fun, but this chat's gonna have to be cut short because Sawyer and I need to get to a meeting."

Worry squeezed her stomach at his grave expression. Whatever it was, it was serious and likely something to do with the terror threat. "O-okay. You guys take care of each other. Love you."

"We always do, and love you too," Ethan said, then

disappeared out of camera range.

Sawyer's dark eyes stared back at her. "Sorry."

"No, don't be silly." She felt cold suddenly, reached for the edge of the quilt to drag it over her. "Just take care of you both."

He nodded. "I will." His gaze flashed left as the sound of a door shutting reached her, then he looked back at her. Ethan had either left the room or gone into the bathroom, she wasn't sure which. "Listen, I—"

He sighed and when he spoke again he dropped his voice to a deep murmur. "I don't have time to say everything I want to, but I just wanted you to know that I've been thinking about us a lot the past few days."

It was exactly what she'd been hoping he'd say, and yet more than she'd expected. Still, she wanted more. She deserved a man who wanted her enough to overcome his own bullshit. "You have?"

"Yeah. I can't stop thinking about you."

Elation thrummed through her and a wide smile spread across her face. "Hmmm. And what have you been thinking?" Because they both knew where she stood on the matter. She didn't know how much time they had until Ethan came back, and she needed to know where they stood before she exploded.

He darted another glance toward wherever Ethan had gone before looking back at her and continuing. "I want to be with you," he blurted. "You and no one else."

Carmela barely kept her mouth from falling open. That was a huge step, and one she didn't want to take unless he truly meant it, was truly ready for it. Even while she was doing the happy dance on the inside, part of her was still skeptical. "What about Ethan?"

"I'm going to talk to him."

Holy crap, if he was willing to face Ethan over this, then he really did mean it. She couldn't help the smile that spread across her face. "What changed your mind?"

"You. Well, that and I've finally pulled my head out of my ass."

She laughed lightly. "It's a damn fine ass, Sawyer, but I'm glad you did." The pleased but slightly embarrassed smile he gave her was too adorable. "You want me to talk to Ethan?"

"No, I'll do it. Has to come from me. First chance I get, I'll tell him about us."

"*No*." He blinked in surprise at the vehemence in her tone, but she continued. "I mean, don't you dare tell him what happened the other night."

Sawyer snorted. "You think I'm insane?"

She laughed. "No. Okay, I was worried that's what you meant. And for the record, I don't want to see anyone but you. In case you were wondering."

The smile he shot her was pure relief and it went straight to her heart. "Good."

Oh, she loved the possessive vibe he was giving off. Just the way he said it in that low, throaty growl got her blood pumping.

He darted another glance in the direction her brother had gone, then said to her, "Come to Virginia for a few days when you get back."

"You mean, right after the cruise?"

He nodded. "I'm going to take a few days' leave when I get back, to let my shoulder heal up. Come away with me. We'll go to someplace on the coast or maybe in the mountains, just the two of us."

Elation kindled in the pit of her stomach. Just the two of them, alone for a few days in some romantic location. She could dispel any lingering worries he might have that their shift in relationship status would change who they were as people. He'd see that she was still her, that she wasn't out to trick or trap him just because they were together.

And the sex they could have. Oh my God, the sex…

Before she could answer, the door off screen opened and Sawyer immediately sobered. "Gotta go. Enjoy the trip to Anchorage."

There were so many things she wanted to say. *Yes, I'll go with you. I can't wait to see you when I get back.*

Or, more honestly, *I love you, Sawyer.*

Because she did. More than he'd ever realize, she'd bet. She got the impression that the situation with Trina and her family had left him feeling unworthy and even cynical of unconditional love. She was determined to prove to him that it not only existed, but that he deserved it and more.

But she couldn't say any of that now so she resolved to tell him in person when she saw him next, either in Seattle or when she met him in Virginia. Because no way was she turning down the opportunity to steal that precious alone time with him. "I will. Bye."

After he was gone Carmela turned off her laptop and closed the lid, then laid back against the pillows with a sappy smile and tears gathering in her eyes. She felt like she should pinch herself just to make sure she wasn't dreaming, hadn't imagined that whole conversation.

Impossible as it had seemed a few days ago, it felt like she was on the brink of seeing her dream come true. Sawyer wanted a future with her, and she couldn't wait to seize that chance.

****

Sawyer rushed through his shower a few hours later, ignoring the burn in his right shoulder as he washed up, impatient to get out of there and back to the hotel so he could call Carmela again. It was late, almost one in the morning Seattle time, but if he knew Mama Cruz, she'd still be going strong at the casino so he'd likely catch Carmela alone.

They'd just come from another op where they'd

arrested more people linked with Aziz's cell. Aziz and all the others were being questioned separately in a facility near Lewis-McChord. He should probably have been more focused on that and whatever intel they would divulge to the interrogators, but right now all he could think about was Carmela.

It had been scary as hell to blurt out what he had and ask her to take a getaway trip with him. He hoped she'd say yes, wouldn't get a decent night's sleep until he knew her answer. His head told him to walk away before he got hurt again but his heart wouldn't let him, and there was no way he would shut her out now.

It was terrifying to put himself out there with her and risk everything that came with having a relationship with her, but it also wasn't fair to punish her for all his fears and insecurities. First chance he got, he was going to apologize for what he'd said that night in the park, tell her he wanted a fresh start with her.

He dried off, dressed, and hurried down the hallway to the locker room where the team had stored all their gear. Reaching into his bag, he pulled out his phone to check for messages. His heart leapt when he saw one from Carmela.

I'd love to go away with you. I'll make it work somehow.

It felt like a two-thousand pound weight had just been lifted off his chest. He exhaled a deep breath and turned to lean his back against the wall of lockers.

A few lockers down, Schroder shut his and eyed him as he shifted the strap of a backpack up higher on his shoulder. Evers was grabbing his gear beside the medic, Blackwell on his left. "Good news?"

"Yeah." The best. He smiled to himself and typed back a response, had just hit send when he noticed Evers reach for the back of Schroder's pack.

"Hey, what's that?" Evers started to yank the zipper

down. Schroder turned away, looking slightly embarrassed, but Evers didn't let go.

"It's nothing," Schroder argued, giving the pack a yank, a slight flush high up on his cheeks.

"No? Then how come you're trying to hide it and turning all red? Huh?" Evers raised both eyebrows and plucked something from the partially open pouch.

Scowling, Schroder grumbled something under his breath and tried to snatch it back, but Evers only held it farther away.

After examining it for a second, Evers gave Schroder an incredulous look. "A coloring book? Seriously?"

Now Sawyer couldn't help but look at the book too, and even Blackwell came over for a closer look. Sure enough, right there on the cover it said *Adult Coloring Book*. What the hell was an adult coloring book? "Is that like, porn or something?" Sawyer asked, wondering why the hell Doc was in possession of something like that. Because if it *was* a porn coloring book, that was some messed-up shit.

Schroder gave him a dirty look and crossed his arms. "No." He stood there glaring at Evers while his teammate flipped through the pages one by one. Pictures of muscle cars mostly, from what Sawyer could see, a few of them colored in. Not a single porn picture in sight. Which was kind of a relief.

Evers looked truly confused as he glanced back at Schroder. "You color?"

"Yeah." Schroder reached out and snatched it from him, taking time to carefully smooth the pages down before closing the book.

"Since when?"

"Since Taya suggested I try it, okay?"

When Evers looked at him, Sawyer shrugged helplessly. "Try it for what?" Evers pressed.

Schroder let out a long-suffering sigh. "To help with

my PTSD issues, all right? What, did you think I'd just resolved all my shit within the space of a few weeks? I'm doing way better, especially with Taya's help, but when I'm away from her things tend to get worse. When I have nightmares and can't sleep I pull this out and do my thing. Gives me something to focus on and helps relax me. It's recommended by therapists all the time to treat different types of trauma, anxiety and depression. Satisfied?"

"Uh, yeah." Evers eyed him as he hefted a duffel strap over one shoulder, shook his head once. "Just when you think you know a guy…"

"Whatever, you're just jealous because you know you could never color as good as me," Schroder told him with a smug smile. "I mean come on, you saw all my shading in there. It's pretty awesome."

When his phone buzzed in his hand, Sawyer tuned the others out and read the text message from Carmela.

What I've got on underneath.

Before his brain could process what that meant, a picture popped up on the screen. His heart momentarily seized and his eyes widened.

Holy motherfucking *hell*. It was Carmela, but only from the neck down. And she was wearing nothing except extremely hot lingerie and the crucifix necklace.

His gaze glued to the mounds of her breasts, pushed up so enticingly by that black lace with the necklace dangling just above her cleavage, then hungrily trailed down over her stomach to the matching black wisp of lace between her thighs.

Despite himself and the fact that Ethan was standing less than fifteen feet away while he was ogling a half-naked picture of his sister, Sawyer couldn't completely smother his grin. He didn't dare answer here in front of the guys so he hit the home button and started to slip the phone back into his pocket.

But when he glanced up, all the others were watching

him intently. "What?" he asked.

"I know that look," Evers said, a grin spreading over his face. "Vance has a hottie on the line."

He shook his head, fought a stab of panic. "No I don't."

Schroder pointed a finger at him, shook it. "He's doing it. That sorry-ass excuse for a poker face." He laughed. "Dude, you're so busted."

"So who is she?" Blackwell asked.

"No one." His heart drummed a frantic rhythm against his ribs.

"No one, huh? Well we'll see about that." Evers moved lightning quick and lunged for the phone.

Sawyer turned at the last second, blocking Evers with his body but his teammate managed to reach around and wrench the phone from him. He suppressed a growl as his shoulder twinged, sending a white-hot burst of pain down his arm. Goddamn stupid tendons.

Evers hit the power button.

Oh shit, oh, shit. Sawyer tried to snag it but Evers danced out of range. Full blown panic hit him. Why had he left the text there and why hadn't he thought to lock his phone fast enough? "Give it back, man."

"In a minute. I just wanna see—" He stopped and stared at the screen, then laughed. "No one, huh? Then how come she's sending you boob shots?"

He clamped his jaw shut while Schroder and Blackwell got in on it, talking dirty smack about the picture.

Then Ethan stepped into the room and Sawyer's heart nearly stopped. Panic ripped through him and he grabbed for the phone, prepared to wrestle it back if need be.

"God dammit, I said give it *back*." He grabbed Evers's wrist, clamped down on it and tried to twist the phone free, but his teammate broke his hold with a quick move that sent a flash of pain through his right shoulder.

The room went silent, all four of the guys staring at Sawyer now. Schroder seemed to cover a wince.

"What's going on?" Ethan asked, walking over.

Evers rubbed his wrist and shot Sawyer a glare. "We were just giving him a hard time about a dirty picture some girl just sent him and he freaked. Jeez, Vance."

Yeah, for fucking good reason.

Ethan frowned at him, gestured for Evers to give him the phone.

Sawyer shot out a hand for it. "Give it here."

Ethan snagged it from Evers and held it away from Sawyer, an evil grin on his face. "Chill, man. What's the problem? She illegal or something—" He glanced down at the screen, and his expression froze.

His smile slowly died away and Sawyer closed his eyes for a second as utter dread swamped him. *No. No no no no…*

But it was too late. The damage was already done.

He opened his eyes to find Ethan studying the picture, his face set in lines of disbelief. There was no way he'd miss the crucifix dangling between those beautiful breasts. No way he'd not recognize it, since he'd been there when Sawyer had given it to Carmela last Christmas.

Ethan sucked in a breath, his entire body stiffening as he put it all together. "Wait." He lifted his gaze to Sawyer, his eyes rounding in outrage. "Is that…my sister?"

The room went utterly, deathly silent.

Ethan's eyes threw daggers at him and the others stared at him with identical expressions of pained sympathy as they realized what had just happened.

Sawyer pushed out a breath and stifled a groan. This wasn't how he'd wanted to broach this subject with Ethan. Not even close.

He met his best friend's livid gaze head on. "Can we talk somewhere private?"

Ethan's expression was murderous. "Fuck you, private, answer the goddamn question. Is that Carm or not?"

"Yeah, it's Carm."

The other guys spun on their heels and made a hasty retreat out of the room, taking the remaining oxygen with them. The door shut behind them with a thud and it was suddenly hard to breathe in the awful silence that followed. Sawyer braced himself for a fist in the jaw, knew he deserved that and more for what he'd done. And there was no way he couldn't come clean now.

Ethan's expression was still enraged as he stared at him. "You're fucking my *sister*?"

"No!" He held up his hands, took a step back as Ethan advanced on him. "No, it's not like that." Technically they hadn't had sex. It had been close though. He'd wanted her for so long and she'd had him so worked up that he'd been a heartbeat away from grabbing her and driving his cock into her. Even now he wasn't sure how he'd stopped himself.

Ethan stopped, his body coiled, ready to spring. "It's not like that? Then why the hell is she sexting you?" He held up the phone in accusation, that furious stare burning right through him.

Sawyer thought fast, knowing he needed to do damage control before things escalated. "I care about her, and it's not a fling. You know I would never do that."

Ethan dragged a hand through his hair, seemed to struggle with himself a moment. "Dammit to fucking hell, Sawyer... What the hell were you two *thinking*?"

Ethan was too pissed to listen to reason now. He wouldn't hear anything Sawyer said until he calmed down. Still, he had to try. "I'm not using her, E. I swear. And you gotta promise me, man." He swallowed, fighting down the fear that threatened to choke him. "You gotta swear to me that this won't change things between us."

Ethan scowled at him. "What the hell's that supposed to mean? You hooked up with my sister, dumbass, of course it changes things between us."

Cold spread through his gut. He prayed Ethan didn't mean that the way it sounded. His pulse thudded a dull rhythm in his ears as he awaited a response. *Don't. Don't cut me out of your life because of this.*

Before he could say anything else the door opened and Evers stuck his head in, dividing a look between the two of them. "Sorry, guys, but DeLuca needs us. Briefing with him and Rycroft right now."

Ethan sent him one last scathing look before spinning around and heading for the door. Sawyer followed, worry gnawing a hole in his stomach. The three of them hurried down the hall to the briefing room, none of them saying a word.

"Hurt her and I'll fucking kill you," Ethan muttered to him right before they stepped through the door, still glaring at him.

Sawyer inclined his head. "I hear you." Shit, he hated that it had gone down like that. Maybe they could talk again later on once Ethan had calmed down and had time to get used to the idea of him and Carm together. Because Sawyer definitely wanted a relationship with her. He hoped Ethan would listen long enough to hear that, anyway.

The rest of the team was already waiting in the room when they walked in. Sawyer asked Bauer what the story was, but the former SEAL didn't know. It had to be related to the Aziz arrests though, and it had to be big. Anticipation hung heavy in the air while they waited.

Sawyer found himself holding his breath when Rycroft strode into the room a moment later, followed by DeLuca, Celida and Travers. It could have been his imagination, but it seemed to Sawyer like they all looked at him and Ethan before taking up positions at the front of the room. It set him even more on edge but he shelved his concern. He needed to keep his head in the game, since it looked like they were about to have another mission.

Rycroft stood at the front of the room and got right to it. "Just got a major break in the investigation. Turns out Aziz was definitely acting on orders from someone back in Saudi Arabia, although we don't know who that is yet. What we do know, is the cell's target." He looked at DeLuca.

"Signal intercepts verify that the cell we've been tracking has been in close contact with another cell working out of Russia. The good news is, for right now we're fairly certain we're not dealing with chemical weapons," their commander said. "The bad news is, we still don't know who the cell leader is, the attack is imminent and the suspected target is a civilian ship already at sea off the U.S. coast."

His gaze shifted first to Ethan, then Sawyer.

Sawyer's muscles tightened as dread slithered through him. The back of his neck began to prickle in warning a moment before DeLuca said the words Sawyer had been dreading.

"Because of the intel pointing to a Russian link, it looks like the target is likely going to be a cruise ship currently off the coast of Alaska."

Chapter Ten

At three minutes before midnight, Wira received the signal he'd been waiting for. A text message saying "May Allah be with you" from the *Mawla*. He slipped out of his bunk and quietly alerted Ali via radio to signal the others, then headed up the stairs on his way to the nav bridge.

The countdown had begun.

Nerves and excitement stirred in his gut. His pulse thudded in his ears along with his booted footsteps as he ascended the carpeted stairs. Three of his men were waiting for him when he reached the lower promenade deck. They nodded at him and followed up the forward staircase without a word. Ali and one other team member were waiting for them on the lido deck.

"Is the captain in his quarters?" Wira asked Ali quietly. There were hardly any passengers around at this hour, which was why they'd chosen it.

"Yes. Everything's as it should be."

Perfect. And he had more than a dozen others placed throughout the ship, armed, ready and waiting. As soon as the attack began, the other teams would take out the key crewmembers who might pose a threat, and help lock down the ship. They'd gone over the plan many times in meetings prior to boarding the ship in Seattle. Each man knew his assignment, knew what precautions to take and what contingencies to use if a problem arose.

Inside the stairwell Wira paused in the surveillance video blind spot their man up on the bridge had created a few minutes ago for them. They'd only have another minute or two before the camera turned back on again. Plenty of time to gear up and get into position.

One of the men stood guard at the bottom of the stairs and one stood above, in case any passengers or other crewmembers came along. Wira signaled to Ali, who began handing out weapons from a bag he'd stowed in a compartment behind a fire extinguisher set into the wall.

They all pulled black balaclavas over their faces and checked their weapons: a military-style knife, two Glock pistols and an AR-17, all fully loaded. Canisters of tear gas, gas masks. Then they donned night vision goggles as well.

Ali hid the bag and set the fire extinguisher back into place, covering the hidden compartment. Then Wira took the radio from his belt and contacted their man on the bridge to ensure everything appeared normal to the other crewmembers. "All clear here. Signing off for the night."

"Roger. Have a good one."

Wira replaced the radio on his belt and nodded at Ali. *Thirty seconds.*

They split into two groups of three, with Wira leading one group and Ali leading the other. The younger man took the lead and started carefully up the stairs toward the bridge while Wira and his men stayed a few steps behind. Once Ali's team breached the bridge, Wira and his men would take the captain.

Ten seconds.

They pulled their goggles into position. Three seconds later, right on cue the lights went out.

Wira raised a hand then swept it sharply downward, signaling Ali to make the assault.

Their rubber-soled boots were nearly silent on the last set of carpeted stairs. Wira's palms were slick and his mouth was dry. Ali waited just long enough for his men to stack up behind him at the door to the bridge, then unlocked it and shoved it open with a clang. Two sharp explosions sounded from the stun grenades Ali had thrown into the room.

Men were shouting but quickly fell silent as rapid gunshots rang out, telling Wira their assault had been unexpected and met with little resistance. He rushed past the entrance to the bridge and made it to the captain's quarters just as the cabin door flung open. Van Slater stood there in pants and bare feet with a pistol in his hand, his face a mask of shock through the green glow of the night vision goggles as Wira lunged for him.

Van Slater shouted and twisted to the side but Wira had the advantage of surprise and the cover of darkness. He grabbed the gun and tackled him to the ground, used the butt of the pistol to stun him with a blow to the side of the head. Van Slater grunted and slumped forward, but was still conscious.

"What…do you…want?" he gasped out.

He firmed his hold. "Your ship." They were taking him prisoner rather than killing him purely for leverage purposes. Keeping him alive might buy them time, and maybe resources from authorities. If he proved a problem later on, they'd kill him too.

Van Slater tried in vain to twist free, straining to see him in the darkness. "Who the hell…are you?"

"The new captain," Wira snarled back, shoving the man's wrists higher up between his shoulder blades.

Emergency lights began to flicker on around them

but Wira wasn't worried. Even if Van Slater recognized him through the balaclava, it didn't matter anymore. He was now a prisoner in his own ship.

Wira pinned Van Slater to the floor while one of Wira's men bound his hands behind him and then his ankles. For good measure they gagged him before securing him to his bunk and barring his door shut from the outside.

Breathing hard, triumph and elation pumping through him, Wira stalked into the bridge. Ali and the others stood over top of the officers' bodies. They would move the captain down to a holding area shortly and post armed guards outside the room to ensure he didn't escape.

News of the siege should reach authorities in the next few minutes, along with their published manifesto. That would aim a spotlight on his brother's plight, a light which would only grow brighter as the hours passed.

Families and loved ones of the passengers and crew aboard would put substantial pressure on their governments to act. Wira's team had already proven their resolve by killing the officers and some of the crew. Once they began killing passengers over the next sixteen hours, the pressure on foreign governments to act would increase dramatically.

And then, with a little help from their Russian sympathizers, he'd be on his way to find Leo. Even if he died in the attempt, the media coverage would ensure someone looked into the case, expose the U.S. and its secret "black" CIA holding facilities that dotted Eastern Europe.

Ignoring the bodies and blood on the floor, Wira grabbed his radio and checked to make sure he was on the right frequency before addressing the rest of his team scattered throughout the ship. "Bridge secured. Bagas, report."

"Officers secured," the man announced proudly.

"Engine room also secured. We have a few passengers in here as well, all locked down. The ship is ours, sir."

Excellent. Wira turned to Ali. "Sound the general alarm and steer us north-northwest."

Ali rushed to do as he said. Time to get the few passengers still up and about back to their staterooms so Wira could enact the next phase of the plan without interference.

****

Carmela settled under the down comforter on the cushy bed with a sigh and reached for the remote, intending to search for a movie.

She was three channels into her surfing when the sound of the keycard in the lock made her look toward the door. It opened and her mother stepped inside the cabin, surprise on her face. "Oh, you're still up."

"Yeah. Have a good time?" Carmela was way too wired to sleep, still elated over Sawyer's change of heart.

"Had a *great* time. Even made seventy bucks." She shot Carmela a supremely self-satisfied smile before setting her purse on the small writing desk set against the wall opposite the beds. "And how was your night?"

"Good. Relaxing." And yet incredibly exciting, too.

"Hmmm," her mother murmured, and began taking off her jewelry. "Did you talk to Sawyer, by chance?"

The question made her instantly suspicious. "I did." She kept her reply nonchalant and left out the via Skype part.

"And? What did he have to say?"

"Not much. I told him about our day, asked how things were going there. He said his shoulder's healing up well."

Her mother paused and met her eyes in the large mirror above the desk. "Nothing else?"

"Nope."

She set down her earrings and turned to face Carmela with an arched brow. "You seriously think you can fool your own mother like that? *Tomar el pelo? No seas pendejo.*" She sounded insulted.

Don't be a dumbass? Carmela pretended not to understand what she was talking about, began randomly flipping through the channels to find something that might catch her interest. Until they officially became a couple, what happened between her and Sawyer was her private business and she didn't want even her own mother to know about it. "Fool you about what?"

Her mom snorted. "Carmela Cruz, you're not fooling anybody, especially not me. I know there's something going on between you two."

Nope. Not admitting to that. If she did, her mom would start fantasizing about a wedding and the pitter patter of little grandchild feet. "*Mami*, there's nothing—"

"Ah! Don't you dare lie right to my face. I know there's something." Not to be deterred, her mother marched forward and planted herself on the side of Carmela's bed so she couldn't ignore her. "Well? Tell me!" She smacked Carmela's shoulder in frustration.

"Ow!" She rubbed at her arm, glared at her mother.

"Come on, just tell me!" Her mother's eyes gleamed with excitement. And vodka.

"Mom, there's nothing to tell." Sawyer would hate it if her mom knew what had happened between them.

"Don't insult my intelligence, young lady. I'm not blind, and I know what I see when I look at you two together. You don't think I noticed the way you two were dancing together the other night?"

Carmela shot her a quelling look. "Which you instigated."

Her mom didn't look the least bit guilty. Or apologetic, for that matter. "Or how you've been texting each other like lovesick teenagers this whole trip?"

"Not the whole trip, and Sawyer and I have been texting back and forth for over a year now. It's nothing new. Also, I texted Ethan just as much the past few days, in case you didn't notice." She'd done it purposely, to help avoid suspicion. *Good work, Einstein.*

Her mother shook her head stubbornly and folded her arms across her chest. "I know what I saw, and I know what I know. And when I know, I *know*."

Carmela rolled her eyes. Her mother was freaking relentless. Like a bulldozer on steroids when she wanted something. Carmela needed to downplay this in case things with Sawyer didn't work out the way she wanted them to. "We both have feelings for each other, but he's got…issues he has to work through before he's going to be ready for a relationship with me."

She frowned. "What, you mean because of Trina?"

"Yes. And because he's worried he'll lose you and Ethan too, if we started dating and it didn't work out. So like I said, there's nothing to tell." Okay, she felt bad even saying that little white lie, but she wanted to let things develop on their own, without more added pressure on Sawyer from Mama Cruz.

Her mother narrowed her eyes. "*Ay, bendito*, that's ridiculous. That boy knows I love him to pieces. I don't believe he'd think something like that."

"Well he does. Just leave it alone, okay? Don't be putting any pressure on him about this. I need him to want me because of *me*, not because he feels obligated to jump into a relationship with me."

Her mother looked annoyed now. "Of course I wouldn't pressure him about it. I just can't believe he's afraid of all that."

"Well he is, so he has to make up his own mind when he's ready—"

Her words were cut off when a series of loud beeps

emitted from the speakers in the room, making her jump. The ship's alarm.

She sat straight up, her heart knocking against her ribs as she listened, trying to remember what that particular sequence of beeps meant. Just an alert? Go back to your room and get ready to evacuate? She glanced at her mom, who'd gone completely still. Had they hit something? She hadn't felt anything.

"Attention all passengers," a male voice announced. "Please return to your staterooms immediately and change into warm clothing. Gather your lifejackets and ship's ID cards and await further instructions. Please remain in your staterooms."

Carmela and her mom stared at each other for a second, then they both jumped up and headed for the cabinet where their life jackets were kept.

"Is there a fire, do you think?" her mom asked.

"Don't know, but I don't hear any fire alarms going off and the power's still on." She started stripping off her pajamas, casting a glance out the large glass door that led to their balcony. They were already a long ways off shore. If they had to abandon ship they'd have a long wait in the water, and the thought of being in the rolling Pacific in the middle of the night was terrifying.

Her mother's forehead was creased with worry as she pulled off her dress and shoes and tugged on jeans and a sweater. Carmela slid into a bra and panties, pulled on yoga pants, warm socks and a sweatshirt before putting on her jacket. She handed her mom a lifejacket, was just reaching for her own when another alarm sounded over the ship's speaker system.

"Attention all passengers. Once you have changed into warm clothing, gather your life jacket and ship's ID and report to your muster stations immediately. Please refrain from using the elevators at this time, and use the stairwells instead. Follow crewmembers' instructions carefully. This is not a drill. Repeat, this is not a drill."

Oh, shit. Had to be a fire, or they'd hit something. A rock or something. Visions of the Titanic disaster flashed through her mind, all those people in the freezing water in the middle of the night.

Calm down. They've got enough lifeboats on this one. But then there'd been that cruise ship that had hit the rocks a few years ago and partially capsized, and people trapped in a compartment below the water line had drowned…

She shuddered, grabbed her ID and phone and shoved them into her jacket pocket. She put on running shoes, donned the lifejacket, snapped it up and turned to look at her mother. They stared at each other for a moment in disbelief, the moment surreal.

People began moving around in the hallway outside their door. Carmela reached for her mother's hand. Her mom grabbed hold and squeezed tight. "It's probably nothing serious. They're just erring on the side of caution," Carmela said with a smile.

Her mom nodded, that frown still in place. "Yes. Let's hope so, anyway."

Holding tight to her mother's hand, Carmela opened their cabin door. Passengers already filled the narrow hallway, all in various states of dress except for their matching lifejackets. Everyone was quiet, their expressions serious.

Couples stayed close together and parents carried sleeping little ones as they filed toward the emergency exits at the ends of the hall. Carmela pulled her mother after her and turned left, heading for the closest exit.

Dwi was already at the end of the hall, wearing his own lifejacket, directing passengers toward the starboard side staircase. He smiled when he saw her and gave her a nod. "Everything's going to be fine, ladies and gentlemen, nothing to worry about. I'm sure you'll all be back in your staterooms and tucked into bed shortly. Everyone stay calm, no need to push. Please, no running."

"Dwi, do you know what's going on?" she called out.

He shook his head and gave her another smile that was warm, but far from reassuring under the circumstances. A big cruise liner like this didn't send its passengers to the lifeboats just for kicks. "I'm sure they'll inform us in due time." He switched his focus to an elderly couple near him, gave them that trademark bright smile. "Hello, Mr. and Mrs. Zawitsky. Can I see your ID cards? Yes, muster station thirteen, right this way, just as you rehearsed on the first day with us. Staff will help direct you to the lower promenade deck."

Carmela filed past him out into another hallway and into the stairwell, which was jammed with more people. The pace suddenly slowed to a crawl, all of them jammed together in the enclosed space. A low murmur of voices grew louder and louder and people up front began to stand on tiptoe to see whatever was happening down below.

It seemed to take forever to make it down five decks to the lower promenade deck, the constant repeat of the ship's alarm adding to the building tension. A blast of cold, salt-tinged air hit them from the open doorways that led out onto the wooden promenade deck. The ship's movement seemed more pronounced to her now, the rolling and pitching more evident. God, she did not want to be out on that water in the dark.

From her position she could see people grouped together at the muster stations, but everyone seemed to be milling around out there in confusion. Now that she thought about it, aside from Dwi and a couple other cabin stewards they'd passed, there'd been a distinct lack of crewmembers on hand to help direct the crowd. Where was everyone?

They were almost to the doors when some sort of commotion broke out on the outside deck, out of view.

Carmela stopped walking as the voices coming from outside grew frantic. People started shouting and then a female scream ripped through the air.

Panic rippled through the crowd like a live wire, spreading like an electrical current.

All around her people began pushing and shoving to get back into the stairwell, a writhing, moving knot of humanity. Fear shot up Carmela's spine and she instinctively turned and began pushing her mother back the way they'd come.

"What are you doing?" her mother demanded, pushed along by Carmela's hands on her shoulders.

"Getting back up those stairs. Something's wrong out there." A fire maybe, but she wasn't sticking around to find out.

The words had barely left her mouth when a man stumbled through the doorway, his face a pale mask of fear, eyes wide. "They've got guns!" he shouted.

Everyone froze for a moment in disbelief.

Pop, pop, pop. The distinctive sounds of gunshots came from out on the deck.

Pandemonium erupted.

Carmela cried out and stumbled to her knees as the crowd surged around her, a mad scramble of limbs as people clambered to get back to the stairs. She shoved to her feet, grabbed her mother and pressed her back against the wall to avoid being trampled.

Ahead of her an elderly woman tripped and fell on the stairs. The crowd went right over top of her. She flailed but couldn't get up, then went still. Carmela cringed but didn't dare move from her spot.

More gunshots sounded outside, closer this time. People began screaming and the chaos turned into a stampede. Men and women slammed into her, knocking her around like clothes in a washing machine.

She threw her elbow at a man's chest, managed to

knock him back enough to clear a space for her to push through. Carmela reached back blindly for her mother, managing to snag the front of her lifejacket, then yanked her into the corner formed by the stairwell wall and glued them to it.

Her mother clung to her while the frightened passengers buffeted past, pinning them in place until Carmela couldn't have moved even if she'd wanted to. Out of the corner of her eye she saw men dressed in ship's uniforms rush through the open doors, their faces covered with black masks.

People cried out and scattered away from them and then she saw the rifles they held. They turned toward the people crowded into the stairwell, weapons aimed on them. A scream trapped in her throat. She shrank up against the wall, trying to make as small a target as possible, her eyes locked on the muzzles of those rifles.

A group of men standing close by tried to rush the attackers. The crewmembers pulled out pistols and opened fire before they'd made it five steps, dropping the men where they stood. Everyone dove to the floor and covered their heads.

Carmela stared in horror at the men lying on the carpeted floor, twitching and gasping, blood pooling around them in shiny red puddles. In the deathly stillness that followed only frightened whimpers and sobs broke the silence.

"No one fucking *move,* or we'll kill all of you!" one of the armed men roared. "We are in control of the ship! Anyone who tries to defy us will die."

A mutiny.

As the unbelievable thought registered, Carmela risked a glance around. She and her fellow passengers at the foot of the stairwell were trapped now, maybe sixty or seventy people gathered into a tight knot. No one else was on the stairs behind her. The attackers must have already herded the majority of the other passengers onto the lifeboats, or trapped them in groups like this one elsewhere aboard the ship.

Cold invaded her body, her heart racing at a sickening pace. It didn't matter what the attackers wanted, she knew that the longer they held the ship, the smaller the chances were that she and the others would survive.

Crouched in the corner, she kept her mother behind her and fumbled in her jacket. She pulled out her phone as discreetly as she could, her fingers trembling as she sent off a desperate message to Sawyer. She didn't know if they were still within range of a cell tower, but she had to try. He was the only one who could help them now, aside from Ethan.

Three more armed men burst in from the outer deck. Carmela quickly shoved the phone beneath her sweatshirt and slid it under the stretchy side band of her bra.

"Everyone put your hands on your heads," the man commanded in a loud voice, he and the other two training black rifles on them.

Heart pounding a bruising rhythm against her chest wall, Carmela did as he said.

"Get up. Stand in single file line, now." He made an abrupt motion with the muzzle of his rifle. People cringed but did as he said.

Ahead of Carmela a little girl around five or so clung to her father, face buried in his neck, her frightened sobs slicing at Carmela's heart. Poor baby, she should never be caught up in something like this.

"Carmela," her mother whispered uncertainly, fingers digging into her waist like claws.

"Shh, *Mami*," she whispered back sharply, and moved to stand behind the man trying to comfort his terrified daughter. Her mind raced frantically. They needed to do everything possible not to draw attention to themselves now.

They had to somehow become invisible, recede into this group until the attackers didn't even notice them. It was their only chance of surviving whatever was coming next.

With barked orders and curt gestures the three gunmen rounded them all up and began herding them toward the stern of the ship where the theater was.

Her legs felt stiff, her body wooden as she followed, afraid one of the men would open fire on them at any moment. She kept waiting for it but there was no answering vibration from the cell tucked against her ribs. Had her message even been delivered? She sent up a silent prayer that her text reached Sawyer in time to save them.

Chapter Eleven

Sawyer's entire body was rigid as he listened to Rycroft, Celida and DeLuca detail what little more intel they had on the cruise ship threat. Then Rycroft's phone rang. He glanced at the screen then left the room as he answered.

The dread inside him morphed into a heavy sense of foreboding. *Don't let it be Carm's ship. Don't let it be Carm's ship.*

A minute later Rycroft reappeared, his body language tense. "Coast Guard just received an emergency transmission about a hostile takeover on the Ocean Freedom."

Fuck!

Ethan was out of his chair like someone had just hit him with a cattle prod. He dragged his hands through his hair and started pacing, his expression tormented.

"Cruzie."

Ethan stopped and looked back at DeLuca.

"You and Vance step outside with me." He motioned toward the door. "Come on."

Sawyer got up and followed Ethan and DeLuca out

into the hallway. Ethan walked a few steps past their commander then stopped and slammed the side of his fist against the wall with a resounding thud. "God *dammit*," he snarled.

Sawyer folded his arms across his chest and fought a silent battle to keep the rage and fear tearing through him at bay. It wasn't easy. Not with Carmela and her mother being held hostage on a cruise ship hundreds of miles away.

"If Gold Team can't get here in time and direct action is authorized, your team will be part of the assault. Tell me straight right now, both of you," DeLuca said, facing them with hands on hips. "Are you both good to go if we get the green light on this one?"

"Yes," they both responded automatically.

DeLuca divided a hard look between them. "You guys both know the drill. If I think your judgment is compromised, I'll pull you, no hesitation."

Ethan nodded and Sawyer inclined his head. "Understood." He would hold his shit together, no matter what. It's what he and Ethan had been trained to do. They would both keep their emotional turmoil hidden from view so they could go on this op. It would kill both of them to be pulled out at a time like this.

His phone vibrated in his pocket. He whipped it out, grief splintering inside him when he saw the message. "It's Carm," he rasped out, emotion slamming into him. The garbled message told him just how scared and frantic she must have been when she typed it.

Ethan and DeLuca whipped around to look at him. "What'd she say?" Ethan demanded.

Sawyer was busy typing back a response, praying she'd get it. *Stay safe baby. Stay down.*

He wanted to say something like "we're on it" or "we're coming" but resisted the urge. If one of the hostage takers found the phone and read that, it would leave her open to being interrogated for what it meant. They'd likely search any or all passengers under their power.

He hit send on the pathetic, abbreviated response, then translated her garbled message. "Gunmen on ship. Hostages. Help." He swallowed, trying and failing not to imagine how afraid she must be right now. The violence she must have witnessed. She'd reached out for him and he couldn't get to her.

A picture popped up on screen a second later. Fuzzy, the lighting poor, but it clearly showed five men wearing black balaclavas and holding what looked like AR-17s. A few men wearing lifejackets lay on the floor at their feet, appearing to be dead or dying. Fear shot through him when he realized how close she must be to the gunmen to get the image.

"She got a picture," he said, pushing the words out of his throat made tight by fear and admiration. His girl had the brains and the balls to not only get word out during what had to have been a terrifying situation, she'd also taken a picture, probably hoping they'd be able to ID the gunmen.

And it hit him like a two-thousand pound JDAM.

He loved her. Loved her so much he ached with it, felt like his chest might explode. Fuck, he wanted to hold her so badly right now. Would have given anything to be there to protect her.

He held the phone out for Ethan and DeLuca to see. His commander glanced at it then rushed to open the briefing room door. "Rycroft. We just heard from Cruzie's sister. The ship's definitely been taken over and she sent a picture of some of the suspects."

Sawyer moved out of the way while DeLuca, Rycroft and Celida all rushed past him down the hall, all on their phones. "How soon can you get Gold Team here?" Rycroft asked DeLuca.

"Six hours, give or take."

"Make it so." Then Rycroft called to Sawyer and Ethan over his shoulder. "You guys get your team and gear rounded up. We're heading over to meet with the ST6 boys."

Sawyer rushed back to the briefing room and opened the door to deliver the news to his teammates. "Guys, gear up. We're moving."

Nobody said anything as they quickly gathered their gear and loaded into the vehicles for the short drive to the base. Rycroft was already there at the temporary command center, waiting for them with the SEALs. Bauer walked over to them and was met with handshakes and backslaps.

Sawyer took a seat next to Ethan, rubbed his hands over his thighs. "I just wanna fucking get moving."

"Tell me about it." He crossed his arms over his chest, his foot tapping a restless rhythm against the concrete floor.

Come on, already, he bitched silently. At least get them on a flight to Alaska so they could get within striking distance in the next few hours. They could work out logistics and everything else on the way, coordinate the takedown of the ship and be ready if they got the call.

DeLuca was over with the SEALs, speaking to their commander and team leader with Tuck. Then he stepped to the front of the room and let out a sharp whistle, getting everyone's attention. "Okay, most of you guys know each other already but we'll save all the other introductions for later. I just got the word from the director. We're a go if the higher-ups decide tactical action is necessary on board the Ocean Freedom. As of right now this is a joint operation between the HRT and ST6.

"Blue Team's here already," he said, nodding toward Sawyer and the others, "and Gold Team's being brought in as well. You'll be transported by C-130 to Coast Guard Base Juneau within the hour, as soon as the aircraft's fueled and the crew files a flight plan. All teams will rendezvous there and get ready to take the ship if necessary."

Thank God. Sawyer couldn't stand waiting around here while knowing Carm and her mom were being held hostage. He had so many questions. Who the attackers were, how many, their motivation, whether any security members on board were still alive.

DeLuca turned the floor over to Celida, who strode over to stand next to him.

"Okay, to bring you guys up to speed, here's what we've got so far. The Ocean Freedom is a cruise ship carrying just under three thousand passengers and crew." She used a remote to pull up a picture onto the screen on the wall behind her. "Most of the passengers are North American and European, and the captain is a Dutch national, former Naval officer. We have to assume he's been killed or captured along with the rest of the ship's officers, or that he's in on it, though I doubt the latter.

"The crew is primarily Indonesian and Malaysian, with some Filipino and Indians as well. A kind of manifesto believed to be from someone in command of this cell was just released, and we're questioning Aziz about it right now."

That fucker. Sawyer's hands squeezed into fists. What he wouldn't give for five minutes alone in the interrogation room with that bastard right now.

"From what we can tell, the attackers on board appear to be Indonesian crewmembers. Analysts are also going over the manifesto they published. Their motivation is not only religious, but to draw attention to some members of theirs who they think were captured by U.S. forces and taken to a secret CIA holding facility in Lithuania.

"We also received a picture from one of the passengers aboard ship shortly after the siege began.

We've already been running the crew's faces through facial recognition software right now, and we're hoping for a match soon."

Damn I love you, Carm. He wished he'd told her that before. What if he never got the chance now?

No. She'll be okay. She's smart. She'll lie low, play it safe.

It was driving him nuts to just sit here, his mind making him crazy as it spun a thousand different scenarios that might be taking place right now, each more horrific than the last. The hostage takers had already shown they were willing to kill passengers. Was she still okay? If they found her phone she wouldn't be.

He shifted restlessly, his whole body drawn taut as a wire while trying to pay attention to all the details Celida was giving. He wanted to send another message but knew it was too risky. Carmela was smart. At least if his response got through she'd know he'd heard her, and she'd figure out that help was on its way.

Even if it was coming too damn slowly for anyone's liking.

Rycroft took over now, talking about the Russian angle. "We're still investigating what their involvement means, but I think we can safely presume they're either backing or actually assisting the terrorists on board. The manifesto they just released says the U.S. government has until tomorrow at sixteen-hundred-hours Eastern time to release the prisoners supposedly being held in Lithuania, or they'll randomly begin killing passengers.

"They're not interested in money or negotiations. These guys mean business, and they're willing to die to get what they want."

Sawyer was more than happy to accommodate their wishes and send them all to Allah the first chance he got.

Rycroft's hard silver gaze scanned the room. "When you draw up your tactical plans for boarding the ship, make sure stealth is one of your paramount concerns. Because these bastards claim to have a failsafe on board that they've threatened to detonate if anyone so much as approaches the ship, taking the vessel and everyone on it to the bottom of the ocean."

****

The theater she and her mother had watched the comedy routine in earlier now served as their prison.

Carmela shifted against the right hand wall to ease the stiffness in her lower back and hip. All the seats had already been full by the time they'd been herded in here, so she was crowded with the remaining passengers against the side walls. Her hands and arms had long since turned numb from being on top of her head.

The outline of her phone dug into her skin, where she'd hidden it beneath the side band of her bra. Before they'd herded everyone into the theater, the hostage takers had searched everyone for electronics. Carmela had been careful to keep her upper arms against her sides while she held her hands up. One man had give her a perfunctory search before shoving her through the doorway.

From what she could see, five armed men stood guard in and around the passengers. She couldn't tell exactly where they were, since they'd turned off all the lights in here. They must have cut power to this part of the ship completely, because the air conditioning wasn't working and the temperature had climbed substantially over the last hour.

Sweat beaded on her forehead and upper lip, rolled down her temples and down her sides. It was already stifling but everyone was too afraid to move or say anything. They'd all seen the way they'd shot the men who'd tried to stop them, and the gunmen had made it clear they would shoot without warning if anyone attempted to leave the theater.

A strong vibration buzzed under her right arm, against her ribs. She froze, her blood pressure plummeting at the humming sound her phone made. Shit, she thought she'd set it to silent, but in her haste to hide it she must have hit the wrong button. The sound seemed over pronounced in the quiet room, making her heart pound.

Her mother hissed in a breath and elbowed her but Carmela didn't dare move. Thankfully her arm, sweater and jacket were enough to conceal the illumination from the screen that would have given her away, and the amount of white noise in the room from all the people crowded in here covered the sound.

Was it Sawyer responding? Had he gotten her message?

Please, please... She needed to know he knew about their plight. Needed to know help was on its way.

After a few minutes when no one said or did anything, she began shrinking down, curling into a ball against the wall. Ignoring her mother's sharp jab in the ribs, she eased one hand beneath her jacket and sweater to reach her phone. Each movement was agonizingly slow, but she dared not move faster. She needed to know if her message had gotten out.

When she had the phone in her hand she kept it tucked beneath her sweater and carefully lowered her other hand to pull the neckline of the sweater away from her body, far enough that she could put her face in the opening. With the screen held against her skin, she hit the home screen button and read the text.

Stay down baby. Stay safe.

Tears clogged her throat but she swallowed them down. Baby. What she wouldn't have given to hear him call her that face to face.

Had he just sent it now? Or had there been a delay? She couldn't risk looking again to check, at least now she knew someone she trusted realized what was happening and would send help. Maybe he'd even be directly involved in the rescue.

The thought of him and Ethan taking the ship with his team filled her with simultaneous hope and fear for their safety. She had a responsibility to provide Sawyer with as much intel as she could.

Five armed men were in the theater but she'd seen more on the way here from the amidships staircase. It was clear they had total control of the ship, as no one had tried to counter the threat in the past hour. At least not down here. And from the way the men had been talking to each other over radios, they seemed to be well organized.

There was no way she could reply to Sawyer without putting herself and everyone around her in more peril, so she silenced the phone, tucked it back under her bra band and settled back into her original position. Next to her the father holding his little daughter let out a deep sigh and shifted her in his arms. The girl was restless, still frightened and Carmela's heart went out to them both. These heartless assholes were the worst sort of cowards, holding and threatening innocent people, even children.

"Daddy, I have to go to the bathroom," the little girl whined in a whisper.

The man shushed her and didn't respond. A minute later the squirming got worse. "Daddy…" Carmela could hear the tears in her little voice.

A bright beam of light hit them. They all froze as one of the gunmen aimed a high-powered flashlight at them. "What are you doing?"

None of them said anything, all frozen in place under the laser-like impact of that light.

"You," the man barked, and started toward them. He had his rifle aimed at them with one hand. "What are you doing?"

The father hesitated a moment, then responded. "My

daughter has to use the bathroom."

He grunted. "She can piss in her pants like the rest of you," he sneered in heavily accented English.

The little girl—Jenny—started to cry softly. Her father tried to comfort her, his own agitation stoking Carmela's anger. *So brave of you, asshole. Standing there pointing an automatic weapon at an unarmed man and his innocent five year old.* The rage churned just beneath the surface, a slow, seething mass under her skin.

Her mother grabbed her sleeve. "Don't," was all she said, her voice nearly imperceptible, but Carmela heard the plea in it all the same.

She needn't have worried.

One of the other men snarled something in a language she didn't understand and started toward them. Carmela shrank away from the father, wishing she could pull Jenny into her arms and make this all go away. Please stay still and be quiet, she silently begged the little girl, who was still crying, the heartbroken sounds slicing at Carmela.

The second gunmen stalked toward them, shoving his way through the crowd. "Nobody move," he growled. "My men have the entire room covered." His boots thudded over the carpet as he neared them, rifle held across his chest.

The people around them seemed to melt away, several of them gasping as he took something from his belt. He held up a bottle of water and twisted it open, his rifle dangling in front of him. "Drink this and let her go in it after," he snapped at the father, who took it without a word.

The gunman pivoted to return to his place but caught the edge of his toe under Carmela's thigh. He barked something at her in another language and gave her a shove with his boot. There was nowhere for her to go, and when she didn't move fast enough, he jabbed the butt of his rifle against her ribs…

Somehow her phone came loose, slid from beneath her top and hit the floor, and the screen lit up like a freaking beacon.

She held her breath. The man froze for a second then grabbed it. He hit the screen and saw Sawyer's message and her heart plummeted to her toes, taking all her blood with it. A wave of cold suffused her, icy terror washing up her spine.

The man turned on her with a furious expression and bent to hiss in her face. "What is this?" he demanded. "Answer me!" he grabbed her chin in a cruel grip, his fingers digging into her cheeks, his face inches from hers.

She didn't answer, terrified that whatever she said would be a death sentence.

"What is it?" one of the others called to him.

He straightened, holding the phone up. "She's been communicating with someone. She was trying to get help." He turned back to her, grabbed a handful of her hair this time. "Who is it? Who sent you this?"

She tried desperately to think of something to say that might save her, came up blank.

The man let out another snarl and yanked her up by her hair. Carmela gasped and shot to her knees, one hand automatically going to his wrist to prevent him from pulling out a handful of her hair. "Get up," he shouted and yanked again.

She stumbled to her feet, her heart slamming so hard she felt sick. Then her mother grabbed her arm. "Carmela, no!"

The man's patience snapped. "Both of you," he ordered, lunging for her mother. Carmela tried to pull out of his hold but it was impossible and within seconds he had her and her mother and was marching them forward toward his teammates. "Call Wira," he called out to them. "We're taking them to him."

Chapter Twelve

Wira got the call from Bagas just as he left the bridge. "What?" he barked, stalking past the men guarding the door. They were on course for international waters, heading for the rendezvous point where the Russian helos would take off from a waiting ship and extract them.

"We have a problem. One of the passengers has been sending messages to someone on shore, and I think you need to see it."

Wira swore. "I told you to search everyone thoroughly. You were supposed to take all the electronics from them."

"We did. Not sure how we missed it."

The messages were probably nothing to worry about, but he could use this to his advantage to keep the other passengers in line. "Are you in the theater now?"

"Yes. We were going to bring her and her mother up to you."

"No. Leave them there, I'll come to you. I'm going to make an example out of them."

"Yes, sir."

Wira jogged down the stairs from the bridge. Three of his men fell in step with him, acting as bodyguards as he made his way down to the promenade deck and toward the theater at the stern of the ship.

On the way he checked in with his remaining men posted in various stations throughout the vessel. The engine room, others posted outside on the deck to watch the loaded lifeboats. Far easier to keep the majority of the passengers contained that way.

By now news of the siege would have reached authorities, and they would know about the manifesto. They'd likely figure out his involvement soon as well, but he doubted they'd be able to make the connection between him and Leo. Not without some very thorough investigative work, and by the time they figured it out, he'd hopefully be halfway to Russia.

When he got to the theater Ali was already waiting outside the doors, holding two women at gunpoint. They looked up at him as he approached and Wira immediately recognized the young woman and her mother he'd seen boarding the ship prior to departing Seattle. From Miami, he remembered.

They both stared at him in shock as they realized who he was, their bodies completely still, kneeling there on the carpeted floor with their hands behind their backs.

"What have you got?" he asked Ali.

His second-in-command handed him the phone. The screen was cracked but once Ali entered the code she must have given him to unlock the screen, the text message exchange was clearly visible. Wira read the messages then met the younger woman's gaze. "Who did you contact?"

She stared back at him for a moment, her golden brown eyes full of a defiance Wira found equally admirable and annoying. "A friend."

He slid the phone into his pocket. "Who?" When she didn't answer immediately he lost patience. He wasn't

KAYLEA CROSS

going to tolerate anyone playing games with him, especially not her.

"Who is it?" he demanded, and withdrew the pistol from the holster on his right hip.

Her face tightened but she still didn't answer.

Rather than aim it at her, Wira pointed it at her mother. "Start talking, or I'll put a bullet in each of her knees and work up from there."

She swallowed. "His name is Sawyer."

A boyfriend? Wira kept the pistol aimed at the mother's knees. "Where is he and what does he do?"

"Seattle. And he's…"

He kept his finger curved around the trigger. Another ounce or two of pressure and the pistol would fire. "He's what?"

She hesitated a fraction before answering. "He's there on a contract job."

The way she'd paused set off warning bells. She was either lying or hiding something, and if she was willing to lie with a weapon pointed at her mother, then his gut said she was covering something important. He tightened his grip on the pistol. "What kind of contract job?" The wording itself made him suspicious.

"For the government," she murmured, eyes downcast.

Now the suspicion turned into alarm. "Is he military?"

Again, she hesitated. Wira was done.

He tilted the pistol a fraction of an inch and fired once. Both women cried out as the bullet slammed into the floor, less than two inches from the mother's left kneecap. "Who does he work for?" he shouted.

The young woman jerked her gaze back to him. "The FBI," she blurted. "He's with the FBI."

Wira clenched his jaw as anger suffused him. His entire plan hinged on having enough time to get within

176

range of those Hind-D helos that were coming for him and his team before the U.S. launched an attack. The time stamp on her first text message was almost two hours before they'd released the manifesto, and that advance notice might screw with his timeline. They were far enough off shore that it would take authorities some time to launch an offensive, and though Wira was willing to use the failsafe before evacuating if necessary, he would only do it as a last resort.

Both women cowered as he loomed over them. He was tempted to shoot them both here and now, but if the younger one had that kind of connection with someone in the FBI, she might yet prove useful to him if he needed to stall for time later on. And she could certainly prove useful to him now in a different way.

He waved the pistol at them. "Get up," he ordered coldly.

They both struggled to their feet, the mother weaving slightly, her chest rising and falling with her rapid breaths. Wira seized the daughter's arm and jerked her toward him. She stumbled but kept her footing, walking quickly to match his pace. Ali grabbed hold of the mother and followed him into the darkened theater.

Once on stage Wira got on the radio to one of his men up on the bridge. "Give me lighting on the stage in the main theater. I want everyone in here to see this."

The cold words sent a wave of foreboding through Carmela.

Moments later, lights came on above and in front of her. She flinched at the sudden brightness and stood there stiffly, her hands secured behind her while Wira's fingers dug into her upper arm. He was her height, around five-feet-six, but strong. His short dark hair was damp with sweat and the way his angry black gaze bored into her was terrifying.

It had been a shock to realize the head of security was the man behind the attack, but the more she thought about it, the more it made sense. The cruise line and crew had obviously trusted him to put him in that position in the first place, giving him the element of surprise when he attacked. A man in his position would know everything about security measures and emergency procedures on board, would know exactly who to take out and what to do in order to seize the ship.

Carmela swallowed, her mouth dry as sand, her pulse roaring in her ears. As the sister of an HRT member, she was used to giving a cover story about what Ethan did. But when Wira had interrogated her she'd told him the truth about Sawyer for two reasons.

One, she'd hoped it would make them think twice about killing any more passengers if he knew American authorities were aware of what was happening, maybe buying them enough time for a rescue attempt. And two, if these guys were capable of taking an entire cruise liner hostage without anyone from the outside world knowing about it, then they likely had the capability to trace Sawyer's number and find out the truth on their own. Maybe her honesty would gain her points with Wira. Maybe he'd see her as a valuable asset now, and want to keep her alive.

Or not.

The man who she assumed was his second-in-command stood a dozen feet away holding her mother, who was watching her and Wira anxiously. All the other passengers sat before them with their hands either bound behind them or placed on top of their heads. Some of them stared at the floor, others at her and Wira. The huge, two-story room was deathly quiet, everyone seeming to hold their breath along with her, waiting to see what he would do.

"You were all warned what would happen if any of you defied my orders," he told them in a harsh voice that sent a shiver of dread through her. Despite the heat in the room her hands were icy cold and a trickle of cold sweat slid down her sides. "This woman was caught sending text messages to an FBI agent. And this is how I deal with people who defy me."

Before Carmela could react he slammed the butt of the pistol into the side of her head. Pain splintered through her skull and she went down, hitting the floor with a thud. She must have blacked out for a few seconds because the next thing she was aware of after opening her eyes was a blur of color and light. Everything was woozy.

She winced and tried to roll over, wanting to get to her knees, but her body wouldn't obey. The bright lights overhead hurt her eyes and the pain in her head made her nauseous. Then Wira was leaning over her, his dark eyebrows drawn together in a fierce scowl, his expression furious as he yelled something at her. His voice was muffled, like she was underwater.

When she didn't respond to whatever he'd said he grabbed her by the hair and yanked her head up. Carmela let out a yelp and tried to scramble to her knees to relieve the pressure. Pain radiated from just behind her temple down the side of her neck and she felt something warm trickling down the side of her face.

He shook her once then jerked her head back, forcing her to meet his gaze. Her vision and hearing cleared instantly. "Do you hear me?" he screamed into her face, the rage in his eyes making her stomach clench. She could hear her mother crying in the background, begging him to let her go. "I'm going to drag you outside, make you watch while I shoot your mother in the head, then I'm going to dump you both overboard and watch you drown."

Terror forked through her. *No!* She wouldn't let him

kill her mother for this. "No, *Mami*, no! Don't hurt her, please—"

The radio on his belt chirped. Wira stilled, then a man's urgent voice came through. "Wira, come in. We've got a situation down here near the engine room. One of our men saw some unsecured crewmembers and he thinks they're trying to organize an attack."

Wira made an irritated sound in the back of his throat and shook her once, making her flinch as the increased pressure on her scalp intensified the pain in her head. Just as quickly he released her with a rough shove and booted her between her shoulder blades for good measure.

She hit the floor hard, her right shoulder and side taking the brunt of the impact, and immediately curled into a ball to try and protect herself from more blows.

"Search them all again for electronics, and keep a close eye on this one because I might use her later." He jabbed her with the toe of his boot. "If anyone gives you trouble, just shoot them," he ordered his men, then stalked for the wide double doors at the top of the stairs, leaving Carmela trembling and bleeding on the floor.

****

Sawyer hitched the straps of his ruck up higher on his shoulders and hustled across the tarmac in the darkness toward the Coast Guard station, barely even noticing the way the weight and friction irritated the stitches in his left shoulder. Ten minutes ago they'd received a green light from the director of the FBI to execute the takedown of the ship. The hostage takers weren't responding to negotiators' attempts to make contact with them, and with so many lives at stake, tactical action was necessary.

He couldn't wait to get there so he and the others could actually *do* something to help the passengers. No one knew how many of them had already been killed during the initial siege. There'd been total radio silence from Carmela since that text, and both he and Ethan were worried sick.

The familiar scent of jet fuel hit him as he fell in line behind Ethan. Behind them the noise of the C-130's engines lowered in pitch as the pilots powered down. Off to his right he spotted four Pavehawks already waiting for them, rotors turning slowly. Their elite Air Force crews would be ready to launch at a moment's notice.

Sawyer hoped DeLuca pulled the trigger fast on this one.

The station was a flurry of activity, people rushing in and out, the commander coming over to greet DeLuca and Rycroft. Out in the lead, Tuck led the way into the building and down a hallway to a quiet room near the back of the station. Their team and the SEALs all squeezed in there together with DeLuca and Rycroft.

"Just got word from Gold Team leader that their flight got delayed due to mechanical problems," DeLuca announced to the packed room. "They'll take the next transport available but with the delay we'll have to do this operation without them because we can't wait."

That didn't worry Sawyer. They had plenty of experienced operators here, ready and raring to go.

DeLuca outlined the relatively new intel. They'd been receiving constant updates from investigators along with satellite images, with Celida and Travers keeping them informed from back in Seattle.

It looked like most of the lifeboats were loaded with passengers and they'd been able to catch a glimpse of a handful of the terrorists. Coast Guard and Navy vessels in the area were also providing what intel they could, giving brief reports while abiding by the terrorists' orders and maintaining a certain distance from the ship, which appeared to be sailing northwest. All signs indicated they were heading for international waters, toward Russia.

Sawyer and the others had to take the ship before they left U.S. waters, or more precious hours would be lost waiting on reams of red tape and diplomatic bullshit to be cleared. They couldn't afford that kind of delay. They had four full hours of darkness left to operate with, and they had to make the most of that window to give them maximum cover.

"Here's what we've got in terms of backup in the area." DeLuca listed all the assets available to them before, during, and after the op. Once Sawyer and the others launched their counter-attack, the Coast Guard would move in close enough to rescue people stranded in the lifeboats.

"There's talk of some Russian helos coming to extract the tangos once they're within range. Our Navy is ready to intercept if they cross the International Boundary. Right now the status of the remaining passengers and crew is unknown, so time is of the essence." DeLuca signaled for Tuck and the ST6 team leader to take the floor. "Okay, let's hear what you've got."

Using the ship's schematics on a screen mounted on the wall behind them, Tuck and the SEAL laid out their best options which they'd all brainstormed during the flight up here. They all knew the layout of the ship by now, knew what each deck contained along with all the entrances and exits.

"We insert via helo drop and move in close with Zodiacs to avoid detection," Tuck said to the room. "At this point we still don't know exactly what the 'failsafe' on board is or where it's located, but our best guess is in or near the engine room. If they detonate it, they're going to want to do as much damage to the hull as possible in an attempt to sink the ship."

Sawyer and the others listened intently while the two team leaders reviewed the primary plan and then the first two contingency plans. Team members tossed several suggestions back and forth, but the final decision lay with Tuck and the SEAL leader.

"We'll board here near the starboard bow," the SEAL, a stocky dark-haired guy said as he pointed to the area on screen, "and HRT will board at the port stern. We take the bridge while HRT secures the engine room and tries to locate the failsafe. Once those objectives are taken care of, we sweep the ship and take out any remaining tangos. Coast Guard and Navy will move in to assist after the ship is secured and help offload passengers and crew. Sniper teams will assist from the air and from the Coast Guard vessel." He looked up at them. "Any questions?"

Everyone shook their head. Ethan shifted in his seat beside him. Sawyer began bouncing his foot up and down, impatient to get going, his entire body tense and his mind racing. *Come on. Let's go.* He was more than fucking ready to do this, and knew the rest of the guys were as well.

"Let's move," Tuck said. "Wheels up in ten minutes."

Thank God.

Sawyer surged to his feet and headed to the door, his mind already in full operational mode. No matter what it took, they were going to take that ship back. He just prayed it would be in time to save Carmela and her mom.

Chapter Thirteen

C armela's head jerked up when she began to doze off. She winced at the sharp pain in her head and shifted uncomfortably on the floor. That Wira guy's second-in-command stood nearby, keeping an eye on her and all the others in his section of the theater. He was sweating too, the facemask long gone, the armpits of his uniform soaked through.

She had no idea how long they'd been in here but it must have been hours since Wira had pistol whipped her and stalked out of the theater. Two guards were keeping watch while people were using a bucket in the corner of the room as a toilet. A humiliating experience, but better than sitting in your own mess.

She rolled her neck in a futile attempt to alleviate the pressure and took a surreptitious look around. It was dark except for over by the makeshift bathroom in the corner where they had a dim light on.

A few feet to her left, her mother appeared to be asleep finally. A blessing, since it looked like they were going to be stuck in here for the foreseeable future. Wira had said he might use her later, and even though Carmela wasn't sure what he'd meant by that, she sure as hell didn't want to find out.

Sawyer had gotten her message hours ago. He would have reported it immediately, and their situation would be working up some chain of command somewhere.

How long until they made a rescue attempt? She was sure protocol normally dictated trying to contact the hostage takers first, attempt to talk them down or at least negotiate, but maybe not in this situation. Which would be a total waste of time and there was no telling what Wira would do if things escalated.

Although why bother holding them prisoner at all if he just planned to kill them all later? That made no sense, so he must be holding them for ransom or as collateral.

Maybe he thought he could use her connection with Sawyer later somehow. There was a possibility Sawyer's team might be either involved in or responding directly to this crisis though, and it would be a cold day in hell before she endangered Sawyer and the others by giving away any other information. Like him and her brother belonging to the HRT.

Her butt and back were hurting almost as much as her head. She stretched her legs out to ease the tension in her muscles and her shoe hit something on the carpet. Hard pieces of something that sounded a lot like glass when she investigated with her foot.

Keeping an eye on where the second-in-command stood, she inched her way over until she was able to reach behind her and feel around with her hands. There. Her fingers touched something smooth and cool and thin, the edges sharp. Glass. Maybe from a champagne flute like the one she'd sipped out of in here during the comedy show just hours before.

She waited until the guard shifted his stance and looked away before scooting carefully toward her mother. Carmela slid a leg out and nudged her mom, who woke with a start and straightened. There was just enough light for Carmela to see the outline of her face. Making sure the guard was still looking elsewhere, she leaned to the side and whispered as loudly as she dared. "Sit back to back with me."

Her mom didn't say anything but after a moment began to shift around until their backs were together. Carmela made sure they were angled to hide their hands behind the row of people in front of them, then reached back for her mom's hands and pressed the sliver of glass into them.

At first her mom seemed not to understand but when Carmela felt around to position the sliver and began discreetly moving her wrists up and down in a sawing motion, her mom got the picture. She held it firmly in place while Carmela added more pressure and kept slicing at the plastic zip tie cutting into her wrists. Her mother blew out a breath. "*No me panikees*," she whispered to herself. Don't panic.

Carmela flinched when the pointed end stabbed into the tender flesh on the inside of one wrist but didn't stop. There wasn't much space between her bound hands to slide the glass between. Suffering a few cuts and slices was a small price to pay if it meant having her hands free though. If the time came that she needed to defend herself again, at least she'd have a chance.

Provided she could slice through this damn hard plastic.

Sweat gathered between her breasts and beneath her arms as she worked. It was hard to make any headway with such tiny movements and the position of her hands and fingers made it awkward. She didn't give up though.

Pausing whenever the guard looked their way, she resumed as soon as it was safe. The muscles in her shoulders, arms and hands ached but she didn't stop, determined to free herself. Then, just when she was beginning to think this whole effort was futile, the ties suddenly gave way. Her wrists popped apart, and a sense of relief swept over her.

Taking the glass from her mother, she reached behind her and began cutting at the ties holding her mother's wrists together. At one point her mom sucked in a sharp breath, telling Carmela she'd accidentally sliced her, but thankfully didn't cry out or give them away.

This time it was quicker and she got the ties cut in just a few minutes. Her mind was working furiously now. She needed to hide that her hands were free while keeping this momentum going.

Moving inch by inch she crept a few feet over to the young father and his little girl. Keeping her back to him she reached around and took hold of his wrists.

When he felt the glass he stiffened, his head jerking around to look at the guard, but then he held them out for her and tried to pull his wrists apart to give her more room to work. Once he was free she pressed the glass into his fingers and then he moved to the person beside him.

Carmela breathed a sigh of relief and leaned back against the wall, her hands now in a much more comfortable position. If enough people could free their hands, they might just have a shot at being able to make an escape attempt if the opportunity presented itself.

Because she wasn't going down without a fight.

*****

"Three minutes," the crew chief announced over the comms.

Sawyer and the others all had their dive gear on. He'd already checked his regulator and adjusted his mask but he did it again, just to be safe, out of habit.

The pulse of the Pavehawk's rotors thudded in his ears as he waited for the next signal. He and the rest of the assault team lined the sides of the darkened helo, every man locked and loaded. Two more birds flew in formation with them, one carrying the SEALs and the other the sniper teams.

The crew chief held up a single finger. "One minute."

Everyone took off their headsets and stood up. The bird began to descend. They formed a single-file line down the center of the fuselage, Tuck in the lead, with Bauer in the rear and Sawyer right in front of him.

The pilots slowed the helo and put it into a hover. Out the side door of the aircraft, Sawyer could see the water moving fifteen feet below them.

At the crew chief's signal, they released the Zodiac from its harness and dropped it into the water. Over to their right, the SEALs did the same. A second later, Tuck jumped in after it, feet first.

One by one they jumped into the dark waves. Sawyer waited until Ethan had surfaced before jumping out. The free fall lasted only a moment, then the water closed over his head. Even with his special dive suit, he felt the chill of the icy water.

He broke the surface and swam a few strokes toward the Zodiac, then stopped to watch Bauer enter the water behind him. Once he surfaced, Sawyer headed for the rubber-hulled boat. He grabbed the side rope and pulled, gritting his teeth as the tendons in his right shoulder seared in protest.

One of the guys reached down to grab him and help drag him over the gunwale. Bauer climbed in a few moments later and Tuck started up the outboard engine.

They motored for fifteen minutes before lowering the throttle to minimize noise. A minute later, the ship finally came into view on the horizon. Sawyer stared at it through his NVGs, his heart beating faster. Carm was on there. She had to be okay. He couldn't even think about the alternative.

Tuck slowed them even further. Sawyer glanced to the left and saw the SEALs just behind them. The lowered throttle reduced the chance of someone hearing them coming but it also slowed them too much. At Tuck's signal they all grabbed oars from inside the boat to paddle the rest of the way in, using all the stealth they could.

The muscles in his shoulder burned but he blocked out the discomfort. This was the most critical part of the op, getting to the ship unseen. They needed to maintain the element of surprise not only to be able to board the vessel without suffering casualties, but also to prevent the hostage takers from blowing up whatever bomb they had aboard.

Everyone was silent, taking care to dip his oar into the water at the same moment, each stroke coordinated to maximize propulsion. Together they fought to keep along the port side of the ship, staying close to the hull, and aimed for the stern. He breathed a little easier when they reached their target and pulled up alongside their entry point.

All of them had experience with maritime operations and boarding vessels, but Bauer was in his fucking element out here. He went first, using grappling hooks to get their boarding ladder in place on the ship, then held it steady while Tuck and Blackwell secured a line from their boat to it.

As usual Tuck led the way, climbing the ladder and slipping over the edge. Once he signaled that the coast was clear, Evers started up. Then Blackwell, Schroder. Then it was Sawyer's turn.

His damn shoulder protested every rung of the ladder but he got up it quick and held it steady for Bauer, who climbed it as easily as an elementary school kid climbs the monkey bars on a playground.

They took up defensive positions while they assessed

the situation and Tuck murmured to the SEAL leader that their team was in position. Using hand signals, Tuck directed them forward. Their goal was the engine room, below the water line.

Sawyer followed close behind Ethan, Bauer guarding their six. Every step they took increased the danger. It was a huge ship. They didn't know how many terrorists they were facing, or where they even were. Everywhere they walked had to be checked carefully to ensure there were no booby traps or other surprises.

Their boots were nearly silent on the wooden surface of the outer deck as they approached the first doorway. Sawyer hung back with the others, providing overwatch while Tuck and Evers used a hand-held mirror wand to check inside the doorway. Thankfully the hallway was clear.

They moved as fast as they were able, to the first staircase and began the descent, watching the stairwell above and below as they went. One floor. Two. Three.

Finally they reached the deck where the engine room was located. Tuck paused to use the mirror again and this time signaled that he had a visual on two tangos, probably near the entrance. Tuck ducked back around the corner and spoke over the comms, his voice barely audible over the hum of the engines coming from down the hall.

"Two tangos, armed with automatic rifles and wearing NVGs." He handed the mirror back to Evers and readied his weapon, raising it to his shoulder. "On my mark. Three."

Sawyer's heart thudded hard, every muscle tensed and ready. Once they secured the engine room and found the "failsafe" mentioned in the manifesto, they could disarm it and clear the rest of the ship so they could start rescuing the hostages.

"Two."

"I got movement behind us," Bauer suddenly

announced, cutting off Tuck's countdown.

They all turned to face the unknown threat approaching, hugging the wall to give them maximum cover. Everyone waited in position, unmoving.

Bauer waited a few more seconds, then waved them forward. They followed him in formation and when they turned the corner Bauer stopped beside a door that was slightly ajar.

With Sawyer covering the other side, he eased the door open with the toe of his boot. Sawyer moved with him, covering all the angles as the doorway opened up to reveal...

Dead bodies. A pile of at least ten people lying in a heap in the center of the small room, a pool of blood staining the carpet beneath them. All crewmembers, all shot through the torso or head at close range. But no gunmen.

After ensuring the room was clear, they stepped back out and communicated with Tuck and the others via hand signals. Bauer once again took the lead and headed down the darkened corridor. Male voices floated toward them, speaking a language Sawyer didn't recognize but guessed was Malay.

Then the voices grew louder and footsteps sounded at the far end of the hallway, near some of the crew quarters. The team froze in position once again and waited. No doubt about it, the men were coming their way. And when they passed the mirror up to Bauer, he verified the two men were armed.

Sawyer and the others were now trapped between the men and their original target. Unable to move, likely going to have to engage and lose the element of surprise completely.

Which put them and everyone else on board at risk if the bastards detonated the failsafe.

Sawyer bit down hard as he waited, butt of his M4

tight against his shoulder, his finger curved around the trigger. Ready to take these assholes out in a heartbeat.

He silently ordered the two men to turn at the last second, take the access stairwell up to the next deck.

It didn't happen.

With no choice but to engage, they waited until the men rounded the corner. The first one saw them, froze for an instant then Bauer hit him with two shots to center mass. He not only didn't go down, he started to raise his weapon, confirming he wore body armor.

Bauer fired again, this time hitting him in the center of the forehead. The second man appeared and Sawyer fired once, dropping him where he stood.

But the shots gave them away.

A split second after Sawyer dropped the second man, shouts came from behind them and in front of them. Tuck spoke over the comm, his voice calm but terse. "We take the engine room, *now*."

Sawyer silently cursed and began walking backward, guarding their six along with Bauer as the team moved back toward the engine room. Running footsteps reached them, then Tuck and maybe Evers started firing. At the same time shots rang out from the hallway behind them and Bauer returned fire.

Another man wheeled around the corner. Sawyer hit him in the side of the neck, dropping him like a puppet with its strings cut. But he could hear more coming, men moving toward them from either side.

Holy shit.

They were in the middle of a hornet's nest and cut off from the nearest exit. No matter which way they moved, they were going to have to fight their way out.

Chapter Fourteen

The radio on Wira's belt squawked. Studying their position on the GPS display up in the bridge, he keyed it and answered in terse Malay. "Go."

"There's a team near the engine room and they're firing at us," one of his men blurted, sounding out of breath.

What? "You told me you had that deck locked down, and that all the crewmembers there were dead."

"We did, and they are. But these men aren't from the crew, they're professionals."

Wira scowled. Impossible. There was no way a team could have boarded the ship. Not without showing up on radar or one of his men picking up on it, and there'd been nothing. He'd just verified that with the man responsible for watching the displays here on the bridge, moments before the radio call. "How do you know that?"

"They're in dive suits, heavily armed and they not only infiltrated the ship without detection, they've killed three of our men so far without taking casualties. They're well trained, must be military." His voice was high-pitched with stress, the sound grating over Wira's nerves.

Had the Navy deployed a team of SEALs to come after them? He'd known they would likely be the ones deployed in this situation, but he'd hoped to have a few more hours lead time before they showed up. He automatically reached down to grab his rifle, slung across his chest. "Is the failsafe still intact?"

"Yes. They haven't breached the holding area yet, but they will soon if you don't send reinforcements."

"Make sure they don't reach it." He glanced at the GPS again, measuring the distance they had to travel.

No. They were so close now. Only another twenty nautical miles from the pickup point. He couldn't be killed or captured now, when he was on the verge of being extracted. He was literally less than twelve hours away from hopefully finding Leo in Lithuania.

He switched channels on the radio to reach all the remaining team members. "An unknown team is attacking our men down by the engine room. Those of you not guarding passengers and crew, get there immediately and attack. Ali, I'm coming down to the theater now. Keep your men there and wait for me."

The failsafe could wait. He still had some time yet before he became desperate enough to use it. They had a contingency plan in place; they would see this operation through to the end.

Before leaving he quickly turned to the three men responsible for monitoring and guarding the bridge, needing to ensure they understood his orders—and the consequences should they disobey.

"You will all stay at your posts and fight to the last man no matter what," he warned them with a severe scowl.

They'd all been paid handsomely up front when they'd agreed to be part of this op. Every man had sworn his loyalty to the *Mawla*. They all hated the injustices that had befallen their fellow Muslims at the hands of the Americans, wanted the chance to strike back and help free their brothers-in-arms being tortured in secret, illegal holding facilities throughout Europe.

And if they died tonight... If they died carrying out this mission, they knew they would have the glory of becoming martyrs for Allah. A reward beyond compare for any devout soldier of Islam. The *Mawla* would grieve him, but would love him even more for his sacrifice.

But a little extra motivation might make the difference at this point. "If not, you will die by my hand when this is over."

With that he whirled and raced from the bridge. His bodyguards covered him while they ran down the several flights of stairs to the promenade deck, then to the theater.

Thankfully they met with no resistance. Wira kept a solid grip on his weapon as one of his men yanked the door open for him. The SEALs' arrival changed everything and sealed the fate of the hostages.

It was time to start killing the passengers.

****

The waiting was excruciating.

Carmela took a surreptitious glance around, straining to see in the dimness. The side of her head throbbed in time with her heartbeat but thankfully the bleeding from her scalp seemed to have stopped. Even so, movement hurt, a piercing headache adding to her misery.

She wasn't sure where the shard of glass was at this point or if anyone was even still using it, but by now there had to be over a dozen people who'd cut their hands free. The guards hadn't yet noticed what they were doing, but something was going on with them because she'd heard Wira's voice come over the radio a minute ago and now the gunmen were clearly agitated, pacing back and forth, their weapons trained on the crowd once again.

Was Wira coming back? He'd said he might use her later, and based on what he'd done to her already, she knew she'd likely die at his hands if he returned. Whatever was happening, it couldn't mean good news for her and the other hostages, and she wanted the hell out of there.

Carmela nudged her mom and the man next to her with the little girl. When she had their attention she sent a subtle but pointed glance toward the exit sign over the closest doorway to them, a dozen feet or so to the right. They'd likely locked it but it was the only way they were getting out of this room so she had to try. She had a bad feeling about the sudden change in energy in the guards and planned to make a break for it at the first sign that things were about to escalate.

Because her gut told her that's exactly what was going to happen.

She thought back to some of the things she'd learned from Ethan over the years about what to do if facing an active shooter. A sad but unfortunately all too common event in today's world—one she'd never imagined being caught up in until now.

She knew that hitting a moving target was harder than hitting a stationary one, and she clearly remembered Ethan saying you had a better chance of surviving if you ran rather than just staying in place. Playing dead amongst a group of wounded sometimes worked too, but Wira would be looking for her so she wasn't going to chance it unless she got trapped again.

She was damn well going to run for it if it came down to that.

With an eye on the second-in-command, who stood about sixty feet away from her in one of the aisles, she eased her way toward that exit. She slid her butt inches at a time across the carpet as the man and his little girl led the way.

Back here at the rear of the crowd at least they had some cover to conceal their movements, as long as they took things slow. Still, with each sideways shift her heart pounded because she was afraid they'd be spotted at any moment.

A few other people must have noticed what they were doing because they began to creep toward the exit as well, but the majority just sat there, too scared to move. Carmela understood their fear but wished she could have urged them to at least try to get away.

Strength in numbers, just as with a herd of antelope when a lion attacked. The more people who made a break for it with her, the higher the chance of survival in the group if the guards began shooting. And they would, she had no doubt. Her skin crawled at the thought.

The second-in-command suddenly shifted his stance and glanced over her way. She stilled instantly but not soon enough. The way his eyes locked on her told her he at least suspected what she'd been up to. Her heart crawled into her throat as she waited, poised to spring up and bolt for the exit if he came at her.

Before she could react, all the lights flashed on, flooding the theater with illumination. As she ducked her head and squinted against the sudden brightness the main doors flung open and Wira stormed in, surrounded by four bodyguards. Carmela pressed her spine hard against the wall and ducked down trying to shrink out of sight.

He scanned the room for a second, then stalked right up the center aisle, grabbed a middle-aged man who was clinging to his wife and dragged him into a clearing in the center of the room while the man begged to be let go and his wife sobbed pitifully.

Carmela's gut clenched. Her mother reached out and caught her hand, squeezed tight.

"Where is she?" Wira snarled at his second-in-command.

The gunman blinked. "Who?"

"The American whore who brought this attack on us all."

At his angry words Carmela held her breath, sheer terror streaking through her. There was no question he meant her and the rage that vibrated in his voice told her he was going to kill her when he found her.

Then a man's voice came through the ship's PA system. "To the American team on board. You have just signed the death warrant for the people you are here to save. *Allahu-akbar!*"

"*Allahu-akbar!*" Wira and the gunmen around the room all roared in unison, rifles raised over their heads.

Despite the news that some kind of team was here to try and rescue them, ice slid through her veins. She didn't speak Arabic but knew enough to recognize that phrase—*God is great*—and that it likely signaled imminent bloodshed.

Instinctively she grabbed her mother's sleeve and started to haul her upward, but then Wira's gaze locked on hers from the center aisle. The sheer hatred in his eyes made her shiver from clear across the room.

"Do you see him? This is *your* doing by contacting the American authorities," he shouted to her over the frightened murmurs of the crowd, that deadly black rifle rising as he spoke. "This and what follows is on *your* conscience."

Without pause he shot the male prisoner in the head at point blank range. The wife started screaming as blood and brain matter sprayed the stunned crowd close to the victim.

The entire room erupted in panic.

Stricken with horror, Carmela watched in slow motion as Wira started to swing the barrel of his weapon toward her. Almost as if the male prisoner's death had been an unspoken signal to the others, the gunmen posted around the room began firing into the crowd.

Run!

It was her only chance.

Without even being conscious of moving, Carmela was on her feet and dragging her mother after her as she lunged for the exit. Everything stayed in slow motion, each slam of her heart echoing in her ears.

Three running steps and her right hand slammed the release bar while the terrible roar of gunfire erupted behind her, a hail of death and destruction tearing through human flesh.

The prickling in her nape told her he had her in his sights. A scream built in her throat, stuck there as the door gave way under the force of her shove and surprisingly flew open. She tumbled out into the darkened hallway and fell to the floor, taking her mom down with her, just as a spray of bullets peppered the wooden wall above their heads.

Hunted. We're being hunted.

Raw terror drove her forward. She stayed low, knowing better than to get back up and run, that it would only make her an easier target.

She made a desperate crawl on her forearms until she could scoot around the first corner of the wall. As soon as she cleared it she shoved to her feet and grabbed her mom's hand, then tore forward into the darkness, wanting to get as far away from the theater as possible.

Her shoes thudded over the carpet as she ran, thigh muscles straining. Out the port side windows the moon hung in the sky, bathing everything in silver.

Lighting her and the others up with a natural spotlight.

She didn't dare stop, didn't look back to see if Wira had made it out of the theater yet. To her left others had already fled out the main double doors at the center of the theater, somehow having escaped the deadly hail of bullets. Behind her, the deafening roar of more gunfire and the blood-curdling screams of the victims told her people were being slaughtered.

Her legs felt like rubber and she was already panting for breath. When the hallway narrowed people slammed into her from all directions, bounced off and around her as they shoved and jostled for an escape route, panic a living thing that crackled through the crowd of fleeing hostages.

Go, go, faster, she urged herself, shoving through a knot of passengers stuck in a narrow passageway between the theater entrance and the casino. A spray of bullets thudded into the roof and walls above her, raining pieces of the ceiling down on them.

Close behind her people screamed in agony. Her lungs seized.

With a strength borne of desperation she forced her way through the mass of people, the fingers of her right hand like claws in her mother's sleeve. As soon as she'd dragged them through the restriction and popped into the clear again, she put her head down and ran, her muscles straining to keep her mom with her.

Seconds later someone raced up beside her. On instinct she turned to swing an elbow at them but stopped when a familiar male voice reached her.

"Where are you going? We can't go up or down, they'll be watching the stairs!" he shouted.

Jenny's father.

Without slowing she risked a glance over at him, saw the little girl clinging to his neck and felt a surge of relief that both were still okay. "To the bow." As fucking far away from the gunmen as she could get, until she could find a place to hide. The ship was huge, there had to be a place they could hide in and wait for rescue.

There is no safe place, the panicked voice in her mind shouted.

Fuck that, she thought savagely. *There has to be a way.*

The herd of panicked passengers thundered behind her, the sound of the gunfire sharp in her ears. Veering hard to the right when she reached the amidships corridor, she raced for the first door she came to and yanked on the handle.

Locked.

Her mother ran ahead and tried another door. "It won't open!" she cried, her voice barely audible over the noise of the frightened crowd surging toward them.

"Keep going!" Swallowing a sob of desperation, shaking all over, Carmela spun and raced for the bow, away from the gunmen chasing them and prayed it would be enough to save them.

She raced ahead of her mother and tried another door handle. Locked. Behind her more terrified cries rang out, along with another burst of fire. It sounded like it was coming from the left but Carmela instinctively flinched and ducked anyway, then frantically ran to the next door. And the next. And the next—

It opened.

Whipping around, she grabbed her mother's arm and towed her into what appeared to be a small storage closet. The man rushed inside as well, Jenny safe in his arms, jamming Carmela up against something hard enough that the breath whooshed out of her. He slammed the door shut behind them and turned the deadbolt on the inside, locking them in.

And everyone else, out.

They were all wedged together so tight there was no room to turn around. Even though it was pitch dark inside Carmela closed her eyes and covered her ears in an attempt to block out the sound of people banging their fists against the door, trying to break inside, their panicked shouts begging to be let in.

Her mother's fingers dug into Carmela's waist like claws as they stood there panting in the darkness. She gritted her teeth and tried futilely to hold back the tears that spilled down her cheeks, praying the gunmen wouldn't find them.

Chapter Fifteen

D own the hall from the engine room Sawyer fired twice, hitting another militant coming out of the crew quarters while Bauer took out the next. Another stuck the muzzle of his weapon out the doorway and began spraying bullets wildly.

Sawyer dropped to a crouch behind Bauer as the bullets zinged past, burying into the wall and floor. Behind them, Tuck and the rest of the guys were engaged with the tangos holed up in the engine room.

Through the noise of gunfire, the SEAL platoon leader's voice suddenly came over their comms. "Bridge secure, but all hell's breaking loose down on the lower promenade deck. Main body of tangos and their leader are executing hostages at random in the theater, pushing them toward the bow. We're heading down to intercept now."

The words made Sawyer's blood pressure plummet even as he took aim and shot the next militant to exit the crew quarters. *Carmela.* God, were her and her mom two of the passengers trapped up there by those assholes?

Simultaneous waves of rage and protectiveness

surged through him. He wanted to charge up there *now*, and kill every last one of those bastards. Only the ingrained discipline from years of rigorous training and his commitment to the team kept him from acting on it.

"Heavy resistance from unknown number of tangos down near the engine room," Tuck replied to the SEAL in between measured shots.

"Suspect we just questioned said more are headed your way."

Shit. Sawyer didn't know if they could hold off another wave of attackers. He shifted the butt of his rifle against his right shoulder. The burn in it was getting worse and these assholes showed no sign of letting up anytime soon. There had to be dozens of them, maybe more.

"Get clear and rendezvous on the lower promenade deck. We've gotta corner the bastards before they can get into a lifeboat," the SEAL ordered.

"Roger that." Then Tuck spoke to their team. "Evers and I will lay down suppressive fire on this side, Bauer and Vance on the other. Head for the aft staircase." There was a hint of frustration in his voice and Sawyer knew it was because this situation had gone to shit in a hurry, and having to scrap finding the bomb put everyone on board at risk.

But they had no choice. Staying here and waiting for the enemy to reinforce itself was not only stupid, it was suicidal.

"*Go.*"

Sawyer was only too happy to obey. He took a knee and fired controlled bursts toward the doorway where the militants had come out of whenever he saw movement, providing cover for his teammates.

"Forward deck five is clear. Moving down to deck four now," the SEAL leader advised them.

Deck four was the upper promenade deck, two decks above where the killings were happening. Sawyer heard his teammates running for the stairs behind him. Moments later Schroder's voice came through. "Stairwell clear."

The suppressive fire was working. None of the remaining militants were charging toward them now.

One by one the team swung around and raced for the stairs. Schroder was in the lead now, his weapon aimed toward the top of the staircase, with Ethan directly behind him. Tuck hurried past them and took point while Bauer moved into position behind Sawyer to bring up the rear. Once everyone was in place they began the ascent.

Sawyer's heart rate was already elevated thinking about what was happening on deck two, several floors above them. Footsteps sounded behind him moments before one of the militants opened fire up the stairwell. Sawyer flattened himself against the wall and turned to help Bauer clear the threat, but his teammate had already taken him out.

Turning to face forward once more, as they reached the top of the third flight of stairs Sawyer heard distant screams, then the crack of automatic gunfire and the thud of many feet racing down the stairs toward them. He braced for another fight.

"Passengers coming our way," Tuck reported, sounding even more frustrated than before.

No gunmen? Sawyer's boot had just hit the top step when he got his first glimpse of the tide of humanity rushing toward them. Panicked passengers all wearing lifejackets were racing for the staircase, trampling each other in their haste to escape. The sheer number of people made it impossible to find a route through them.

There goes our chance of reaching deck two in time to help, Sawyer thought with a sinking heart.

"FBI! Get back!" Tuck shouted at them, trying to stem the tide flowing toward them. "It's not safe down here, there are more gunmen below. Turn around!"

More screams. Some people near the front dove to

the floor and covered their heads, further clogging the way out.

It was still dark in the ship, but the moonlight and ambient light gave his NVGs plenty to work with and he could see perfectly. Stuck for the moment, he couldn't help but scan the crowd for Carmela or her mom, but didn't see them.

As Bauer fired twice behind him, more panic broke out up the stairs. The passengers on the floor now stood up and began pushing their way toward the bow, away from Sawyer's team, probably thinking they were more terrorists.

Swearing under his breath, Sawyer bulldozed his way through the mass of terrified passengers with his teammates, using brute strength. It would take the SEALs at least a few more minutes to reach them on their way down from the nav deck. He felt like a salmon fighting his way upstream against a heavy current, with a pack of hungry grizzly bears waiting to pick them off above.

As well as below.

Though the shooters seemed to have mysteriously disappeared over the past few minutes. Either they'd run out of manpower, or they'd retreated back to guard the engine room.

It should have made it easier for the team to reach their objective but tactically speaking, they were screwed in these conditions. It was utter fucking chaos in here and they still had one more flight of stairs to take before they reached the main body of gunmen on deck two.

He was sweating and breathing hard by the time they finally reached the lower promenade deck, where the sounds of terror and gunshots were a continual roar. The crowding was even worse here, people fueled by terror following the ingrained instinct to flee from the source of danger.

He scanned a few faces as they passed by but still

didn't see Carm. The good news was, from the direction the escaping passengers were moving, it was obvious the gunmen were coming at them from the stern, which gave his team a chance to cut them off.

A sea of men, women and children flooded past them in the darkness, most veering away screaming when they saw him and the others coming toward them brandishing weapons. Sawyer and the others kept directing them toward the bow as they moved, trying to clear a path for themselves.

The gunshots were getting closer. Any moment now the gunmen would come into view.

"Contact, ten-o'clock," Tuck reported.

Sawyer swung his head around to follow the line of sight and caught a glimpse of a handful of what appeared to be armed men slipping out an exit on the port side. One of them in the rear of the group stopped in the doorway to spray bullets into the retreating crowd. People in front of the deadly hail of fire fell to the deck, either wounded or playing dead, Sawyer couldn't tell.

Fuck. His finger stayed curved around the trigger. He wanted a chance to take out these assholes but he still didn't have a clear view and there were too many innocent people in the way.

"Moving forward to see if I can get a clear shot," Tuck said, and began to force his way through another tangle of passengers.

Sawyer's heart sank. There was no way Tuck or any of them could get a shot off in here, not without hitting passengers. These bastards were using the confusion to cover their movements, enabling them to slip out to the lifeboats. There hadn't been time to disable or guard the boats, not with so many militants attacking.

Fuck that, he thought savagely, biting down hard. These cowardly bastards were going down.

Tense seconds ticked past as Sawyer and the others

pushed their way around the bend in the staircase but by then it was too late. The men had already slipped outside onto the deck.

"Hold tight," Tuck ordered, and they all stopped, stacked in position against the wall now hiding them from the gunmen's view. He reported their position to the SEALs and explained the situation.

"We're on the lower promenade deck now, starboard side aft of the bow," the SEAL leader responded a moment later. "Moving your way now."

"Copy," Tuck replied. "Get ready," he said to the team. "We've gotta keep them from launching the lifeboats."

Every second they waited cost them. With an unknown number of militants still out there and just under three thousand passengers and crew clogging this deck, they couldn't divide the team up in these circumstances. It was too risky, and with the sheer volume of bodies around them they needed every man to help protect the team.

Sawyer stayed right on Blackwell's ass as they started across the hallway toward the door the gunmen had slipped out of, frustration and adrenaline pumping through him.

He could smell the blood as they moved toward the doors and he tried like hell to block out what was happening around him. Several wounded people grabbed at his legs as he passed by, begged him to help them, but he didn't stop, didn't look at them. He couldn't. His team had a mission to complete.

The terrorists had to be taken out before they escaped. Only then could he help the wounded and search for Carmela.

****

Wira's heart raced as he rushed for the port side door that led to the lifeboats. They were definitely under attack from an unknown number of forces but he wasn't giving up yet.

Denial and regret filled him. His plan to reach the pickup point while onboard the vessel wasn't going to happen now. His only chance to get to his brother now was to abandon ship and attempt to get within range of the incoming helicopters. He had to make it that far.

Had to.

Images of Leo and their mother's weary and sickness-ravaged features filled his mind, galvanizing him. The *Mawla* would be devastated if he failed. He owed it to them to fight to the end for the chance to locate his brother.

He would never surrender, no matter what.

It wasn't ideal and certainly not his first choice, but surviving long enough to reach the point where the helicopters could hoist them out of the water was paramount now. The pilots knew to look for lifeboat twelve if there were boats in the water when they arrived.

Completing the mission and getting to Leo was his first priority. Taking down the ship was second.

Whatever teams had boarded the ship to attack them, they were well trained. Had to be the Navy SEALs. The bridge was now lost and he didn't know how many of his men down by the engine room were either wounded or dead. But none of that really mattered now that they were going to evacuate.

When his man on the bridge had made that announcement over the ship's PA system prior to the executions in the theater, it had been a signal to the others to begin shooting and enact their escape plan. Right now every surviving member was heading for lifeboat number twelve, located off the port side.

Turning the final corner that led to the doors, safe as

he could get for the moment in the center of the group of bodyguards clustered around him, he spotted the lifeboat through the large windows. Several had already been lowered into the water, he saw, no doubt passengers and remaining crew attempting to save themselves.

Ali was already at the prearranged lifeboat, pulling the remaining passengers out of it, dumping them unceremoniously on the deck. Some dead or wounded, others scrambling away in the opposite direction as fast as they could.

The cold, salt-tinged air hit Wira the moment he stepped outside onto the wooden deck, clearing the tide of adrenaline and bloodlust from his head. He and the others kept firing at intervals, effectively herding the terrified passengers steadily toward the bow, winning him and his men space and time to make their escape.

But when he took another step toward the boat, he saw his point man freeze in place a dozen yards ahead.

"The Americans!" he shouted, and wheeled around, lunging behind the safety of a steel bulkhead set into the port side.

Up ahead in the moonlight, through the crowd of fleeing passengers Wira caught a glimpse of a man dressed in a black dive suit and carrying a rifle. A split second later he was gone, disappeared around a distant bulkhead.

The first stirrings of fear hit him. They were close. Too close.

"Go!" he shouted, shoving the man in front of him to make him move faster.

They had only seconds now to reach the boat, and they had to cross the entire distance without any cover. With no one around them to shield them and in this moonlight, they'd be easy targets.

The door behind them pushed open and a small group of passengers rushed out. They all skidded to a stop when they saw Wira and his men, but not fast enough.

Wira seized one of them—a woman—around the neck and yanked her back against him. She screamed and struggled for a moment but went limp when he put the muzzle of his pistol to her head.

"No, don't," she blubbered, shaking so hard it was difficult to hold onto her.

"Stay still," he snarled at her, ducking his head down behind her shoulder so the SEALs couldn't get a head shot.

He dragged her with him along the deck, moving as fast as he could while holding his hostage. His heart thundered in his ears. So close now, only another thirty yards or so.

Four of his men raced past him for the boat. The two in the lead cried out and fell as bullets slammed into them. Wira jerked to the side and ran faster, practically carrying the woman, holding her in a chokehold so she couldn't break free.

Blood rushed in his ears as he ran, his boots thudding over the hardwood. Only twenty yards to go. He couldn't take a different boat—all the others they'd passed were crowded with passengers and he didn't have time to clear them out.

But as they ran toward it, more shots rang out. The man out front cried out and pitched forward, landing facedown on the deck, twitching once before he stilled.

Wira cursed and flattened himself against the wall behind a steel reinforcement beam, breathing hard. He hadn't seen the shooter through the crowd of scrambling bodies, but he knew there were more out there.

The woman began clawing at his arms and kicking his legs, twisting like a wildcat in his grip. "Let me go! You bastard, let me go!"

Wira increased the pressure of his forearm across her windpipe. She stilled instantly, her hands now locked

211

around his forearm as she choked and gasped.

He didn't care if she suffocated in the next minute, all he needed was for her to act as a shield long enough to get him to the boat.

He darted a glance to the right, saw two more of his men make a desperate dash to the boat. One was cut down but the other dove inside it.

"Come on!" he yelled, waving his free arm wildly, then stuck the muzzle of his weapon out the side and began returning fire in the direction of the American shooter. The remaining crowd of passengers caught in between scattered like ants in an effort to evade the bullets, increasing the confusion and hopefully impeding the American's sights.

Taking several deep breaths, Wira locked his gaze on the lifeboat and prepared to make the final run. Saying a silent prayer to Allah for protection, he burst out from behind cover and ran.

Chapter Sixteen

"Contact, two o'clock, forty meters."

Crouched behind cover near the center staircase on deck two, Sawyer immediately turned to see three more men slip out the far exit near the stern.

The crowd of running passengers in this part of the ship had slowed to a trickle now, most of the remaining ones huddling in small groups in the corners, too afraid to move. Sawyer pushed it all from his mind as he crept up behind Ethan and laid a hand on his shoulder to alert his buddy of his position.

"Tangos are heading for a lifeboat on the port side. We're cut off by the passengers and don't have a clear shot. Report." The SEAL platoon leader's voice was crystal clear over their comms now that the noise had died down.

"Roger that. Moving in for a closer look." Tuck used hand signals to direct the team toward the far door. No one shot at them, a good indication that all the tangos were already outside, but they weren't taking any chances and were careful to guard the team as they moved.

They kept to the shadows to help camouflage them. Tuck held up a fist and they stopped while he snuck a look out a port-side window. "Got a visual. Five of them about twenty-five yards forward." He paused a moment, checking the tangos' position. "Cruzie, Vance and Bauer go out first while we provide overwatch. Fire only if you have a clear shot."

They all responded in the affirmative. Sawyer followed Ethan, Bauer close behind as they eased up to where Tuck and the others took up defensive positions around the doorway in case any more shooters came at them from inside. "We'll cover you," Tuck said. "On my mark. Three."

Sawyer leaned his weight forward onto the balls of his feet, his hands steady around the grips.

"Two."

Ethan moved a step closer to the doorway and Sawyer followed suit.

"One."

His heart rate slowed a few notches. A sense of calmness overtook him as it always did just before an assault. His team was tight and the guys were all highly skilled operators. For the few seconds after he cleared that door his life would be in their hands, but he wouldn't want anyone else watching his back.

"*Go.*"

Evers kicked the door open. Ethan rushed through it then crouched slightly just outside it, pausing to assess the threat outside while Sawyer stood over top of him, his weapon tight to his shoulder, eye to the sight.

Everything slowed down, as if each second was broken into a separate frame on a movie reel. The gunmen were all running for one of the lifeboats. Some turned around and spotted them but one of them had a hostage held in front of him as he backed toward a boat.

A woman. Her face was turned away from him but

Sawyer could see she had long dark hair and his heart seized.

Carmela.

****

"Behind us!"

Wira whirled around, his hostage held close in front of him. She'd lost consciousness a minute ago and now hung like a dead weight in the crook of his arm. He strained to keep her upright. *You stupid bitch*, he cursed her silently, then turned to confront whatever his man had seen behind them.

He saw nothing but empty deck and shadows. But before he could turn away again, two shots rang out in rapid succession. Both men standing between him and the door fell.

A bolt of terror flashed through him. The enemy was closing in on him from both sides.

I have to get out. Have to get the lifeboat to where the pilots can reach me.

Leo was counting on him. His entire family was counting on him to succeed.

He swung around so his back was to the railing and half dragged, half carried his prisoner, the burden of her dead weight slowing him down. Whoever was shooting at them wouldn't be able to get a clear shot of him if he positioned the hostage properly. Only a few more yards until he reached the boat and his human shield seemed to be working so far.

But when he got less than ten running strides away from it, Ali began to lower it to the water.

"*No!*" He roared it, overcome with rage and betrayal. He couldn't believe it.

Ali and those other cowardly bastards were going to leave without him to save their own skins, abandoning him to face the American teams alone. Abandoning Leo and their brothers-in-arms to rot in the hellholes they were trapped in. Spitting in the face of the oath they'd all sworn to the *Mawla*.

I'll kill them. Kill those traitors for doing this.

Shaking with fury he raised his pistol and fired three shots, hitting the windshield of the lifeboat. The men inside ducked down as the bullets smashed through the glass but didn't stop lowering the boat.

The effort of holding the hostage up was draining him. Wira couldn't carry the woman and make it to the boat in time. He needed to do something else to buy time.

The failsafe.

He'd planned to detonate it when the helicopters arrived anyway. Now the bomb was his only hope, it might distract the American team long enough to buy him another few seconds so he could reach the boat that was rapidly descending out of reach.

Snarling his fury at being forced into this situation, he dumped his human shield and grabbed the remote trigger from a pouch on his vest, firing his pistol in the direction of the shooters at the same time.

He rushed for the boat, feeling like he was moving through quicksand. Everything was happening too slowly. His hand had just closed around it when a bullet hit him between the shoulder blades.

He grunted at the impact and staggered forward, a feral growl issuing from his throat. His vest had prevented the bullet from going through him but it knocked the air from his lungs.

His gaze sought the lifeboat. It was below the railing now. He could still make it if he jumped.

He straightened, put on a burst of speed, desperation driving him forward.

A bullet slammed into his neck, tearing through the front of it. Screaming, he dropped his pistol and fell to his knees. Through the waves of agony tearing through him he could hear men behind him shouting at him in English to stay down and put his hands over his head.

Never.

He'd never let them take him alive. He would not allow himself to be taken captive only to rot in a secret prison like the one Leo was trapped in.

Blood pumped out of his ruined throat, out of his gasping mouth. He choked, managed to turn his head and saw the lifeboat slip out of sight below the railing. Already he could feel his strength fading.

It's over.

He'd failed Leo, the *Mawla* and his family. Failed *himself.*

The best he could hope for now was for someone else to pick up the torch he'd carried this far. Defeat crashed through him, then resignation, followed quickly by a sense of peace.

Leo's plight would have worldwide attention now. There was still a chance he might be freed if politicians at home and abroad put enough pressure on the Americans.

He couldn't see anymore. Running footsteps thudded on the deck behind him, more male shouts reached his ears.

Hearing really is the last sense to go when you die.

He was out of time.

Calling on the last of his will, Wira commanded his limp fingers to curl around the device, each millimeter of movement taxing his endurance. His heartbeat was sluggish, his lungs no longer drawing in air.

Have to detonate the failsafe. Once he did the ship would be mortally wounded and go down within the hour. Taking all its wealthy Westerner passengers down with it.

Fervent prayers filled his head. He was ready now. Ready to die after this one last act.

With his remaining strength he curled his fingers

around the trigger and hit the detonator.

He never even felt the bullet that slammed into the back of his head a split second later.

****

The tango was dead and the woman he'd been holding hostage wasn't Carmela.

Sawyer's lungs started working again the second he realized it, but his gut clenched at the muffled boom from below and the way the deck rolled beneath his feet.

Fuck, he'd been a second too late with the headshot.

He charged straight for the dead man, Ethan hot on his heels while Bauer stopped to check the female hostage. The dead tango was lying on his stomach, eyes still open in his now misshapen face, the front of his skull blown away.

And the fucking trigger was lying on the deck inches from his open hand.

"God dammit," Sawyer snarled at himself as he knelt and picked it up. He hadn't seen it in the bastard's hand until it was too late. "Tango down," he snapped into his comm.

Tuck and the others jogged over, scanning for more threats as they ran. But it appeared the gunmen that had been on deck were either all dead or already in boats in the water. Sawyer spotted at least a dozen of them motoring away from the ship off the port side.

He handed over the trigger to Tuck, furious with himself.

"Hey," Bauer said, slapping a hand on Sawyer's back. "There had to be more than this one trigger out there. One of the others would have blown it at some point anyhow. I didn't see it in his hand either until the last second."

The words didn't soothe his conscience one iota. Sawyer clenched his jaw and didn't answer, sending a silent look at Ethan, who was scanning the crowd anxiously, probably for his sister and mother. They both turned around as the SEALs ran up to join them.

"Deck's secure," the platoon leader said. "For now, at least. But that sounded like one hell of an explosion down there."

No shit, Sawyer thought sourly. He scanned the deck now too, watching as passengers continued to scramble into the remaining lifeboats. How the hell were he and Ethan going to find Carmela and Mama Cruz now?

"How long do you think we've got?" Tuck asked the platoon leader, already pulling out his radio.

"An hour, tops. Probably less."

Jesus Christ, and Carmela might still be on board somewhere. Sawyer pushed out a frustrated breath and dragged a hand down his face. He wanted to punch something. Mainly himself. He'd never felt so helpless in his life and he hated it.

"We need to evacuate the passengers then do another sweep of the ship up to the water line," the SEAL ordered them. "Wright, alert the helos to pick us up when we've cleared the ship," he said to one of his men before looking at Sawyer's team. "We'll break into two-man teams and get these boats filled. You guys start sweeping the lower decks to clear them and look for passengers stuck down there. The water could be rising fast. Let's move out."

It killed him to know he wouldn't be able to search for Carmela or her mother now.

Heart in his throat, Sawyer paired off with Ethan and ran back to the door they'd just come through. They were locked in a deadly race against time and every second counted.

Please be okay, Carm. Please, baby, I couldn't stand it if I lost you.

Chapter Seventeen

Wedged tight inside the pitch black closet with the others, Carmela sucked in a sharp breath when a loud boom resonated from somewhere below. The floor shook beneath her feet.

"What the hell was that?" the man, John, whispered.

"I don't know." But it couldn't be good. Sounded like an explosion of some kind. The rescue team fighting the gunmen, maybe?

She held her breath and waited a minute longer, straining to hear anything more. The darkness and confined space made her breathing seem overly loud. Beneath her lifejacket her sweater was soaked with sweat but she felt cold all over. When was this nightmare going to end?

In front of her, her mother was whispering fervent prayers in Spanish. Normally Carmela would find those familiar prayers soothing, but now the fearful whispers only reminded her that they were trapped in a life and death situation.

"Haven't heard anything for a few minutes now," John murmured. "I think they're gone. We should get out of here."

And go where? "Not yet. They might come back." And she was afraid that anyone around her would become a target if Wira was still out there somewhere. If he spotted her, he would kill her without hesitation.

The floor seemed to tilt a little beneath her. Maybe she was dizzy from the blow to the head or maybe being trapped in the dark like this had disoriented her. Either way, it seemed like the ship was beginning to lean to the right. She put a hand out to brace herself against the wall, hoping the dizziness would pass. A minute later something rolled off a shelf behind her and hit the floor.

Her heart lurched as a new fear took root. "Is it just me, or are we tilting?"

John swallowed audibly. "I think so."

There was only one reason she could think of for that, and it was just as terrifying as facing the gunmen somewhere outside this door. She shifted her stance to counteract the change in angle, trying to fight the fear exploding inside her. Was the ship sinking?

"Okay, let's stay calm and think this through. We'll just stay here until—" She broke off abruptly when her shoe made a distinct squishing sound on the carpet as she widened her stance.

Oh, God, no...

She tapped her foot on the floor just to be sure and a wet slapping sound answered.

Water. Sea water. They were sinking.

"Oh my God," she breathed, automatically pushing forward between her mother and John to reach for the doorknob. Her fingers found the deadbolt and twisted it hard. "We have to get to the lifeboats. *Now*."

"But what about the gunmen?" her mother asked, her voice frantic.

"We can't stay in here."

"She's right," John said.

"Daddy…" Jenny quavered, then began to cry again. "What's happening? Are the bad men still out there? I don't want to go out there if the bad men are there."

"No, baby, they're gone," he said, and neither Carmela nor her mom corrected him. That poor child had already gone through enough trauma to last her three lifetimes.

"It's time for us to take another boat ride now, Jenny," she said instead, hand poised on the knob. Once she opened it, there was no telling what they'd find, no telling what would happen. "Do you remember the little boats we took to shore the day we docked in Juneau?"

Jenny made a frightened sound that Carmela took to be an affirmative.

"The bad men are gone but now we have to take one of the little boats back to shore. It'll be fine, just close your eyes and hold on to your daddy. We won't let anything bad happen to you."

She prayed she would be able to keep that promise. It was quiet enough outside the closet that she wondered if maybe the terrorists had fled the ship using the lifeboats.

A sudden voice booming out of the ship's PA system made her jump.

"Attention ladies and gentlemen. This is Captain Goddard of the U.S. Navy SEALs. The ship is now secure but all passengers must evacuate immediately. Proceed to the lifeboats located on deck two. Repeat, proceed to the lifeboats on deck two immediately."

Carmela didn't have to be told twice. She pushed down on the handle and shoved the door open. Out in the wide hallway people were running in small groups toward the doors at either side of the ship.

"Come on." She grabbed hold of the front of her mother's life vest and hurried for the first outside door on the right.

People were stacked up a dozen deep waiting to get

into the lifeboats, many of which had already been launched. The entire deck was crowded with passengers standing shoulder to shoulder.

"There are some boats being loaded one deck down," John yelled to her over the noise.

She immediately turned to follow him to the nearest staircase on the port side. They couldn't take the starboard side since the ship was already listing to starboard and the water already soaking the floor there. Partway down the steps John jerked to a halt.

A moment later, Carmela saw why.

The emergency lights flickered on, illuminating a film of water on the deck below. Her mom grabbed her wrist and hauled her back up the way they'd come.

"This side," Carmela called out to John, who was cradling Jenny to him as they dodged the mass of passengers now fighting to find a lifeboat that had space. Together they hurried out a port side door and turned right, toward the bow.

Someone screamed up ahead. Carmela froze, her gaze instantly colliding with a big man holding a rifle next to a lifeboat.

"Look out!" Everyone around her ducked down, but when the man didn't turn and fire on them, instead seemed to be helping people into the boat, she realized he must be with the SEALs. She didn't see any others around though. Her heart knocked crazily against her ribcage as the sharp spike of terror subsided.

They got caught up in the crowd once more, slowing them to a stop. Claustrophobia closed in on her, making it hard to breathe. The ship listed further onto its starboard side. Frightened cries rang out among the crowd.

Carmela shifted her weight to keep from staggering into the port side wall. Shit, they were taking on water way too fast. They needed to get off this ship *now*, or they'd face having to jump into the water to save themselves.

The crowd surged around them, carrying them along the deck toward the bow. All the lifeboats they passed were either full or already being lowered into the water.

"The starboard side," Carmela shouted over the noise. "Get around to the other side!"

They fought their way out of the mass of bodies and began the race around the stern to reach the right side of the ship. The soles of her shoes skidded on the deck, the change in angle making it hard for her to keep her balance.

A middle-aged woman grabbed hold of Carmela's shoulders, her face pinched, her eyes stark with terror. "My son—I can't find my son!" She cast a frantic look around, her panic making Carmela's heart twist. "David! David, where are you?"

"I'm sorry, I don't know who—" Her words cut off abruptly when someone behind her shoved her forward, knocking the woman's hold loose. The woman's frantic cries raised the hair on her nape as they hurried for the stern.

When they made it around to the starboard side, another crowd blocked their way to the boats. The ship continued to roll by degrees as they slowly crept forward. One by one, the remaining boats were filled with passengers.

It felt like an invisible fist was crushing her chest, squeezing tighter and tighter with each shallow breath she took. She did *not* want to have to jump into the water. Even if the sheer terror of it didn't kill her, hypothermia likely would, long before anyone rescued her.

"There, look!"

At her mother's shout, Carmela followed to where she was pointing out to sea. The lights of another ship came into view and hope buoyed her spirits. Now, even if she had to do the unthinkable and jump in the water to save herself, she might still be saved.

A creaking/groaning sound rolled up from the belly of the ship. The vessel took a sudden lurch, twisting harder onto its side. Carmela and the others slipped over the wood and slammed into the railing. She grunted at the impact and immediately turned to brace herself against the metal railing.

She pushed at her mother's shoulders. "Go, go!"

They kept heading toward the bow, passing boat after boat too full to take on any more passengers. *This must be what the passengers on the Titanic felt like, knowing there weren't enough lifeboats to save everyone on board.*

Carmela watched in horror as people climbed onto the railing and jumped into the water. She imagined what it felt like to plunge into the icy water, try to swim away from the sinking ship. She shuddered, her throat dry, and cast a frantic look ahead of them.

Two lifeboats up, a wide-shouldered man in a dive suit and a rifle slung across his chest was helping people inside. Carmela made a beeline for it but when she finally reached it they were already lowering it into the water.

"Keep heading toward the bow," he told her, already turning to usher the remaining passengers forward. "Everybody stay calm. There's another ship coming."

She didn't believe him. She rushed for the next one, but it too was full. There were only three boats left that she could see and her heart sank. Was she really going to have to make the choice to jump into the freezing water in the darkness?

"Miss Cruz!"

Her head snapped around. Dwi, their cabin steward, stood near one of the remaining boats, which was now dangling at an odd angle over the water. He waved them over, the motion of his arm frantic. Carmela used the railing to help keep her balance and rushed over with a group of passengers.

"In here," he shouted, and reached for her. Carmela clamped her fingers around his hand as he pulled her inward, toward the boat. His other shoulder had a bandage wound around it, the entire length of his arm soaked with blood as it hung at his side. He must have been wounded by one of the gunmen.

"Are you all right?" she asked, still gripping his hand.

Nodding, he pulled free and reached for her mother. "I'll be fine. Hurry now." He helped her into the boat and she turned to reach for Jenny, whom John had to peel away from his neck.

With the little girl safe in her arms, Carmela moved as far back into the crowded boat as possible and sat on a bench-style seat. Her mom climbed in next to her, then John, and Jenny immediately scrambled back into her father's lap.

On deck Dwi was still busy shepherding passengers into the boat. Carmela set an arm around her mom's shoulders and rested her cheek on top of her head, watching the people as they boarded. Everyone was tense, all of them afraid, some bleeding from bullet wounds.

She cast a glance out the right hand window, peered down at the midnight-dark waves only a matter of yards below them. She gasped when someone plunged past the window—too desperate to wait any longer to abandon ship—and hit the water a second later.

Pressing her hands to the glass, she peered down anxiously and saw a head appear above the surface. In the moonlight she caught a glimpse of his face and realized he was no more than a teenager. He began to swim away, his movements panicked and uncoordinated.

That could have been me, she thought with a shiver, sending a prayer out for the boy. She continued to watch his painfully slow process toward the other lifeboats. *Swim*, she urged him. *Come on, swim! You can do it.*

Don't give up. You can't give up now, not after all this…

But already his movements were slowing. The cold had to be terrible. And she already knew the other lifeboats probably wouldn't pick him up, for fear of swamping the boat.

More than the attack, more than the terror of the ship sinking out from beneath them, knowing he would likely die broke something inside her.

Carmela turned away, her heart shredded.

A strange numbness began to take hold as Dwi packed the boat tight. When it was jammed full he climbed aboard, fought off a man trying to force his way on board with his two young children.

"We're already overfull!" Dwi shouted at him, kicking out to prevent him from climbing on board. "Any more and we risk sinking!" He managed to dislodge the man and quickly slammed the door shut in his face, then scrambled up to the driver's seat.

It was too much.

Carmela closed her eyes to avoid witnessing any more but the man and his children's faces were now burned into her mind. A wave of nausea and guilt slammed into her.

She squeezed her eyes shut, her face crumpling as she buried her face in her mom's hair. Out on deck someone began lowering their boat into the water. She felt the moment the hull brushed the waves, then the wires holding them released and they plunged into the water.

Several sharp cries of fear rang out. Her mom grabbed her hand, squeezed until Carmela's bones ached, but she still didn't open her eyes.

All those people. All those poor people trapped on deck or in the water. That teenage boy. That father and his kids and so many others.

A sob ripped through her and she didn't bother trying to hold it back.

"It's all right now, ladies and gentlemen," Dwi said from up front, sounding tired and out of breath. "I'm getting you all to safety now." He started up the engine and turned them away from the ship. People all around them began to cry in relief, in grief and horror at having to leave others behind.

Her mother began to weep, her entire body shuddering with each harsh sob. Carmela kept her eyes shut and let the tears flow, thanking God that she'd lived through the harrowing ordeal.

She reached for the crucifix around her neck and thought of Sawyer, likely still back in Seattle, and clung to the image of his face she held in her mind as they chugged their way toward the other ship. He'd asked her to go away with him and after this she needed that more than ever. He'd be frantic when he found out what had happened on board. She wanted to reach out to him so badly, just to hear his voice, tell her she was okay.

I need you, Sawyer. God, I need you so much.

****

The icy water was already up to his thighs. His legs and feet were already numb from the cold.

Sawyer panted for breath as he and Ethan finished their sweep of the starboard side of deck two. The emergency lights had gone out around fifteen minutes ago, likely shorted out by the water. Everyone they'd found down here was already dead. And anyone trapped beneath the water line would be dead by now too.

"Vance, Cruz, report." Tuck's voice was terse in his ear.

"No one down here," Ethan answered in between breaths. "We're coming up to deck three now."

"Copy. All but a handful of passengers have been evacuated. Helos are inbound, ETA six minutes. There's no time to take the tangos' bodies with us. Coast Guard ship is on its way but the survivors can't wait that long. Head up to the nav deck for extraction."

"Roger that," Sawyer gasped out, sloshing through the water as fast as he could on the way to the forward staircase.

He and Ethan didn't speak as they struggled through the icy water, then up the stairs to deck three. He couldn't stop himself from scanning the victims lying on the carpet, soon to be swallowed by the rising water. Carm wasn't one of them, and he thanked God for that because he couldn't handle finding her body.

He needed to believe she'd been one of the lucky ones. That she'd gotten off the ship safely in one of the boats. It twisted his gut to think of her terrified and desperate enough to be one of the people to leap overboard in an attempt to save herself. Water that cold would kill her long before anyone could fish her out of it. It killed him to know she was close by but not know if she was even alive.

She is, he told himself forcefully. He refused to let himself think otherwise.

The ship was eerily quiet on the inside except for the occasional groan as metal and wood shifted under the strain of the water flooding on board. That bomb had blown a huge hole in the starboard hull, large enough that the ship would likely be completely underwater in the next half an hour.

The muscles in his thighs and ass burned as they climbed flight after flight, making their way up to the navigation deck. At the top Sawyer paused a moment near the doorway to bend over, hands on his knees as he caught his breath. Ethan did the same, both of them panting, weak with fatigue and the adrenaline crash.

But then the tension inside him became too much. He reached out and put a hand on his buddy's shoulder, bringing Ethan's head up. Their gazes locked and Sawyer felt a crushing weight on his chest. "They're probably on one of the lifeboats," he gasped out.

Ethan nodded and looked at the floor. "Yeah."

There was nothing else Sawyer could say that wouldn't make this already epic goatfuck of a situation even worse. He squeezed Ethan's shoulder in reassurance. "Come on, let's go get the rest of those passengers off this boat."

Outside on the sharply tilted deck, their team waited with the SEALs and a group of about twenty remaining passengers. None of them were Carm or her mom, but he'd already assumed that because Tuck hadn't told them otherwise.

All of them looked exhausted, passengers and operators alike.

Sawyer gazed out at the water, at the people swimming or now floating motionless in the waves. The lifeboats were almost at the Coast Guard ship now, and he knew a Navy vessel wasn't far behind. They'd be the ones responsible for cleanup and retrieval of the bodies during the recovery mission that was no doubt being planned even now.

The cold wind whipped around him. His teeth began chattering, shivers wracking his body despite the insulation of the dive suit. A few minutes later the beat of rotors reached him. Overhead the silhouette of four Pavehawks crossed over the face of the moon. They circled overhead, moving into formation, then one of them broke away and descended toward the deck.

He stood back while a few of the SEALs helped load some passengers aboard. A second helo dropped down and hovered above the deck close to him. The remaining passengers rushed over.

A crewmember from the helo lowered a hoist and Sawyer and Ethan helped secure the first passenger. A woman holding an infant. She was crying, clearly in shock. In her state Sawyer didn't trust that she wouldn't drop the baby, and with the deck tilted like this there was no way for the helo to land and make it easier for her to get aboard.

"I'll go up with her," he shouted to Ethan, handing him his rifle and turning back to the woman. The rotor wash beat down on them, intensifying the cold. He got them secured in the harness and wrapped his arms around her, sandwiching the screaming baby between them.

The crew hoisted them up to the doorway. The airman waiting there took the baby and handed it to a medic aboard, then it was the mother's turn. A sharp pain lanced through Sawyer's right shoulder as he helped maneuver her into the helo. He hissed in a breath and cradled his arm as they lowered him back to the deck.

It took another twenty minutes for them to load the last of the passengers aboard the birds, which flew them over to the waiting Coast Guard vessel and offloaded them the same way.

The minutes dragged past as they waited for the helos to return for them. They huddled together on the listing deck for warmth, none of them speaking. Below them, the waterline was already less than ten meters down.

Finally two birds lifted away from the Coast Guard ship and turned back toward them. Sawyer took what felt like his first full breath since he'd boarded the ship—

Metal groaned and popped as the ship took a sharp turn to starboard. Sawyer threw out his right arm to catch the railing and the sudden pain in his shoulder made him light headed. His mind felt hazy as the two helos dropped into a hover above them. The hoist was too slow, they had to use the fast ropes.

One by one the SEALs began climbing up the rope of the first bird while Tuck held theirs and ushered Evers upward. Sawyer cradled his arm across his chest and waited his turn, his heart thudding hard. If the ship turned any more, they'd all be thrown into the water and he *really* didn't want that to happen.

Blackwell was next, climbing one hand over the other up the rope, then Bauer. Schroder went next, then Ethan. Sawyer moved to the base of the rope, waited until his buddy was aboard before gripping the rope. Just hold out long enough to get me inside, he told his shoulder, and reached for the rope.

The deck tilted abruptly beneath his feet. He swore as his feet slipped, and grabbed the rope, tweaking the already damaged tendons in his shoulder. A cry of pain locked in his throat.

Tuck caught him around the waist to steady him and gave him a shove to get back to the rope. "She's going over, hurry!"

Pressing his lips together, Sawyer grasped the rope and hauled himself upward. Ethan's face was sticking out the open side door of the helo above him, along with Schroder and Bauer. They were all yelling at him, reaching their hands out for him.

Climb, you bastard, he ordered himself. *Climb before you fall and knock Tuck into the water with you.*

His fists clenched tight around the rope as he wound his feet around it. The first few pulls hurt like a bitch, the next five torture, and by the time he neared the top his right shoulder was a mass of searing agony.

Ethan was reaching for him, straining to get his hand close to Sawyer's, his face a mask of concern, mouth open as he yelled something Sawyer couldn't hear.

There was no way his right arm could make the final pull, but he had no choice. Clamping his jaw tight, knowing it would hurt like a mother, Sawyer flung up his hand for Ethan.

Ethan caught it, locked his fingers tight around his

hand and hauled upward, his face screwing up with the effort of lifting Sawyer's weight. It was the last thing Sawyer saw for the next minute.

He screamed as something popped and tore in his shoulder, screamed again as Ethan relentlessly hauled him up and into the belly of the helo. White-hot agony ripped through the joint, like someone had stabbed him with a glowing red brand.

Someone else grabbed hold of his other arm and pulled him along the deck. Sawyer curled into himself and cradled his shoulder, gagging at the relentless pain.

Hands started to roll him over. He snarled at whoever it was but they just kept going until he was on his back. When he managed to pry his eyes open at last he was panting, shaking all over from the pain. Schroder and Ethan were both staring down at him in concern.

"Your shoulder?" Doc asked.

He forced a nod and bared his teeth in warning, his left hand cupping the joint protectively. "Don't fucking touch it," he spat.

Schroder's eyes widened and he held up both hands in surrender. "Okay, I won't." He shot Ethan a *can-you-believe-this-guy* look.

More of the guys crowded around, all staring down at him. "What's wrong?" Tuck shouted over the pulse of the rotors. Sawyer wasn't sure but he assumed from the motion they were already flying back to shore.

"Fucked up his shoulder," Ethan told him, setting a comforting hand on Sawyer's good arm and giving it a squeeze.

Sawyer ignored them all, struggling with the pain outside as well as within. Through the fiery bursts of agony he made himself turn his head to see out the open doorway, just in time to see the Coast Guard ship as they flew over it.

His heart sank. More than even making the pain in

his shoulder go away in that instant, he needed to find Carmela. Or at least know that she was okay.

The hand on his left arm tightened and he looked up into Ethan's face. "We're gonna find them, man," his buddy promised him. "I know they're fine and we're gonna find out where they are as soon as we get to shore."

Sawyer laid his head back against the deck and closed his eyes, still cradling his shoulder, and prayed Ethan was right.

Chapter Eighteen

The weight of exhaustion made it nearly impossible to keep her eyes open.

Carmela shifted on the cot and lowered the ice pack one of the medics had given her earlier for her head. It had been over four hours since the Coast Guard ship had brought them to shore, where the FBI had bussed all the passengers to this high school gym in Anchorage currently serving as a triage station for everyone.

She and her mom had already been checked over and treated for their injuries. A few cuts, scrapes and bruises, which could have been so much worse.

The true damage was on the inside. The horrors of what she'd witnessed over the past few hours would never be erased.

Carmela had received a couple stitches in her scalp and a painkiller since she hadn't shown signs of a concussion.

Apparently she had a thick skull.

They'd given their information to an Army nurse and then FBI agents had come to talk to them. When they'd found out she'd been face-to-face with Wira, they'd asked question after question until her mind began to spin. They'd told her the SEALs had rescued the captain of the ship. She'd asked them about Ethan and Sawyer, had begged them to contact them, but the agents had been far more interested in whatever intel she could give them about what had happened on board.

At this point she didn't know where he was. Seattle? L.A.? When he found out they were in Anchorage, would he and Ethan fly here? She wasn't even sure if they could get the time off to do that right now.

Her mom sat at the end of the cot, one hand absently trailing up and down Carmela's calf. All around them people were receiving medical attention and being reunited with loved ones.

The anxious expressions on the faces of those still waiting to see their family and friends were hard to bear. They knew as well as she did that many people would not be coming through those gym doors, either killed by the gunmen or having succumbed to the frigid water when they jumped into the sea.

Someone came by and offered them sedatives to help them sleep. Carmela refused it but her mother took one and stretched out on the cot beside her to sleep.

Carmela laid on her back and stared at the ceiling, unable to bear the strained faces around her as they waited for news of their missing loved ones, and unable to close her eyes because images from tonight kept flashing back at her.

Wira's face just before he pistol whipped her. The man he'd killed in cold blood. The father and children's faces when Dwi forced them away from the lifeboat. The teenage boy who'd plunged into the water and probably died of hypothermia before he reached the Coast Guard ship.

She rolled to the side and conjured up an image of

Sawyer to focus on instead. She wanted to see him so badly, needed to feel his arms around her. More than anyone except for Ethan, he would understand what tonight had been like for her. He knew what it was like to face gunfire and the instinct to flee, to survive.

He would know all about mental trauma and survivor's guilt.

"Miss Cruz?"

She rolled over and looked up at the soldier standing beside her cot. "Yes?"

"Your brother's here and is asking to see you."

Ethan? She gasped and jackknifed into a sitting position, searched for him. Then she saw him, winding his way toward them, dressed in his fatigues, a huge smile breaking over his face when he saw them.

She reached out and batted her mom's shoulder. "Mom! Ethan's here."

Her mom sat up instantly and gasped when she spotted her son. "*¡Wepa!*"she cried.

They both rushed to him. Carmela flung her arms around his neck and closed her eyes, hugging tight while their mom clung to his waist. His big arms enfolded them and for a moment he didn't say anything.

She lifted her head to search his eyes. "When did you get here?"

"Just now. They would still have us in a debriefing if we hadn't insisted on coming here to find you guys."

"We? You mean your team? Were you guys called in for this?"

He nodded. "We were on the ship."

Oh, God, and she hadn't even known. She stepped back, still holding onto his shoulders, and scanned the length of him. "Are you okay?"

"I'm fine. You?"

"Little worse for wear, but yeah, I'm okay. And what about Sawyer?"

"Like you. A little worse for wear," he said, his gaze shifting to the right, "but otherwise okay."

Carmela automatically followed his gaze over to the door. Sawyer was standing there, looking around, his arm in a sling.

Without even thinking she gasped and tore away from her brother, shouting Sawyer's name as she raced toward him.

****

"Sawyer!"

He whipped his head around, saw her running toward him and something in his heart cracked wide open. Sheer relief almost dropped him to his knees where he stood. Instantly he teared up. His legs ate up the distance between them, and then she was in his arms. Or arm, to be exact.

He banded his left arm around her back and lifted her off the ground, burying his face in her hair. "God, Carm," he choked out, squeezing her probably too hard but he couldn't help himself, all too aware of how close he'd come to losing her tonight.

She clung to him fiercely, her arms trembling with the force. "Don't let go," she whispered.

Swallowing hard past the thickness in his throat, he promised, "I won't." *Not ever*, he vowed to himself. *Not ever again.* He'd been so stupid in holding back before. Life was too unpredictable, could be cut short in an instant and he knew that better than most. His feelings for Carmela eclipsed what he'd felt for any other woman, even Trina.

They stayed like that for a few minutes, just holding on to one another. Finally she lifted her head from his neck and looked up into his eyes as one of her hands gently touched the sling holding his arm across his chest.

"You're hurt. Were you…did they shoot you?"

"No, just wrecked something in the joint when we were being extracted. Was only a matter of time, I guess." Tendons for sure, but maybe ligaments and the labrum, Schroder had figured. He now had bursitis because of it, but they wouldn't know how bad the damage to the joint was until he could get a CT scan or MRI when they got back to Quantico. It hurt like a bitch but somehow the pain was less now that he was holding her.

Not that he really gave a shit about his shoulder at the moment.

He set her down and brushed the fingers of his left hand over the side of her cheek, which was wet with tears, her beautiful golden brown eyes brimming with them. And she had a few stitches in her scalp. "You okay?"

"I am now," she murmured, settling back against him and laying her cheek on his chest. "I didn't even know you guys were on board until Ethan told me."

"They flew us up here with the ST6 guys as soon as the news broke." He kissed the top of her head, careful to avoid her cut and ran his hand up and down her back. She felt so tiny and delicate in his embrace.

"It was a nightmare. I was there through the whole thing but I can't even believe it really happened." She shivered.

He held her closer. "Shock," he murmured into her hair. But yeah, he knew what a nightmare it had been. It was going to be a long while before he shook this one off. He wanted so badly to tell her he loved her but he wanted to do it when she wasn't overwhelmed by the trauma of the attack and everything that had happened.

"I can't believe you're really here," she said with a shaky smile.

He smiled in turn and bent his head to cover her lips with his. Her hands linked around the back of his neck. They kissed slowly, gently, a gesture of claiming but also one of comfort and reassurance.

After a minute she drew back and wiped at her damp cheeks. "So what happens from here?"

"They're going to bus you to a hotel for the night. Once the FBI takes everyone's information and statements down they'll make arrangements for you to fly back to Seattle and then home. The cruise line is covering the cost."

She snorted. "I should freaking hope so." Boy, was she going to write the most heated, negative review in the history of reviews when she got home. "What about you guys?"

"We'll be here for the night in meetings, maybe part of tomorrow, but then we'll head back to Quantico." He cupped her cheek once more, ran his thumb across her cheekbone. His reasons for being afraid to open his heart to this woman seemed so ridiculous now. "Can you still come out to see me, or…" He trailed off when she glanced behind them where Mama Cruz was still hugging Ethan.

"I want to, but don't think I should leave her yet. It was…really hard tonight," she finished, a tremor in her voice.

Ah, baby. "I know it was. I'm so damn thankful you guys are okay." He didn't know exactly what they'd been through, but he could guess well enough and it still made him sick to think of them enduring all that. "Listen, if you can't come to me, then I'll come to you. I can't work with my shoulder like this right now anyway, so I'll fly down to Miami as soon as I can get clearance. Maybe in a few days."

Her smile was full of relief. "Okay. I'd like that." She glanced behind her at her mom and brother. "And so would my mom."

"I'd like it too." He'd love to spend some time with the two women who meant the most to him in the world. But mostly, he wanted Carmela to himself for a few days at least. "Think she'd mind if we snuck away on our own for a while when I'm down there?"

She snuggled up against him once more, her arms around his waist, cheek resting over his heart. Right where she belonged. "I think she could be persuaded to let me go for a few days," she teased.

"Good." He kissed her forehead, met Ethan's gaze across the room. Mama Cruz was smiling at him. He waved at her, received a blown kiss in return. Ethan nodded at him. Time to go. "Sweetheart, we gotta get back to base now," he murmured.

Carmela lifted her head and gazed up at him with the same disappointment he was feeling. "Now?"

"Yeah. DeLuca gave us an hour to get here and back and our time's up."

To his horror she bit her lip and tears filled her eyes. "Don't cry," he begged. He didn't think he had the strength to leave her if she broke down in front of him.

She sniffed, wiped impatiently at the tears. "Can you come by the hotel later?"

"I'll try." He'd move heaven and earth to make it happen, but it all depended on whether or not they could get all the briefings done before they had to catch a flight back to Seattle in the morning.

Her chin came up and her shoulders straightened, that inner strength he admired so much shining through. And he couldn't help but smile. "Come on, babygirl," he said, wrapping his arm around her shoulders. "Let's get you the hell out of here."

Once she'd collected herself fully, he tucked her under his good arm and led her outside. Buses were lined up at the curb, ready to take the passengers to a local hotel for the night, maybe longer. He hated like hell to let her go so soon though.

Outside in the school parking lot an FBI agent held an umbrella over them to shield Carmela from the cold drizzle as they made their way to the first bus in line. The cruise line was facing one hell of an undertaking with arranging transportation home for everyone, not to mention cooperating with the salvage operation and paying for damages.

Not that money had ever brought back a dead loved one. Sawyer hated to think of what the victims' families were going through right now.

Carmela looked up at him with a worried expression. "Are you sure about this? I'd rather stay with you until we get everything sorted out."

He shook his head. "Wish I could stay but we've gotta go. We're gonna have a long night getting everything tied off on our end." And he needed to get his shoulder looked at by someone other than Schroder, get x-rays, all that. It hurt almost as much as the thought of letting Carmela go in another minute. "You go on to the hotel and we'll come see you guys as soon as we can, okay?"

She searched his eyes for a moment, then nodded. "All right."

He hugged her, gave her one last kiss then helped her up onto the first step before letting her go. When he turned around, Ethan was walking Mama Cruz toward the bus.

Her face crumpled when she saw him. "Oh, Sawyer…"

Without a word he reached for her, pulled her into a one-armed hug. "It's okay now. Everything's gonna be okay."

She cried against his chest and squeezed him for all she was worth, this little woman with a giant heart who he loved so much. After a minute she pulled back, wiped her eyes and tried a smile. "We'll see you before you leave, right?"

"Absolutely." He'd make it happen somehow.

Ethan hugged her and pressed a kiss to the top of her

head. "See you in a while, *Mami*."

"Okay," she murmured, her gaze immediately going to Sawyer.

He smiled, gave her a reassuring nod. "Take care of Carm for me until I can do it myself later."

Her expression softened with total adoration at the mention of her daughter. "I will, *pequeño*," she told him.

Little one. Even though he towered over her and outweighed her by who knew how much. A lot. The ridiculous endearment made him smile.

She got on the bus, looking as reluctant as Carmela had, and moved toward the back. When it pulled away, he stood on the curb with Ethan as the drizzle coated them. There were so many things he needed to say to his buddy, he didn't even know where to begin.

A long silence stretched out as he gathered his thoughts, then Ethan let out a deep breath and spoke. "So I guess I owe you an apology."

Huh? Sawyer shot him a confused look. "For what?"

"You and Carm. I didn't realize things were that serious. I understand now that I misjudged the situation between you guys." He put his hands in his pockets, his gaze still on the retreating bus.

"Well it was...I didn't mean for you to find out like that."

His buddy shrugged. "I saw the way she ran to you the moment you set foot in that gym. That right there tells me everything I need to know."

"Oh. Not everything, though."

Ethan looked his way, frowned. "What do you mean?"

"I love her. Plain and simple. I'd do anything for her." Anything but walk away, because that would kill him.

Now a smile tugged at Ethan's lips. "Well that's ...kinda cool, actually. Especially since it's obvious she loves you back."

Sawyer grinned too. "Yeah. I feel like I just won the lottery *and* the Superbowl."

Ethan nodded, looking pleased. "Good, that's the way you're supposed to feel. I'm happy for you guys."

Sawyer's expression turned wary. "So you're okay with it?"

"As long as you treat her right."

His gaze sharpened on Ethan, old insecurities flaring to life. "I'll be good to her, you know I will." He rubbed a hand over the back of his neck. "But look, whatever happens with her and I down the road, no matter what I just need to know that you and I will still—"

Ethan snorted and shook his head. "You're telling me you'll be good to her, yet in the next breath you're talking about the possibility of you guys not working out. What the hell am I supposed to read into that?"

Sawyer blew out a breath and glanced away, fighting those long-buried fears trying to scrape to the surface once more. "I want it to work. I do, and I have every intention of making it work between us. I'll do whatever it takes and I want to make her happy. But I'm just saying, *what if?*" He shook his head, then added softly, "I couldn't take it if I lost you because of that."

"Aw, hell. Seriously?" Ethan shook his head in exasperation, looking equal parts insulted and baffled. "I'm not Danny, dickwad."

Sawyer fought a smile at that. "I know."

"Well then don't lump me in the same category as him. Jesus, that just pisses me off." Ethan stared through the drizzle at the bus as it turned the corner. "Can't lie that thinking of you two together doesn't ick me out a little though." He made a face and Sawyer nearly laughed.

"What? Seriously? You've had, what, almost twenty-four hours to get used to the idea. Adapt already."

"Give a guy some slack, man. It's been a helluva

couple days." Ethan nudged him with an elbow and grinned. "Hey. As long as you treat her right, you and I won't ever have a problem, no matter what happens. Okay? Satisfied?"

Sawyer let out a relieved breath, finally feeling like his world was balanced again. "You don't ever have to worry about that."

Ethan nodded. "I know. I *know* it, man. So if for some reason you and her don't work out in the long run— which, come on, is just totally ridiculous—well…" He shrugged. "Look, bottom line, unless you dick her around, which I know you'd never do, you've got nothing to worry about with me. You're part of the family, you know that."

Christ, now he was getting choked up. He cleared his throat brusquely, glanced away for a second, then back at him. "Thanks, man. I appreciate it."

Ethan stared at him now and shook his head, those golden eyes so like his sister's. "You're like a brother to me, dammit."

Hell, his damn eyes were starting to sting. He turned his head to stare at the spot where the bus had just disappeared, flooded with relief and gratitude, and nodded. "Same here." He paused a second, shot Ethan a sideways glance and raised his eyebrows. "So we're good?"

Ethan grinned that familiar grin, and Sawyer knew everything was cool between them. "Yeah. We're good." He slapped him on his good shoulder. "Now let's get back to HQ. Sooner we finish up there, the sooner we can see my mom and Carm again."

Sawyer was *so* down with that plan.

Chapter Nineteen

After watching the first five minutes of the news broadcast, Summer Blackwell couldn't take it anymore. The reporter in Anchorage was talking to some of the passengers who'd been aboard the cruise ship that had been attacked by terrorists. The male passenger had mentioned seeing an American military team on board and Summer *knew,* even without being told.

Adam and his team had been in Seattle when the attack had commenced. Only a few hours' flight from Alaska. And taking back a cruise ship from armed terrorists was exactly the type of mission they trained for.

There'd been a lot of casualties. The passenger described seeing dead bodies all over the place.

She left the TV on and went into the kitchen to grab her phone, which she'd left charging on the counter. He hadn't called, but that wasn't surprising given the situation there in Alaska, and not given the state of their marriage.

She just needed to know he was okay.

After dialing his cell she sat on one of the stools at

the center island, the fingertips of her free hand drumming on the cool granite. He wouldn't answer, but if she left a message he'd probably call her back.

Maybe.

"Summer?"

She was so startled by him answering that it took her a moment to respond. "Yeah, hi. I…are you okay?"

"I'm fine."

Relief slid through her. She let out the breath she'd been holding. "Are you just saying that to make me feel better?"

"No," he said, and she could hear the hint of a smile in his voice. "I'm really okay."

"Thank God." She rubbed at her forehead for a second, suddenly feeling nervous. Which was crazy. She'd been married to this man for almost eight years.

Then her gaze strayed to the envelope containing the paperwork on the kitchen table. The damning evidence right there to remind her of how bad things had gotten.

He didn't know she'd been talking to a lawyer to see about a legal separation and she didn't plan on telling him until after he got back. They should probably have split a long time ago but they just couldn't seem to let each other go. And the last time they'd spoken, the other night, he'd sounded like he missed her.

Which was likely wishful and ridiculous thinking on her part. But the truth was, she still loved him. Would always love him, because he was the love of her life, no matter what had happened over the past two years. Even if she did leave and file for separation, she knew in her heart she'd never get over him.

Well it sure seems like he's gotten over you.

She pushed the crushing thought aside. "I was just watching the news and thought you guys must have been involved in the rescue mission of that cruise ship," she continued, refusing to feel guilty. It wasn't like she'd actually filed for separation, she was just exploring the options and what was involved, legally speaking.

Just so she knew what to be prepared for if it came to that.

"It was a joint op, but yeah, we were."

He sounded tired. "And the rest of the guys are all right too?"

"Vance screwed up his shoulder pretty bad during the extraction, but everyone else is okay."

She nodded, then realized he couldn't see her. "Glad to hear that. I'm just sorry we didn't find out what the attack was going to be or who the leader of the cell was in time to stop it." The ensuing silence made her shift restlessly on the stool. There was an invisible wall between them now. A slow but steady construction they'd both participated in, brick by brick.

Neither of them was blameless in this. And she knew she'd purposely withdrawn from him emotionally over the past few months. Ever since...

Automatically she put a hand to her abdomen, fought the all too familiar surge of sadness and anger. *No. Don't go there again. The past is in the past. You have to move on.*

But that was exactly the problem. He'd moved on and she hadn't. Not really. And for her the struggle was still very real.

"Think you'll be coming home soon?" she finally asked, hating the uncertainty the question created inside her.

"Hopefully in a few days. What about you, will you still be in town?"

Another stab of guilt made her mentally wince. "Ah, actually, no. My boss wants me to go with him to London for a series of meetings with MI6." He didn't need to know that she'd volunteered for it after finding out Adam planned to come home in the next day or two.

Purely because she was a coward and didn't want to face the reality that their marriage might be over. She was so afraid that when Adam came home next he would end it, tell her he was leaving.

"Ah." Just one syllable, but now his voice was flat with resignation and it made her stomach corkscrew.

"But I'll be back early next week," she added quickly.

She heard voices in the background and Adam muttering a response to whoever it was. Then to her, "I gotta go."

Summer blinked at the abrupt tone, feeling even more awkward. "Oh. Okay." The hesitancy, the tentativeness she felt now was foreign. And she didn't like it.

"Another briefing."

"Sure, I understand." But he was no doubt relieved to have a reason to end the call.

And just like that, tears stung her eyes. She thought of the newscast, the cruise ship he and his teammates had taken from dozens of armed militants. What was pride compared to what he'd just been through? *Are you going to give up, or are you going to fight for your man?*

Her heart pounded. "I miss you, Adam." Saying that out loud was both terrifying and liberating at the same time.

He let out a heavy sigh, heavy with a mix of relief and frustration. "I miss you, too."

The warmth was back in his voice again and gave her hope. It also made her eyes sting. "I'll see you when I get back from London then." She was amazed at how normal her voice sounded when it felt like an invisible fist was squeezing her heart. "Safe travels."

"You too, doll. Bye."

The "doll" bit made her feel slightly better, but not much. "Bye."

She ended the call, slid her phone away and dropped her head onto her folded arms atop the counter, and let the tears come. Before Adam, she'd never known love could hurt this much.

****

Nothing on TV captured her interest and when she flipped past a news station Carmela caught a glimpse of Wira's face along with the headline Terror At Sea.

She quickly turned it off and tossed the remote onto the bedside table. The hotel had had food waiting for them when they arrived a couple hours ago. Carmela made sure her mom was settled before coming to her own room and taking a long, hot shower.

Her stitches were sore and her head hurt but more than anything she was exhausted and wanted to see Sawyer again. He'd texted a while ago to say they were wrapping up another meeting and that he'd try to come by if he could sneak away so she'd given him her hotel room number and had been waiting ever since.

It was almost ten in the morning and she hadn't slept since the night before the attack. Her eyes burned, her lids too heavy to keep open any longer so she laid down and drifted off.

The sound of a keycard in the lock made her eyes fly open. She shot to her feet, heart thudded, anticipation curling inside her. The door pushed open a few inches and Sawyer appeared there in jeans and a T-shirt, his wide shoulders blocking most of the light from the hallway.

A look of pure relief came over his face when he saw her. He stepped inside and let the door shut behind him and she noticed his arm bound in a more secure sling. "Hey, babygirl."

She couldn't hold herself back another second.

With a glad cry she ran at him. Sawyer caught her

around the waist with his good arm and hoisted her up. She wrapped her legs around his hips and grabbed his face between her hands, covering his mouth with a desperate kiss.

He groaned and shifted her higher, turning her until her back was against the wall and pinned her there with his weight. His erection swelled rock hard against her abdomen, his big body vibrating with the same tension running through her own.

Their mouths met hungrily, tongues stroking, his hips moving against her core in a rhythm that made her desperate for more. His heat, the powerful, solid feel of his muscles, made her feel safe. She reveled in the taste and feel of him, drank in his obvious need for her.

But it wasn't enough; she desperately needed all of him, right now.

Tightening her legs around him she released his face and leaned back just enough to drag her shirt up and off, then tore off her bra, her hands unsteady in her haste. Her breasts spilled free and Sawyer's eyes darkened with lust.

She grabbed hold of his head and arched her back, pushing her breasts up toward his mouth. He rubbed his face against her, the slight prickle of his goatee and the stubble around it adding to the layers of sensation. Then his mouth closed around one tight nipple and her entire body shook. Her head snapped back and she held his face to her, a sob of need and longing coming out of her.

More. She needed more. Everything he had to give. She wanted his weight on top of her, holding her down, anchoring her and keeping her safe while he drove into her body and made her completely his. Obliterating the images from last night she was trying to hold at bay.

God, he felt good. The throb between her legs was becoming unbearable. She rolled her hips against him, let the sensations careen through her. "Sawyer, need you," she blurted.

He lifted his head and sealed his lips to hers in a full body kiss that left her shaking. She didn't even realize he'd moved until she no longer felt the wall against her back. She kissed him with every bit of need and passion inside her.

Then he was bending to lay her back on the bed, the sheets cool and soft beneath her fevered skin. She released him only long enough to strip out of her yoga pants and panties, then sat up to help him undress. He managed to wrench off his boots and socks one-handed, but winced when he took off the sling and tried to pull the sleeve of his shirt over his sore shoulder.

"Let me," she whispered, and gently got it off him, then undid his pants and pushed them down his long legs along with his boxers. She helped him secure his sore arm back in the sling, then reached for him.

"Wait, stop for a second and look at me."

She did, wondering why he was stopping. The chance to be with him after everything they had gone through was a gift she intended to experience to the fullest.

He was kneeling in front of her on the bed now. Cupping her chin in his hand, he held her gaze, his dark eyes filled with emotion. "I love you. I have for a long time and I should have told you that long before now. I'm sorry I didn't man up sooner."

She gave him a wobbly smile, her eyes filling with tears. "You're forgiven. And I love you too."

He smiled down at her, slipped his arm back into the sling and paused to cup the side of her face with his free hand, his dark gaze delving into hers. "Don't know how I got so lucky," he murmured, leaning in to kiss her.

Carmela closed her eyes and let herself get lost in it.

Sawyer laid her back against the sheets. His lips were soft, the only soft part about him, and he kissed her like he couldn't get enough. He blazed a fiery path over her jaw and down her throat, back to her breasts, dropping his hand to her hip in a possessive grip. The feel of his hot mouth on her sensitive flesh made her writhe in his hold.

"You're mine, Carm," he rasped against her breast, his voice deeper than she'd ever heard it. "All mine."

She nodded, in complete agreement, loving the way he said it. She'd wanted this man for a long time, had been through so much and now she'd finally won his trust—his love. That meant the world to her. "Yours," she whispered back, holding him tighter to her breast. And he was hers.

Her fingers dug into his scalp as he gave her what she wanted, sucking and licking at her sensitive nipples, the pleasure twisting higher with each pull of his lips and the glide of his tongue. Impatient, she slid one hand down to grasp the length of his erection. He hissed in a breath when she curled her fingers around his naked length and squeezed.

Desperation drove her, a frantic need to have him claim her. "Want you inside me," she panted, lifting her hips and curling her legs around his thighs to pull him where she needed him.

Inside her was exactly where he wanted to be.

Sawyer's hand shook as he curled his fist around himself and guided it to the soft flesh between Carmela's open thighs. She was gripping his good shoulder with one hand, her elegant fingers slipping down to stroke her clit and he almost lost it the instant the head of his cock touched her entrance.

She made a soft needy sound and pressed her hips upward, trying to force him inside her.

He set his hand on her hip, his fingers squeezing before he paused, staring down into her gorgeous amber eyes.

Carmela was beautiful and brave and loving. He'd dreamed of this moment for months and now it was finally happening. He was finally claiming her for his own. She'd been taken hostage, pistol whipped and barely escaped the sinking ship. He loved her with everything in him and it killed him to know what she'd been through, that he could have lost her.

His heart thundered in his ears as he eased forward a little, just enough until her folds enveloped the head of his cock. Pure pleasure shot up his spine.

A ragged moan spilled free as he leaned in and gave her more of him, letting gravity do the work. His gaze slid down to where his rigid flesh disappeared into her body. He shuddered at the hot, tight perfection of being inside her. Face awash with pleasure, she whimpered and rocked her hips against him.

"So good," she moaned, arching her neck back. He fucking loved how sensual she was, how she let him see how the pleasure affected her. She tugged at his good shoulder. "More. I want more. Stop teasing."

Something primal flared to life inside him at her demand. Something that wanted to imprint himself on her on the deepest level. She was his woman and he wanted her to feel his claim in every cell of her body.

With a firm grip on her hip he surged deep in one thrust, burying himself completely inside her. Her answering cry echoed off the ceiling, pushing his arousal to the breaking point. Sawyer bowed his head and gasped in a breath, his muscles shaking. He was finally inside his woman and she was clearly loving every second of it.

Now that he was completely buried inside her, the wild desperation he'd felt when he'd walked in the door suddenly fell away. Everything slowed and calmed, the most primal side of him soothed by their joining.

There was no rush now, only this intimate moment to be savored. He allowed the sensation to flow through him and began to pump into her, watching her face so he knew what she liked. He kept his rhythm steady, each tender, slick stroke into her body making the pleasure flow through his veins like warm honey.

Sawyer leaned down to seal their mouths together, absorbing every breathless moan and cry she made, wishing only that he could use both arms to hold her, cradle her tight to him while he made love to her. But she didn't seem to mind stroking herself for him and God, it was hot.

Her breathing grew shallow, her face tight as she neared her release. He kissed her slow and deep, gliding in and out of her with tender strokes while she caressed her clit. The tiny mewls she made grew louder, more desperate, then he felt her clamp down on his cock, felt the first shudders start.

"*Sawyer.*"

The way she called his name made him shudder. A growl of pure possessiveness locked in his throat. She was *his*, goddamn it, and only his. No one was ever taking her from him.

He groaned in satisfaction as she started to come and nipped at her jaw, pressed kisses to her face as she went wild beneath him, her fingernails dug into his back. Her hips moved frantically, increasing the friction along his swollen cock.

Sawyer closed his eyes and pressed his face against her temple, his thrusts harder now, forceful, taking what he needed more than he needed his next breath.

He chased hard and fast after the release hovering so close, plunging deep and locking there as it exploded. His hand clamped down on her hip as he roared his pleasure when it hit, his entire body shuddering with the force of it.

Carmela's hands were cradling his head now, her lips raining tender kisses across his face, over his cheek to his jaw, his mouth. On a groan he turned to meet those soft lips, let himself get lost in the kiss. In her.

Gradually the pleasure faded, and his injured shoulder reminded him of its displeasure with a constant throb that now registered an eight on his one-to-ten pain scale. He pushed himself up with his good arm, wincing as his right shoulder twinged, and slowly withdrew from the warmth of her body.

Carmela sat up and reached for him, drawing him onto the bed next to her. "Lie down," she told him, dropping a kiss on the tip of his nose. He stretched out on his back while she got up and went into the bathroom.

She came back with a warm cloth and gently washed his groin then pulled the covers over them both and curled up against his side, her cheek cradled in the hollow of his left shoulder.

Despite the pain, a wave of peace and gratitude overcame him. He'd never felt this contented. Just holding her like this filled him with joy. She was a light in his soul, filling him with a warmth he'd never known before.

Her hand trailed gently across his chest, careful to avoid bumping his right arm in the sling. "Did you take anything for the pain?" she murmured.

"Yeah. It's not helping much though."

She made a sympathetic sound and kept stroking him, her touch light and soothing. "What did Schroder say?"

"He thinks it's bursitis with a second degree tear of one of the rotator cuff tendons, probably some ligament damage too."

"Will you need surgery?"

"Hoping not, but we'll see. I'm gonna need some time off to see if it settles down and then go from there. But I don't want to talk about my shoulder right now." All he cared about was being here, having her naked body up against his.

With his good arm he pulled her closer, bent to

nuzzle the side of her neck with his nose. "I just want to lie here and hold you and never let you go."

She hummed in agreement and snuggled even closer, draping one thigh over his. "I'm down with that plan."

He meant it literally that he never wanted to let her go, though he didn't say it. It was too soon. But he'd come so close to losing her forever yesterday and it scared the hell out of him. He couldn't seem to shake the fear, kept remembering the way the ship had listed as it rolled onto its side and how he'd wondered if she was trapped under the water somewhere.

Yeah, he was going to have nightmares about that for a while. He squeezed her tight. "What do you need right now, baby?"

"Just this. Just you. I feel safe with your arms around me."

He raised his head to kiss her temple, gently, in deference to the swollen lump close by. "Good, because you are safe now." He already knew it was going to be hard to let her out of his sight after this, at least for the next while. Which sucked, since she lived a thousands miles away from him. "Think you're up to a few days away with me when you get home?"

"Yes. I thought about it when I was trying to find a lifeboat. I kept thinking of you and the chance to start a life with you…" Her voice thickened, slicing him inside as she detailed what had happened on board the ship. The terrorist leader singling her out for execution made his blood run cold and he tightened his arm around her.

"I kept thinking I couldn't die because I had you there waiting for me but then the ship started to slide and I didn't know if we'd get free, I thought we might have to jump into the water like the others."

Sawyer closed his eyes and cradled her as her tears dampened his skin, his own eyes stinging. "But we both got out. And now we've got each other."

She let out a quiet sob, her shoulders shaking with the force of it. He didn't try to quiet her, just held her tight as he could with one arm, absorbing her warmth while she vented her pain and fear. His heart broke for what she'd gone through. But his lady was strong. She had survived and she would get through this, with him at her side.

After a few minutes she finally quieted, a weary sigh leaving her. She seemed to melt against him then, clearly exhausted.

"I love you so much," she told him quietly.

He'd never ever get tired of hearing those words from her. "I know, baby. I love you too." There was no way he could ever live without her now. She'd already been his family, but now she was his reason for breathing.

"Did you ever get the chance to talk to Ethan about us?"

"Yeah. He saw the half-naked picture you sent me."

She let out a shocked gasp and raised her head to stare down at him, her expression full of horror as she wiped the traces of tears from her face. "No," she breathed.

He cracked a grin at her appalled tone. "It was tense there for a while after he found out," he said. *That being an understatement.* "But after all this and the way you and I reacted when we finally saw each other this morning, he told me he's okay with it. Does your mom know?"

"Are you kidding? She was trying to pull strings behind the scenes from the day we arrived in Seattle. She's thrilled."

Sawyer smiled, but it quickly faded as reality intruded. He'd finally gotten everything he'd ever wanted: Carmela and her entire family. But after their short getaway together he'd be returning to his life in Quantico and she'd be staying in Miami.

How the hell was he going to live that far away from her now? He wanted to fall asleep beside her each night he could and wake up next to her every morning, come home to her at night.

"After our trip, what are we going to do about us?" he asked her.

She settled her head back on his shoulder. "I don't know, what do you want to happen?"

"I don't want you to stay in Miami. I want you to move in with me."

He felt her still in surprise, her fingers pausing on his chest. "You sure?"

He frowned at the hesitance in her voice. "Hell yeah, I'm sure. You're my baby. There's no way I can handle being that far away from you all the time."

A light chuckle shook her, full of what he hoped was relief. "Then I guess I'll be putting in for a permanent transfer to Virginia as soon as I get home."

At her words something deep inside him seemed to break free, as if a weight he'd been carrying around had suddenly vanished. "Thank God," he said, and rolled partially on top of her, covering her with his body, putting himself between her and the rest of the world.

****

Alex Rycroft woke from a deep sleep when his cell rang. He rolled over, snatched it from the nightstand without turning on the light. He knew that ringtone. Zahra. His right hand woman, one of the best cryptologists he'd ever seen in all his years with the NSA, and the closest thing he had to a daughter.

Alex could use the sound of a friendly voice right now. "Hey, Zahr. What's up?"

"Sorry to wake you. I know you've had a long night."

It'd been a *hell* of a long night. He and his team had spent it interviewing survivors and examining the bodies of the dead terrorists. More than three hundred civilians had been killed in the attack, and hundreds of others were wounded or missing. In short, it was a fucking nightmare, not to mention the headache of trying to coordinate multiple government agencies for the investigation. The only useful thing they'd learned was the identity of the man leading the attack—Wira Tejda, the head of security, from Java.

May the bastard rot in hell.

"It's okay," Alex said.

"I would have let you get some more sleep but I thought you'd want to know what we just uncovered."

He slid one arm behind his head. "Okay, shoot."

"Did Aziz start talking yet?"

"Nope. Sealed up tighter than a drum of the oil that made him such a rich asshole. He denies knowing anyone involved with the attack, says he didn't know any of the attackers." And maybe he hadn't, at least on a personal basis. "But he was definitely bankrolling it and providing material support." Which made him equally as guilty for the massacre.

"Well, doesn't much matter anymore. We know who the *Mawla* is."

At that he sat bolt upright, a sense of urgency and excitement building in his gut. "What? How?" They'd been investigating every angle and come up with nothing so far.

"Because we're amazing," she said with a laugh, referring to her team of analysts working back at Fort Meade.

"So are you going to make me guess? Because I'm all out of guesses."

"Are you sitting down?"

"Yeah."

"Okay, well, the *Mawla*, as it turns out, is…"

An Indonesian. Had to be. Every call they'd traced going to and from Aziz in the last three days prior to his arrest had been from in or around Jakarta or Surabaya.

"Wira Tejda's mother."

Alex's mouth fell open. It wasn't often he was surprised anymore, but he definitely was this time. "What?" The *Mawla* was a woman? How the hell had that worked with a hardened terror cell full of hardcore Islamist males? How could she possibly have pulled that off without any intelligence agency picking up on it? Maybe some of the cell members hadn't known they were swearing allegiance to a woman, but Wira must have known his mother was the *Mawla*. It would have made him even more determined to carry out the mission.

"Yes, I know, but when we started putting the pieces together it all made sense. It turns out she had a son before Wira, with a different man. Leo Chandra."

He sucked in a breath. "The guy the manifesto claims was taken prisoner by us and put into a secret CIA facility in Vilnius." Another jihadi captured in Syria last year. Had they really hidden him in Lithuania?

"Well, it looks like they may be right about that part. Sealed records show he was captured in a raid last year by our SOF members. We're investigating several leads right now."

"I'll contact my sources and get on it right away." A lot of high-power people in Washington owed him favors. It was time to start cashing them in. "Now I get the connection with Wira and why he wanted to carry out the attack. He wanted to tell the world about his brother, have the Russians help him locate Leo."

"And set him free."

Right. "Have you alerted a team in Jakarta yet?"

"Yes, but there may be an issue with the arrest."

He frowned. "Why?"

"Because Mrs. Tejda has just been diagnosed with terminal ovarian cancer and was moved to palliative care in Surabaya three days ago. She's not expected to survive more than a few days."

Alex rubbed at his forehead. "Is she responsive?"

"Not at this time, no."

He pursed his lips. "Thanks for the intel. I'll get on this."

"Okay. Take care. Grace and I miss you like crazy."

A picture of his wife formed in his mind, made him smile. "I miss you guys, too."

He hung up, staring into the darkness for a long moment. Unreal. The head of the terror cell that had pulled off the biggest terrorist attack against America since 9/11 was an elderly, terminally ill woman living in Surabaya.

Just when he thought the world couldn't get any more fucked up than it already was, the world proved him wrong.

Good thing he and others like him would always be here to take action, determined to fight that kind of evil wherever it surfaced.

Epilogue

Eleven weeks later

"Hey, easy there. You've gotta be gentle with me, it's only my second time."

One side of his mouth tipping upward, Sawyer turned in the saddle to look behind him and check on Carmela, who'd resorted to talking to her horse. True, she'd only ridden for the first time yesterday, but she was doing fine, sitting regal as a queen atop the palomino he'd saddled for her. "He's just impatient because he doesn't like it when he's not in charge."

"Hmm, sounds like someone else I know," she said, sending him a sardonic look.

He raised an eyebrow. "You love it when I'm in charge."

The crisp late November air had already put a healthy pink flush in her cheeks but now it deepened even more. "In the bedroom, maybe."

No maybe about it. She loved it when he "went alpha" as she called it, in bed. "And in the kitchen, and the bathroom…"

She laughed at him. "Wow, holy ego, Sawyer. I might have to knock it down a peg. Or three."

He shrugged, mighty pleased with himself. "Hey, it's not ego if it's the truth." His nearly healed shoulder gave a faint twinge when he shifted the reins to his right hand.

The physiotherapists and doctors didn't think he'd need another surgery, but he was off work until the ligaments and tendons healed completely. He had at least a few more weeks of rehab to go before he'd be cleared for duty again. His team was on support rotation right now, so that made it a little easier to be sidelined. He'd have hated to be laid up during an ops cycle.

During that same time Carmela had been busy juggling her job while trying to arrange a move to Virginia and many appointments with a psychiatrist. She seemed to be doing better in how she was dealing with what had happened, but still suffered nightmares. Thankfully she never hesitated to call him in the middle of the night if they were apart. Talking about it helped both of them and Sawyer was glad she wanted to turn to him when she needed comfort.

At his response she nudged her gelding and brought the horse alongside him and threw him a meaningful look to make her point. "I'm your equal in every way, and don't you ever forget it."

"No, ma'am, I won't," he promised and guided his gelding up the path that led to the spot he'd chosen. It felt great to be out here on horseback with her, even if she wasn't completely comfortable in the saddle yet.

"Where are you taking me, anyway?"

"You'll see in a bit."

They rode side by side in silence for a while, the horses' hooves a steady but muffled clip-clop on the leaf-strewn path. He noticed the way she kept watching him, was secretly pleased by the admiration in her eyes.

"God, you have no idea how freaking sexy you are right now," she told him with a shake of her head.

He smothered a grin, that look in her eyes telling him she was thinking about riding him the first chance they got. "Am I?" Some guys were in their element on the football or baseball field, or in a boardroom calling the shots and closing a deal. His element was this, being atop a horse with her beside him, surrounded by a hundred and sixty acres of land worked by the hands of his ancestors and passed down in his family from generation to generation.

"Well you are. You look like you should be in a Marlboro man ad."

He smiled at her. "You look pretty sexy yourself right now." She wasn't wearing a hat but she had on a sheepskin coat and snug jeans that hugged her ass in a way that made him want to groan.

She turned her attention back to their surroundings, a little smile of contentment on her lips. "It's so pretty out here."

"One of my favorite spots on earth." The fields and small groves of trees they passed were damp with dew, catching the last rays of light from the sun in glimmers of pink and gold. After a whirlwind trip to Miami where they'd snuck a few days away together in the Keys, he'd returned to Quantico and had his surgery the following week. Since then she'd put in for a transfer with her company, which was supposed to come through any day now.

"Feels good to get out here, just the two of us."

"Sure does." It had been hard, being apart for weeks at a time, only spending two or three days together at a stretch over the past two months.

They'd spent Thanksgiving down in Miami with her mom, Ethan and Marisol before coming here to Oklahoma for a few days before he was due back in

Quantico. He'd warned Carmela ahead of time that his dad wasn't the warmest of men, but even his gruff old man seemed to have fallen in love with her since they'd arrived three days ago.

At the crest of the next rise he turned them east and their destination came into view. Carmela let out a gasp. "Oh, wow, it's gorgeous."

It was. The small clearing was surrounded by a grove of huge live oaks, planted almost two hundred years earlier by one of his ancestors. In the center stood a small white summerhouse, its windows and brick chimney reflecting the rosy glow of the sunset. Built by one of his ancestors over a hundred and thirty years before.

"Wait here a minute," he told her, then dismounted and grabbed the saddlebags before going inside.

Once he had the fire going in the hearth he laid out the blanket he'd brought in front of the fireplace and went back outside. After helping Carmela down he hobbled the horses to let them graze and took her by the hand to lead her inside.

She made a sound of wonder as she glanced around the cozy little room. "This is amazing."

No, you're *amazing*, he thought, watching her glance around. Every day he fell more in love with her. Her resilience after the trauma she'd been through amazed him. Her sharp brain, her sense of fun and her incredible capacity for love awed him.

"What is this place?" she asked, turning in a slow circle to look around.

"My great, great, great-grandfather built it for his bride in the late 1800s."

"It's beautiful."

"Here, come sit by the fire." He settled her on the blanket in front of the fire and turned back to the small table where he'd placed the thermos of hot chocolate. After pouring them both a mug, he handed her one and stretched out beside her, admiring the way the firelight flickered over her smooth skin.

A happy smile curved her lips as she inhaled the scent of the hot chocolate and let out a blissful sigh. Outside the windows the sky was beginning to turn purple with the coming twilight. "This is so romantic."

And it was about to get even more romantic.

Setting down his mug, Sawyer reached up to cup the side of her face and draw her down for a slow, thorough kiss. She put her mug aside and took hold of his face, making an enthusiastic hum in the back of her throat. Her response made him grin and before things could get out of hand, he drew away.

She frowned at him but he sat up and got onto one knee before her. When he took her hand and gazed into her eyes, he saw the surprise there, the almost breathless anticipation.

"I never knew love could be like this," he told her softly, the crackle of the fire providing a soothing backdrop. Things had moved fast between them but he didn't question it because it didn't feel fast. They'd been friends long before they'd become more and the basis of their relationship was rock solid because of that.

"I know I couldn't ask your dad, but on Thanksgiving I asked Ethan and your mom for your hand instead. I hope that'll do." Reaching into his front jeans pocket, he pulled out the diamond solitaire he'd bought last week in Miami and held it out to her.

Carmela gasped, both hands flying to her mouth. She stared at the ring, then up at him and lowered her hands, her front teeth digging into her bottom lip.

His heart swelled with love for her. The first time he'd done this he'd been so nervous he could hardly get the words out. Because some part of him had known even then that he was making a huge mistake. This time there were no nerves, no questions or whispers of doubt. Only a bone deep rightness that they were meant to be together forever.

He'd finally found someone to love and accept him as he was, to support and lean on him. Someone who'd taught him what unconditional love felt like. And he wanted to spend the rest of his life with her, protect her, come home to her, show her every day how much he loved her. "Will you marry me, Carm?"

Her lips trembled and her eyes shone with tears. "Yes." She reached for him, wound her arms around his shoulders and let out a joyous laugh. "Yes."

Grinning, Sawyer slid the ring on her finger then caught her face between his hands and sealed his promise to cherish her forever with a deep kiss. Then he laid her down on that thick pallet of blankets in front of the fireplace and demonstrated with his body just how much he loved her.

Later, when the fire had died down to glowing embers, they got dressed and rode back to the barn under the silvery light of a half moon. Together they unsaddled then groomed the horses, chatting about wedding plans. She wanted a big, traditional church wedding, and he was willing to make that wish come true for her. Personally though, he'd have been okay with just an officiant and a single witness. A quick and easy ceremony that made her his under the eyes of the law.

The sound of a vehicle crunching over the gravel outside the barn reached him. Frowning, Sawyer set down the curry brush he'd been using and headed for the door. Wasn't his father, not this time of night.

He stepped outside in time to see a man climb out of a new model pickup. When the visitor rounded the hood, he spotted Sawyer and stopped for a moment, tipping up his hat. The moonlight cut across his face.

Danny.

Sawyer was so shocked he didn't move, for a second

wondering if he was looking at a ghost. They hadn't seen or spoken to each other since the day after he'd broken things off with Trina.

Carmela stepped up beside him and slid her arm around his waist without a word, casting him a curious glance. He wrapped an arm around her shoulders and hugged her tight into the side of his body. Whatever Danny wanted, Sawyer wasn't going to let him ruin the most perfect night of his life.

Danny took a few steps toward them and stopped, nodding. "Hi."

"Hi." He couldn't help the way he tensed, his body subconsciously bracing for a blow.

Danny stuck his hands into his pockets. "Your dad said I could find you out here."

The silence stretched out for a few seconds, until Sawyer had had enough. "What do you want, Danny?"

His former best friend's gaze slid from him to Carmela and back. "I heard you were in town for a few days so I wanted to come by."

Clearly reading the awkwardness of the situation, Carmela squeezed him once then gently eased away. "I'm going to head inside. It's cold out here."

That's not why she was leaving. "You don't need to leave," he told her, still looking at Danny.

"Yes, I do. It's okay. I'll see you in a little bit." She stretched up on tiptoe to kiss his cheek then walked away.

Sawyer set his hands on his hips and faced Danny. "Okay, so what did you come by for?" He didn't want to deal with Danny, he wanted to go inside and share the joy of this night with Carmela. See his dad's shocked expression when they announced the news, listen to Mama Cruz squeal and then probably cry when they called to tell her.

Danny sighed. "I wanted to come by and tell you something, face to face. What I did wasn't right. I was an asshole. I'm not sure if your dad told you but I'm going through a divorce right now."

"Sorry to hear that," Sawyer said, impatient to get back to Carmela.

"Thanks." Danny cleared his throat. "Thing is, I get it now. Why you broke up with Trina before the wedding."

Sawyer didn't answer, just waited, already surprised by where this was going.

"Deep down I knew that getting married to Heather probably wasn't a good idea but everyone expected it and it just seemed easier to go through with it than to get out. Anyway, I should've listened to my gut, because getting married was a mistake. One we're both paying for now, as well as both our families. It's a total shit show." He shifted his stance, straightened his shoulders and met Sawyer's gaze head on. "I should've done what you did. I understand now why you broke things off when you did, and I wish the hell I'd had the sense to do the same." He drew in a deep breath. "I'm here to say I'm sorry."

The apology eased something inside Sawyer. He nodded once in acceptance. "Thank you." He could forgive, but he wouldn't forget. Danny and his family had burned their bridges with him a long time ago. They were in the past. His future was waiting for him right now inside his father's house and he couldn't wait to get back to her.

When Sawyer didn't say anything else or start up a conversation to fill the awkward gap that followed, Danny took the hint. He lowered his gaze and nodded once, regret passing over his features. "Well. You take care, man." He stepped forward and held out a hand.

Sawyer shook it once. "You too."

But when Danny reached his truck, guilt got the better of him. "Danny, wait."

Danny stopped and turned back to him. "Yeah?"

"I'm only in town for another couple days, but…maybe we can go grab a coffee or something before I go." It felt like a pathetic thing to say to a man he'd once trusted with his life, but at least it was a start. Maybe they might never regain the friendship they'd lost, but Sawyer didn't hate the guy. He was willing to see how things went.

A relieved smile spread across Danny's face. "I'd like that." He looked toward the house. "Sorry I didn't get a chance to officially meet your girl."

"My fiancée. I just popped the question a couple hours ago." He still couldn't believe how lucky he was.

"Congratulations, man. I'd like to meet her, if you're cool with that."

Sawyer nodded. He'd meet up with Danny on his own first, then, if things were smooth enough, they could maybe all go out for dinner together before he and Carm left. "I'll call you."

He stood in front of the barn and waited while Danny got in his truck and drove down the driveway, filled with a sense of peace. Extending that olive branch had been the right thing to do. Whether anything came of it, only time would tell.

When the truck's taillights disappeared around the first bend, Sawyer headed inside.

Carmela was at the kitchen table with his father. They both looked up when he came in through the mudroom. "Everything okay?" Carm asked with a little smile.

"Yeah, it's fine." He walked over and wrapped his arms around her from behind, his stomach against the back of her chair, and looked at his dad. "Well?"

His old man's harsh features melted into a wry smile. "I can't believe she said yes."

"Believe it," Sawyer told him, smiling as he set his chin against the top of her hair. "She's all mine."

Those dark eyes so like his were warm as they regarded him. "She's definitely a keeper, son." He got up and came around the table to bend and kiss Carmela's cheek. Then he straightened and shook Sawyer's hand, holding his gaze. "I'm happy for you both. Congratulations." He turned and headed up the stairs, leaving them alone in the quiet kitchen.

Carmela swiveled in her seat to look up at him with a worried expression. "You sure you're okay?"

"Yeah. He came by to apologize, and I accepted. But we're not going to be friends again, and I think he was hoping we might be." He took her left hand, raised it to his lips to kiss the diamond on her finger. "I've got my family already."

She pushed up from her chair with a huge smile on her face, wrapped her arms around his neck and kissed him soundly on the lips. "That's right. You were already one of us but this'll just make it official." Her eyes gleamed with excitement. "Now, do you want to call my mom to tell her the news, or should I?"

"You go ahead." He folded his arms across his chest and waited. He wanted to see this and enjoy it to the fullest.

Carm dialed, barely got out, "Hi, *Mami*. Guess what? I said yes", when an ear-piercing shriek made her jerk the phone away from her ear. Then a female scream came through the phone, loud enough that his father probably heard it upstairs.

Sawyer grinned. Carmela held the phone away from her and laughed up at him. "I guess that means she's excited."

He set his hands on her shoulders and leaned over the phone, that high-pitch squeal still coming through loud and clear. "Hi, Mama Cruz," he called out.

He wasn't sure how she heard him, but she must have because she cried out his name and started babbling away in Spanish, the words so fast it was like they were being fired out of a minigun. The only one he caught her screaming over and over was *"¡Wepa!"*, which even he knew was an expression of joy.

Carmela rolled her eyes and shook her head, a fond expression on her face. "Mom, *English*, if you want him to understand you," she told her, eyes sparkling up at him.

Sawyer wrapped his arms around her and listened to his adoptive mother's delirious tears, filled with so much happiness his chest felt tight. He finally had his forever family. He would cherish that for the rest of his life.

—The End—

Thank you for reading SEIZED. I really hope you enjoyed it and that you'll consider leaving a review at one of your favorite online retailers. It's a great way to help other readers discover new books.

If you liked SEIZED and would like to read more, turn the page for a list of my other books. And if you don't want to miss any future releases, please feel free to join my newsletter: http://kayleacross.com/v2/newsletter/

Complete Booklist

<u>**Romantic Suspense**</u>
Hostage Rescue Team Series
Marked
Targeted
Hunted
Disavowed
Avenged
Exposed
Seized

Titanium Security Series
Ignited
Singed
Burned
Extinguished
Rekindled

Bagram Special Ops Series
Deadly Descent
Tactical Strike
Lethal Pursuit
Danger Close
Collateral Damage

Suspense Series
Out of Her League
Cover of Darkness
No Turning Back
Relentless
Absolution

<u>**Paranormal Romance**</u>
Empowered Series
Darkest Caress

Historical Romance
The Vacant Chair

Erotic Romance (writing as *Callie Croix*)
Deacon's Touch
Dillon's Claim
No Holds Barred
Touch Me
Let Me In
Covert Seduction

Acknowledgements

Many thanks to my team for helping me with this story! My editors Deb and Joan, Katie Reus my fabulous critique partner and bestie. And DH, for lending me your eagle eyes.

Couldn't have done it without you guys!

About the Author

NY Times and USA Today Bestselling author Kaylea Cross writes edge-of-your-seat military romantic suspense. Her work has won many awards and has been nominated for both the Daphne du Maurier and the National Readers' Choice Awards. A Registered Massage Therapist by trade, Kaylea is also an avid gardener, artist, Civil War buff, Special Ops aficionado, belly dance enthusiast and former nationally-carded softball pitcher. She lives in Vancouver, BC with her husband and family.

You can visit Kaylea at **www.kayleacross.com.** If you would like to be notified of future releases, please join her newsletter. **http://kayleacross.com/v2/contact/**

Made in the USA
Middletown, DE
22 January 2023

22828037R00170